To Ruth

THE TALE OF
ARCHIE SMITH

Best wishes
Enid Mavor

Enid Mavor

Published by Lyvit Publishing, Cornwall

www.lyvit.com

ISBN 978-0-9957979-4-9

To my grandsons

Matthew, Thomas, Jacob and Louis

Acknowledgements

Many thanks to my two daughters, Fiona and Alison for the help they have given me again over the last few months.

And to my sister Pat Opie for her companionship and encouragement.

THE TALE OF

ARCHIE SMITH

CHAPTER ONE

If someone had told me my life was about to go haywire when I got back from Brazil, I'd not have believed them. But here I am. Archie Smith, still unattached, sitting at the office computer, jet-lagged and hungry. I yawn and look at my watch. It's almost eight o'clock in the evening. A long time since I'd landed at Heathrow in the early hours, taken a taxi to my flat and had that short nap. Then the tube to the office to get this thing wrapped up.

Strange how quickly you adapt; one day deep in the rain forest of Brazil, the next, rattling along beneath the city. One day tropical rain bucketing down through the tree canopy with a roar like an express train. Tonight, soft April drizzle smudging the window panes.

I shook my head. I had to concentrate. It was a bit of luck getting back home in time for the monthly meeting. Another hour and I'd have finished writing up the whole project. And tomorrow I'll be able to walk in to the office and toss it on the table. One up on Kitchener and I grinned as I pictured my rival's annoyance. Good mates, they were, but there was always fierce competition between us, we members of the team. Which was the reason for our firm's success.

My stomach growled, remembering that last in-flight meal. I leaned back and as I flexed my muscles I thought I heard the whine of the lift. Strange. Everyone had gone home hours ago. Even the cleaners had rattled and banged their way out long since. Maybe one of the boys had come back to drag me off for a drink. But no one came into the office and I turned back to my notebook. This would all have been a piece of cake if my work's laptop had survived. The flash flood that'd

1

come raging through the camp, tearing at the flimsy huts had caused a lot of damage, the worst being the loss of the computer. But my scribbled notebook had saved the day. Not for the first time.

No one came to the door so I carried on working with my notes. At last I reached the end. I printed all the work, stacked the papers together and stowed them in my own laptop briefcase. First thing in the morning I'd check them through, but now, I'd be away to find something to eat. And some English beer. Or maybe some Scotch.

I closed down the computer and pulled on my jacket. Switched off the lights and stood for a moment beside the window. In the daytime the tenth-floor block gave you a bird's eye view of London. Now there was the blur of lights from the traffic flowing non-stop through the streets. No stars except these man-made ones in the tall buildings all around. If I closed my eyes I knew I'd see again the blaze of the tropic sky above the clearing, stars pulsing, seeming close enough to touch, bright enough to dazzle. I shivered. Disorientated. Lonely.

Food. That's what I needed. I swung away from the window and headed for the corridor. But half-way along I stopped. There *was* someone else working up here. Light spilled from beneath one of the doors and I could hear the sound of electronic equipment in use. I scowled. Was this more industrial espionage?

I took a deep breath and approached the door quietly. Gripped the handle. And suddenly flung the door open yelling 'What the fu…?'

The person standing by the photocopier spun round to face me, her hands flying to her mouth. I stopped abruptly. I'd expected to see a man. One man at least. But a female! Before she could catch her breath to speak, I strode across the room and picked up a sheet of paper and swiftly scanned the page. Then I turned to her and accusingly growled, 'What's this? The German rock drill details! All this stuff's secret.'

She took her hands away from her mouth and answered me. 'I know it is. And who d'you think you are anyway, bursting in like that and scaring me witless?'

'I'm Archie Smith. I work here. Now, what's going on?'

'Oh! You're the one just back from South America.' She seemed to relax, then she paused and pushed her hair off her forehead. Red hair, I noticed. And I saw that all the colour had left her face leaving a scatter of freckles afloat on the whiteness. 'Identification please,' she said and held out her hand imperiously.

Disconcerted, I delved into my pocket for the office pass and held it out to her, noticing her hand trembled as she took the plastic. She examined it carefully, then looked up. 'OK then. I'm Jo Saunders. I'm a translator. Freelance. I've been working here lately. Your boss David Phillips phoned me at home this evening and asked if I could translate this paper and get copies out ready for tomorrow's ten o'clock meeting.' While she spoke she handed me back my pass, picked up her handbag and pulled out a pass of her own and held it out to me.

I bit my lip in embarrassment, but played my part and duly checked her name. Gave her back the card and turned my hands up in defeat. 'Look. What can I say? I'm sorry to have given you such a fright.' And then, into the awkward pause, my stomach gave a ferocious rumbling growl. I felt the heat of the first blush I'd known since my teens and suddenly she laughed.

She threw back her head and crowed with mirth. 'Oh dear! Sorry to laugh. But you did give me such a fright!

3

This is a reaction I think,' and she pulled out a tissue and dabbed her eyes. 'You can make amends by walking me to my car.'

I found I was smiling back, embarrassment swept away by her laughter. 'Sure. What about all these papers though?'

'I'll lock them in the safe. OK?'

When she had at last made everything secure, I switched out the light and followed her to the lift. She shrugged on a loose purple overcoat and as we walked outside and the rain pounced on us, she unfolded a large multi-coloured golf umbrella and handed it to me. 'Plenty of room for both of us under this.'

And I found myself brushing shoulders with her, strolling along the wet pavements and not minding the occasional splash from passing traffic. 'Where's your car?' I asked.

I could hear the frown in her voice. 'That's the trouble. I knew the staff car park would be closed. And all these streets have yellow lines. So I parked in The Feathers' car park.'

'The Feathers!' I was astonished. 'You do like to live dangerously, don't you?'

'Yes, I know. I know it's a tough place. But at seven o'clock it seemed like a good idea. I didn't expect to be so long.' She turned to me. 'But I did buy a couple of bottles of beer to pay for my parking.' There was a smile in her voice.

'Oh well. Not far now. Perhaps all the roughnecks will still be inside drinking.'

But just as we drew near enough to hear the beat of drums from the pub, a group of youths spilled from the lighted doorway and turned towards us. Were they heading this way, or were we their target?

She grabbed my arm. 'My car is just over there,' and

4

she pointed to the far end of the car park. We'd have to pass the gang to get there, and I could see she was nervous.

But just then a car came roaring along the street, driving fast. Too fast. It swerved towards the pavement and through a large puddle, sending a wave of water over the approaching group.

'Aw Jesus! Me new jeans! Shit! Bastard!' The yells of rage merged into a torrent of obscenity and blasphemy. But shaking their soaked limbs, they turned away. 'That was fucking Sidney Frank's car. We'll get the sodding bastard!' And they jostled each other back to the pub to dry out and plot their vengeance.

'Phew!' Jo blew out her cheeks. 'Come on, the car's over there. Let's get out of here!' And moments later we dived into her yellow mini.

As we strapped ourselves in, she turned to me. 'Sorry if I seemed a bit too nervous. But when I came home for Christmas to stay with my parents, I went out one evening with Sue, a friend of mine. When we went past a pub, a bunch of lads who'd just come out, grabbed us and pinned us against the wall and demanded our cash and our phones. Thankfully, just as we were handing them over, a police car came along the road and the boys ran for it.'

'Did they get what they'd asked for?'

'My phone and my cash, yes. Sue's purse fell onto the pavement and her phone was still in her hand. But it has made me nervous of groups of lads.' She gave an embarrassed laugh. 'That was my second scare tonight.'

I felt guilty. 'Yes. I am so sorry that it looked like I was about to attack you in the office. It's just that we've been on the lookout for industrial espionage lately.'

'I know,' she said. 'I quite understand why you acted the way you did. So now, where do you want to go?' As she asked she turned the car out of the pub's parking and headed for the lights and traffic on the busy road.

'Where do I want to go?' I replied. 'Well, as you no doubt guessed, I'm starving!' and I gave a wry laugh. 'So let's make it somewhere to eat, and I hope you'll join me so I can make amends for giving you such a fright back at the office.'

'Great! I'm hungry too. There's that nice Italian place near here. That do?'

And when I agreed it'd be fine, she swung the car on to a side road and drew up near a small restaurant. 'Oh look, there's one parking place left! They're always busy but we won't have to wait too long.'

And for once I didn't mind having to wait.

CHAPTER TWO

Jo asked for tonic water and I chose my favourite whisky and when the drinks came, she begged for a sip of my drink to 'settle my butterflies'.

As she handed back my glass she laughed. 'That's my ration of alcohol when I'm driving.' I could see she was looking at me with curiosity. 'You must be absolutely knackered! You only got back today, didn't you?'

I nodded. 'Yep. Early hours. I got a bit of a sleep though before I came into work. I wanted to get things ready for tomorrow.' I grinned. 'It's a co-incidence getting back just before the monthly meeting, but too good a chance to miss out, being able to walk in tomorrow morning with the whole project wrapped up, ready to set it out before them.'

She smiled back and nodded. 'They do sort of encourage enthusiasm, don't they, your old boys.'

I sipped my drink. 'It's the reason they're such a success. When the three of them should have been thinking about retirement, they decided that a 'pool of know-how' as they put it, was needed. And they started the firm. And now they've got a great name. They send us engineers off to the four corners of the world at a moment's notice. As trouble-shooters or consultants or sometimes even salesmen. Whatever. We're most of us fairly young. And unattached. Have to be, the kind of lives we live.'

Her hair, darkened by the rain, was beginning to dry and curl in red tendrils round her forehead. I noticed colour had come back to her cheeks and the freckles no longer stood out. Her eyes were dark grey. I could feel my own hair plastered on my forehead and I pushed it back, thinking maybe it might have been easier to trace my parentage if I'd had unusual colouring like this girl. But there, I'm just ordinary; dark hair, blue eyes, average height... I leaned back in my seat, tiredness in my bones, but no longer wanting just to fall into bed and sleep.

'You were in Brazil, weren't you?'

'Yeah. Deep in the rainforest.'

She asked a lot of questions. About the jungle. About the people. About how they coped in extreme conditions. And about the equipment I'd used. And I began to doubt her again.

Suddenly she reached out and touched my hand. 'It's OK. Really! I'm not a spy. Ask your boss David Phillips tomorrow. He's known me and my family for years. It was David who got in touch and asked me to do some work for your firm.'

I gave an awkward smile. I liked the feel of her hand on mine for that brief moment. I relaxed and looked at her again with interest. 'Where did you work before?' I asked.

Her eyes shadowed and she looked down at her hands. 'I've been living in Germany for a couple of years. Working there. My married sister lives in Munich. I went out to be near her and brush up my German.'

The waiter came just then with our food, just as I felt she was hiding something. But by the time we began to eat, she was smiling again and open.

The food was good. Lasagne for me, mushroom risotto for her. Hot, piquant. I bit into my garlic bread with relish. 'God, I was so hungry! I'll remember this place, Jo. Put it on my list of specials.' It was the first time I'd used her name and I liked the feeling of intimacy it gave. She was easy to talk to, smiling, her eyes reflecting sparkles of light from the candles on the table.

'What about your family, what do they make of all these trips of yours?' she looked across at me.

I felt the familiar defences spring up; the old reluctance to talk to anyone about my background. But suddenly, I shrugged. 'No family. I'm an orphan.' I spoke with assumed nonchalance.

'Oh. Poor you!' As if she sensed my difficulty, she steered the conversation away from me. 'I'm the opposite.' She laughed. 'Parents, grandparents, one sister and two brothers. Not to mention the niece and three nephews!'

And then, to my astonishment, unbidden, I found myself telling her about my childhood; the children's homes, the fosterings, the changes of school... The transience of it all.

I didn't tell her about my loneliness; I didn't have to. I knew she heard it through my sudden silences. Each time I paused so abruptly, she made small talk, asked casual questions, covered the yawning abyss I faced. And all with a friendly normality that encouraged me to go on.

'Your name, Archie.' She said at last in one of the silences. 'Who gave you all those Christian names? If I remember there were several on your identity disc.'

I grinned wryly. 'Archibald Ensor Gregory Smith. Yes, quite a mouthful isn't it? When I was left in the foyer of the hospital, the names were on a card pinned to my shawl. With the message "Please take care of me for my mother"'.

'Oh, how sad,' she said quietly. 'How very sad.'

The sympathy in her voice was almost too much. I finished my whisky in a gulp and ordered another from the passing waiter in a voice harsher than I meant. Maybe it was the jet-lag. Or perhaps the release of tension after the strain of the last few months. More likely it was talking about the past. But suddenly I knew if I stayed any longer, talked any more, I'd be breaking all my self-imposed taboos; that I'd be moving into forbidden territory, allowing some other person into the privacy of my personal life.

I pushed back my chair. Remembered the drink I'd just ordered. The bill to be paid. Sat down again and began to search for my wallet.

Jo gathered her coat from the back of the chair. 'Look. Thanks for the meal. I've really enjoyed it. You're sure I can't pay my whack?'

Safe ground again. 'Sure I'm sure!' I smiled at her. 'You can buy me a coffee tomorrow.' I pulled on my own coat, gulped down my whisky and as I paid the bill I asked the waiter for the phone number of a local taxi firm. I used my mobile to call for a cab as I walked her out to her car. It had stopped raining and the air had a chill that made me shiver and fasten my coat.

'I'll drop you off if you like to cancel that call.' She'd climbed into the car and wound down the window, peering up at me, her hair eerily whitened by the orange glow of the overhead lights.

'Josephine Saunders, it's nearly midnight. D'you want this car to turn into a pumpkin half-way home?'

She laughed, shaking her head. And I felt a sudden urge to reach through the window and cradle her face in my hands. To brush her lips with mine... But she'd already started the engine and was moving off, waving a cheerful farewell and calling back, 'See you tomorrow then, Archie. Ni-night.'

And after I'd waved my hand, I stood, waiting for my taxi to arrive, my head light with tiredness, whisky and something else... I stood beneath the starless sky, waiting, waiting for tomorrow, my mouth wide with an unfamiliar maudlin smile.

CHAPTER THREE

I thought of her as I woke next day. I lay for several minutes huddled beneath the quilt going over our evening together, remembering the way she smiled, her pale skin. The freckles. Then my clock radio came to life and I leapt out of bed with a curse. The shower took an age to run bearably hot but by the time I'd shaved, the water was passable and I set the coffee to drip while I dressed. There was a stack of mail on the table which I'd ignored yesterday when I got back - I'd had that short sleep and then shot off to the office. Now I glanced through the pile while I drank the coffee. Most of it I binned; circulars and appeals already a couple of months out of date. But there were several cards and letters which I stowed in my briefcase to read on the tube. Gulping down the last of the coffee, I picked up the gifts I'd brought for my two neighbours, the other occupants of the house.

My flat is on the top floor of this tall narrow building. Peter Watson lives below and Mrs White, our landlady, reigns over the ground floor. They're both early risers and were expecting me. After five years of sharing the building they still called me Mr Smith most of the time, although sometimes Mrs White responded to my Mrs Double-u and managed a self-conscious 'Archie'. Occasionally, when I'm not at work, I'd join them in the small garden at the back and trim the shrubs while Watson cut the grass and Mrs White weeded. And we'd sit around in companionable silence while Watson smoked the pipe that was forbidden indoors. Undemanding. Unintrusive. They suited me and they suited each other.

This morning in honour of my return, Watson followed me down the hall and waited while I tapped on Mrs White's door. When she came, professing surprise that I was back 'so soon', I gave her the box of chocolate brazils and an illustrated guide to the country knowing this would delight her. My landlady, thanks to the collection of such books I'd had given her over the years, was something of an expert on a number of far-off lands. She pored over every one, engrossed in the pictures and maps and script, an elderly woman who travelled vicariously, the only way she could.

For Peter Watson there were more chocolates. And a solid pack of tobacco to fumigate the back yard for weeks to come. I grinned at their smiling faces, pleased to see I'd struck the right note once more. But there was no time to stay and I was soon hurrying down to the underground station, thinking of Jo again.

On the train I opened the briefcase and dug out the letters. A couple from engineering colleagues. Some insurance bumph. And no less than three letters from Ethel Miners! I sorted them into date order and read the first.

My dear Archie,

I couldn't believe my eyes when I saw this in the paper. What do you make of it? I'll send you the whole page so you can see the date and such. Let me know what you think and what are you going to do about it? I hope you've not gone off overseas again. Not just now.

Your friend, Ethel

Mystified I unfolded the attached sheet of newsprint.

My name sprang from the page.

'Archibald Ensor Gregory Smith. Died 7ᵗʰ March 2017'

My mouth was suddenly dry and I closed my eyes. My name. My death notice! But no, someone else. Some other person with this stupid cumbrous bloody name! I turned to the page again and read the complete announcement:

Archibald Ensor Gregory Smith died 7ᵗʰ March 2017 at St. Hayes, Cornwall.
Will persons with an interest in the estate of the above contact the Treasury
Solicitor - GOV.UK - failing which the Treasury Solicitor may take steps to administer the estate.

The impact of the announcement was like a physical blow. I sat staring a the paper in a daze, barely conscious of the train stopping and starting and people jostling and pushing to and fro. What did it mean? Was it some bizarre joke? Or was this truly a namesake? Just a weird coincidence or did this connect in some way with me? The train jolted to a standstill in another station and my case almost slid from my lap. As I grabbed it I remembered Ethel's other letters and quickly opened them.

One was an impatient note asking me to get in touch. What did it mean, Archie? But the last letter was longer and after reading it I stared through my reflection in the window with a lump in my throat. I knew how frail she'd become; so different now from the strong acerbic woman who'd ruled over the kitchens of Wilton Hall where I'd spent a lot of those difficult childhood years.

A strange friendship ours had been; a friendship that had lasted ever since. And now she'd done this for me! I read the letter again.

When I got your card from Brazil I couldn't wait any longer. I knew I wouldn't get anywhere with the Treasury Solicitor people so I went to St. Hayes in Cornwall. I went to the Council Offices and looked through the voters register. So many Smiths. But I found it in the end.

I meant to visit the house and find out what I could, but there, that leg of mine, you know what that's like. I couldn't walk that far from what I was told. So I had to come back on the train. Anyway, you said on your card that you'd be home soon so you better get on to it right away. It's got to mean something. Some family thing I mean. The address is Keyes Lane House, St. Hayes. I wish I could do more.

With a start I saw I'd overshot my stop. I jumped out at the next station, ran to the opposite platform and leapt through the closing doors of the departing train. So much for my plan to be early! But suddenly work was less important. This newspaper cutting. What could it mean? The picture of Jo suddenly came into mind. Jeezus! If it was a family thing! To be able to find out! To know for sure! To shed this feeling of being different, unable to live like everyone else for fear of what might crawl out of the woodwork of the unknown past…

But as soon as I reached the office, I took a deep breath and thrust my confused thoughts aside to concentrate on the works' meeting.

CHAPTER FOUR

The meeting was lively. As well as me, there were two other engineers recently back from overseas stints. And the three elderly partners, on the ball as always, were roaring with enjoyment as they listened to the reports of the triumphs and near-disasters of we three younger men. My paper which I'd re-read last night before I slept, featured strongly as they discussed the pros and cons of the new equipment I'd been trying out; equipment tested to the full in the heart of the rain forest.

But no Jo. I kept looking at the door while forcing my mind back to work. Then, half an hour into the meeting, there was a tap on the door and in answer to David Phillips' shout of 'come!', she came in carrying a stack of magazines as well as her briefcase. She smiled her apologies for being late. 'Flat battery,' she said.

The senior partner stood up and gave her a hug. 'Jo, my dear. Good to see you. Sit down, sit down. I think you know everyone here. All except Archie of course. Archie, this is Jo, our new translator. Known her since she was a tot.'

I got to my feet and held out my hand, smiling. 'As a matter of fact we bumped into each other last night. But nice to see you again, Jo.' And she too smiled as she formally shook my hand, colour rising in her cheeks.

We all got back to work. Jo's skills were swiftly needed as we went through several overseas trade magazines and once or twice she referred to a couple of heavy engineering dictionaries as she wrote up her notes. I must say I was impressed by her thoroughness, her professionalism.

15

'Right, you boys can go off and get Jo a cup of coffee.' David Phillips waved us away. 'Come back in half an hour or so. We'll tell you what we've decided then. Need a private word with Adrian first.'

'Who's Adrian?' Jo asked as we walked along the corridor heading for the coffee bar.

'He's the accountant.' I'd fallen into step beside her, neatly cutting out my colleagues. 'Did you come in by cab? D'you want me to come and sort out your car this evening?'

She laughed. 'No. And no. I caught a bus in. And the garage are sending someone round this morning to fix the car.'

'Good line that, Archie.' The comment came from colleague Jim Black. 'But it won't work. Nothing works with Jo,' and the youngest member of the team tweaked her hair as he grinned down at her. 'Come on boys, I can see Sandra and Eve. Might get somewhere there, eh?' But as the others went on ahead I noticed again that troubled shadow cross her face.

'Archie.' I turned to see David Phillips beckoning from the doorway of the conference room we'd just left.

'Go and see what he wants,' Jo said. 'I'll grab a table and order your coffee.'

'Archie.' The boss looked directly at me as Jo disappeared. 'Listen. Thought I'd better tell you. Young Jo. Lost her husband two years ago. Tragic. Childhood sweethearts, y'know. Went to stay with her sister in Germany for a time. Parents asked me to find her some demanding work at home. Go on. Go on. Just don't put your foot in it.'

And before I could make any reply, he swung on his heel and went back into the room. So that was it. Poor kid. That lost look of hers. I made my way slowly along the corridor to the bar.

She'd claimed a table by putting her jacket on it and was collecting a tray as I joined her. Perhaps she suspected what David Phillips had been saying about her because she seemed stiff and remote as we pulled out our chairs and sat down. And then, with a sudden jolt of my heart, I remembered the newspaper cutting. I pulled out my wallet and took out the piece of paper, knowing this would break the ice.

'What do you make of this, Jo? A friend sent it to me.' And I handed her the cutting.

'Good God! It's your name. Died... Ugh. It's made me go quite cold.' She re-read the paper carefully and looked across the table at me. 'But I thought you said you have no relations.'

I nodded, slowly stirring my coffee. 'Absolutely none. Zilch. And then this, out of the blue. Look, read Ethel's letters. She's an old friend of mine. She was cook at the place where I lived for eight years while I was at school. A bloody good friend too. The best.' And remembering those grim days at the Hall, I recognised, none better, how much I owed to her.

She bent her bright head over the letters and presently looked up. 'What are you going to do about it Archie?'

I shook my head. 'Don't know yet. I haven't had the time to take it in. It does seem to be one hell of a coincidence to have exactly the same name though.' I sipped my coffee and made a face. 'Yuck! What is this stuff? If you gave it to a dog the RSPCA would have you in court for cruelty.'

Jo grinned. 'One way to get the staff back to work.' She stood up as she spoke. 'Come on. Duty calls.' But as we walked along the corridor she turned to me. 'I know it's not my business, but can I make a suggestion? Apart from the Treasury Solicitor, I mean.

17

If I were you I'd get hold of this man's death certificate. If you go to St. Hayes as your friend suggested, you could get a copy from the local registry office. It might give you some information about his family. You can get it online of course, but it takes a couple of weeks. And you might find out more on the spot.'

'Good idea.' We were outside the conference room now and I frowned. 'I think I'll have to take some time off and go and find the place. Not only get the death certificate, but visit the house Edith wanted to go to.' I turned to her. 'You couldn't come with me, I suppose?'

She bit her lip. 'I've got a lot of work on at the moment. Not only here, I mean. I help at the local school three afternoons a week and today is one of them. I really am interested in what you have to do though. I'll give you a ring this evening if you let me have your number.'

'Great.' I took out my mobile and we sorted out our numbers as we made our way back to the meeting.

We joined the others back at the conference table and I had to force myself to concentrate. But each time I looked up and saw her busy with her notebook my heart lifted. And when David Phillips asked me if I could defer the leave I was due to take for a couple of weeks, I was torn. Part of me wanted to use the time to look into this weird matter of the newspaper advert, but part was glad of the chance to see more of Jo each day.

I compromised. 'I've got a couple of personal things to clear up, David. Might need a day or two away, but apart from that, yes, sure I'll stay.'

When the meeting ended I was sorry to see Jo wave her hand to say cheerio to us all as she left just before lunch. But I immediately found a quiet spot where I could go on line to the Treasury Solicitor using the

18

information in the newspaper cutting.

CHAPTER FIVE

I phoned her that evening, too impatient to wait for her to call me. She was eager to hear what I'd found out and told me to go ahead while she turned down her cooker.

'That's the trouble. I've got nowhere. When I went online, I found the office was there to deal with estates which had no will or no known family. To make enquiries, you had to give proof of your relationship. Well, I can't do that, can I?'

'Mm. That is a nuisance. Because I really feel there must be a reason for you having been given that unusual name. An unmarried mum, perhaps? Girls didn't always get much help then. Still don't from some families, do they?'

'Well, could be, I suppose. I think I'd better ask David if I can take a couple of days off and go to St. Hayes like you suggested.' And after a little more chat, Jo said rather reluctantly that she had to go, the pan was boiling over.

David Phillips was quite happy for me to take a couple of days off. I was entitled to a break anyway after the long stint abroad though I often preferred to stay at work, enjoying the company of my fellow engineers rather than going off on my own.

'If you take tomorrow and Friday, you'll be able to add the weekend if you need it for whatever business you have to complete. As long as it's not an interview with another firm?' And he looked enquiringly at me as he spoke.

'No, of course not.' I grinned. 'No, this is a personal

thing. I…'

'Alright, alright. I didn't mean to butt into your plans. But it's good to be sure you don't intend to leave us.'

So off I went and called my old friend Ethel once more. She'd been so pleased when I'd phoned the day after I got back to talk about the newspaper cutting and I'd promised to keep her up to date with what I might find out. 'I'm sure that man who died is related to you Archie,' she said. 'I know it's not about getting money from the estate. You'll just want to know who you really are. Like I would if I was in your shoes.'

And then another chat with Jo on the phone. She was sorry she couldn't go with me - it was such a terrific search to make. Once again, we both seemed reluctant to end our talk and chatted about this and that until we finally said our cheerios.

I hired a car and set off at six o'clock on Thursday morning. The sun was shining as I drove and once out of the city, I pulled over and used my iPhone to find the best route to my destination; Keyes Lane House, St. Hayes.

It was just before eleven o'clock that morning when I slowed up outside the gates of the place I was looking for. On the tall granite gateposts I could just make out the name of the house, almost hidden under the branches of an evergreen tree. The drive was usable, though the gravel base was weed strewn and the edges overgrown by shrubs and just as I turned the car from the road, the sun vanished behind a looming cloud and I felt I was driving along a tunnel of gloom. Soon there was an open space in front of the large double fronted house and I pulled up and stared around.

It was like a child's drawing of a house; five windows along the top floor, two each side of the front door which was protected by a pillared porch. I climbed slowly out and walked towards the door, my heart sinking as I could see there were closed wooden shutters behind all the downstairs front windows and curtains drawn across all of the upstairs.

Feeling it a waste of time to ring the bell, I walked round to the back and saw that on this side the curtains were open and there was a full bottle of milk on the back doorstep. With a lift of the heart, I mounted the three steps and rang the large bell. I could hear it ring inside and thought I heard a movement, but then total silence. After a brief wait, I tried again, and knocked on the fading blue paint of the wooden door. Silence followed. I tried a couple more times, sure there was someone inside, but finally, reluctantly I made my way back to the car, noticing how the large garden which had obviously once been landscaped, was now unkempt and overgrown. And there was a great view of the sea from the front of this house.

Back in the car, I sat for a few minutes, drumming my fingers on the steering wheel. At last, with a sigh, I swung the car round and drove back out to the road. Left or right? Once more I shrugged and turned left and a mile or so farther on, spotted a pub. Aware now of my body's need of a drink, I turned into the parking space and climbed out, stretching to try and remove the tension which had spread through my body. There were picnic benches outside, but with the sun still behind that great grey cloud, I decided to stay indoors.

There were half a dozen or so men inside seated round a table playing some card game. They looked up as I came in and I gave them a casual nod as I walked past them to the bar.

'Well sir, what would you like? Bit early for lunch, but would you fancy a bacon buttie with your drink, whatever that might be?' The barman was a large and friendly-looking guy.

'You must be a mind reader,' I grinned at him. 'A bacon buttie would be great. And seeing I'm driving, just a half pint of beer and a strong black coffee.'

When he brought the sandwich and the drinks, the bar tender chatted about the weather, naturally liking a talk with his customers, and I took the chance to ask a question. 'Did you know the man who died a while ago, the bloke with the long name, Archibald Ensor Gregory something?'

'Greg Smith? Oh yes. He was a nice guy. Ran an iron foundry in town. I know his workmen are all worried about what's going to happen to the place when it finally gets sorted out.'

'Mm. Interesting.' I was frankly astonished to hear my namesake had also been an engineer. And owned a foundry! I concentrated on my food for a bit and then told him I'd called round at the old man's house but no one answered the door, even though I'd really thought there was someone there.

'Hm. That'd be his housekeeper, the Julian woman. Nasty piece of work she is. We couldn't understand why he never got rid of her. But there, he always felt responsible for his staff.' He reached over to the bar and began to polish a couple of glasses while I carried on eating my buttie. 'Needed to get some information at the house, did you?' The bar tender was obviously liking a bit of gossip.

Thinking of what he'd said, I jumped at the chance of asking another question. 'Well, I work for an engineering company and we'd like a few details of this iron foundry of his.' I pulled out my notebook and asked for directions to go there. After scribbling them down, I turned back to my food again while the innkeeper hung over me, ready to ask his own questions. Luckily, a couple of new customers came through the door into the bar just then and reluctantly the bar tender turned away.

I quickly finished my meal, but as I paid my bill, I casually asked if they happened to have Greg Smith's home phone number. 'Yes, 'course we have. He used to book a meal here quite often.' The landlord turned to pick up a notebook and flicked through the pages. 'Yep, here you are. Got your phone?'

I nodded, mobile already in my hand, while he hovered over his own notepad. And a few minutes later I was driving back along the road towards Keyes Lane House. I pulled into a lay-by and dialled the number, tense while it rang and rang. Unanswered. At last I sighed and tucked the phone away. Another drumming on the steering wheel, until I decided to go into the town and find the Registry Office.

I followed the signs to a large half-empty car park and as I collected a ticket, I spotted an assistant and asked him for the directions I needed. Ten minutes later I entered a reception room, gave my name and request, and was asked to wait my turn. I'd been about to give the name I used all the time, Archie Smith, but instead, I gave my full name which made the secretary look up in surprise. Ten minutes later two people left and I was beckoned into a small office.

The registrar, a grey-haired man nearing retirement, introduced himself and glanced at the piece of paper his secretary had handed him. 'Good Lord!' He stood up and held out his hand. 'I never knew Greg had family. I'm Roger Baker, by the way.'

I shook hands and nodded back at him. 'Well, I never knew either. In fact I still don't. But you knew him?'

'Yes indeed. We were both members of the Rotary

Club and met quite often. But sit down while I get this copy you requested.' He turned to sort out the paper work but was obviously curious about my presence. 'Mind if I ask you your age, Mr Smith? Or do you call yourself Gregory Smith like my friend and his brother both did.'

I pricked up my ears. 'He's got a brother?'

The registrar shook his head. 'He was called Hannibal Ensor Gregory Smith. But sadly he died in Africa aged thirty-eight.' He glanced up at me. 'You're not his son, by any chance?'

I shrugged. 'No idea. When did he die? If it helps, I'm thirty this year.'

'Thirty. Hm. I'll have to look it up. But hang on. My youngest son is thirty and I know Hannibal died four or five years before my Tim was born. So you can't be his.' He frowned. 'But Greg's son too was born thirty years ago. You wouldn't like to give me your date of birth, I suppose?'

'Of course.' I reached across for the piece of paper I'd already written on and added the dates.

Roger Baker looked stunned. Without a word, he turned to the archive and searched for his record book. He flicked through and then paused and looked up once more. 'I know you've asked for a copy of Greg's death certificate, but if I were in your shoes, I'd like two more; one is the record of the child's birth, the same date as yours, and the other is the baby's death next day.'

I felt the hairs on my neck stand up. The registrar was staring at me, his face reddened. 'It's not my job to tell people what to do, Mr Smith. But Greg was a good friend of mine and I know he'd want to know who you are.'

'Well, Mr Baker. I have no idea who I am. Except for

the name pinned to my shawl as a day-old baby.'

The registrar called his secretary and asked her to make a couple of cups of coffee. She looked surprised but said alright seeing there was no one waiting at the moment. And by the time we'd finished the coffee and I'd told him all I knew, I had three certificates in my hand and I thanked the registrar for giving me this surprising information.

Baker shook my hand again. 'Good luck with your search, Mr Smith. I'd be very interested to hear what you find out,' and he turned and picked up a card. 'There's my name and phone number. That's if you ever have the time to call.'

I nodded. 'Thanks. I'm grateful to you for all this extra information that I'd never have had a clue about, and I will let you know if I ever do find out who I am.' And off I went on the way back to my car.

Back in the car park and feeling a surge of unexpected confidence, I phoned the number given to me by the pub landlord once again, and this time, after a number of rings, a woman answered.

'Good afternoon, Mrs Julian. I wonder if I could call and have a chat with you?'

'What? Who are you?'

'Well, that's the problem. I'm not sure. But my name is the same as your late employer. I'm Archibald Ensor Gregory Smith.'

'Rubbish. You're just another of them trying to get his estate.'

'Not at all. I would just like to know who I am; a baby with that name pinned to his shawl in a hospital thirty years ago.'

There was an icy silence. Then she spoke, her voice tight with tension. 'What hospital? You're making this up.'

Trying to calm her down, I asked again if I could call and chat to her. I felt I would like to be talking to her face to face, rather than on the phone. Another long silence until at last she spoke. 'I can't have a visitor today. Give me your address.'

Surprised, I spelt it out and just as I knew she was about to hang up on me, I said, 'You know, I can't help thinking I might actually be his son.'

The phone slammed down after a silent moment and I sat back, amazed at what I'd just said. What I felt could be true.

CHAPTER SIX

Sitting in the car, I sat reading and re-reading the certificates I'd just been given. How in hell's name... What a co-incidence to learn another child was born the same day. And for it to die straight away - a child with two parents, while, I, Archie, with no known parents, survived. The idea that perhaps it was my twin, wouldn't work; I was found in a hospital about a hundred miles away. In Devon. Hardly possible...

I took a deep breath and stowed the certificates away in my case and pulled out my notebook. Where should I go now, to the iron foundry? But just as I turned the pages to find the address the pub landlord had given me, my phone rang.

It was David Phillips. 'Archie. Thank goodness we caught you. I'm sorry to have to ask you this, but could you possibly give up your days off? Justin's had an accident at the Blue Rock West Africa mine, the one you've been to several times. And Gordon's wife's baby is due any minute, so we haven't got anyone else to go out there. And it is a bit urgent. D'you think you could do that?'

I answered right away. Yes of course I could and I asked how Justin was. 'He's OK, but he's broken his arm and has to stay there in the hospital to have it checked again tomorrow.'

'Good. As long as it wasn't anything serious. I'll be back in five or six hours or so.'

David thanked me with relief in his voice, and said he'd book the early morning flight for tomorrow.

I put away my notebook and phone and started up the car. These visits could wait. My job had been priority in my life for years and I'd always enjoyed working at Blue Rock. The only snag was I'd not be able to see Jo. This fact hit me hard and while driving back towards the motorway, I kept wondering how long I'd have to stay away. Often these emergency trips didn't last very long and I hoped this would be one of them because I didn't like the idea of not seeing Jo…

Back at the office the rest of the late afternoon was taken up with checking details of Justin's work and together with David Phillips we were pretty sure there wasn't a lot more to do at the Blue Rock mine. So hopefully I'd would be back in a week or so.

Before I left I asked Jo if she'd like a coffee and while sitting together, I showed her the certificates I'd collected at St. Hayes. She was just as astonished as I was. 'I think you will be able to find out why you were put up for adoption. You've already discovered such a lot about this family name.' Jo nodded her head sagely. 'I know you'll have to set it aside until you get back from Africa, but then you'll have to make sure you take time off to look into it all.'

I smiled. I was watching her face as she spoke, watching the shining red hair, the warmth of her grey eyes… I'd never felt like this about anyone before. And I wasn't at all sure the friendship she was showing was anything more than interest in the strange facts I'd discovered. She was still mourning her husband. I mustn't let her know how I was feeling in case it put her off completely. And then two of our colleagues joined us and when I'd finished my coffee, I stood up and said I'd got to go, 'Things to do at home, packing and so on. See you all when I get back,' and as I left I was glad to go without putting any pressure on Jo, because if my mates hadn't joined us, I didn't think I'd be able to hide the way I was feeling.

It took eight days in all. As soon as I reached the camp I met up with Justin who was lounging on a chair on the hospital veranda. Justin joked about his fall, tripping over a dog, though I could see he was pale and obviously in painful discomfort. We agreed to travel back together as soon as I'd finished checking the last set of machinery which had just been installed. And for the next few days I worked with some of the miners I'd known from my previous visits. Each night as I went to bed, I realised how little time I'd had to think about my namesake. But I also knew I'd thought about Jo so many times; imagining bringing her with me on a working visit. After all there was a lot of German machinery and it would be handy having her there to interpret instead of trying things out in different ways. But would she want to be with me...? And back it came, the feeling I'd always had that without knowing my background, it wouldn't be right to have a relationship and possibly a child which might be carrying some bad problems in its genes...

The days went by quickly and Justin was looking better each evening as I talked over with him all the things that'd been done during the day. We had a few drinks with some of the miners on the last night before we left and next morning were off flying home together.

When we got back, instead of being able to take some time off again, I felt I must stay on at work as Gordon's wife had had a difficult childbirth and their baby was still in hospital with both his parents by his side. And Justin too, was due time off and after his accident he needed a rest more than I did. Well, those were the reasons I gave myself, but I knew beneath it all that I wanted to be at work so I could see Jo on the days she was there. She'd suggested I go online to follow up what I'd found out from the Registrar, but I felt I'd rather go to the town and meet face to face those I wanted to question. After all, would the Registrar have given me all that information if I'd just asked for that death certificate online? Jo reluctantly agreed that it probably would be better that way, but said she couldn't understand why I was so patient. I was glad she hadn't guessed that she was the reason I was so determined to stay at work in the office.

CHAPTER SEVEN

A couple of days later, Jim Black, one of my colleagues called across the room. 'Hi Archie. Call for you,' and he held out the receiver to me.

I got up and strolled over to answer the call, looking across the room to where Jo was busy on the computer. 'Yep, Archie Smith speaking.'

'Ah good. This is PC Major. We would like you to return to your home at once, Mr Smith. There's been an explosion. And Mrs White, who tells us she's your landlady, won't leave the premises unless you come. And it's very dangerous.'

'What! What are you talking about!' my attention was now focussed. 'Sorry, but is this some kind of joke?' I saw Jo's head come up and her face turned towards me.

'Certainly it's not, sir. If you like to call your local police station they will confirm my identity. The number is…'

'No! No! It's alright. I'll get round there straight away.' I put down the phone, frowning.

Jo read my face. 'Trouble?'

I nodded. 'Seems so. Unless it's some kind of twisted joke. A policeman.' I waved at the phone. 'Says there's been an explosion at my place. I've got to get there right away. Let's hope there's a cab handy.'

Jo stood up. 'I'll drive you. My car's down below in the car park. I can finish this when I get back.'

And quickly explaining what was happening to the other staff in the office, we hurried off together.

Ten minutes late Jo's car was stopped at the end of my road by a uniformed officer. As the policeman bent to speak to her through the window, I clambered out from the passenger door. 'Sorry, but the road's closed,' the officer said turning his attention to me as I stood gazing down the street. 'Can't go down there, sir. Been an explosion.'

'Yes. I know. I've been told to come by Constable Major.'

'Oh, right then. You'll have to go round to the back as the front is blocked. And you can't stay here miss.' he added, turning back to Jo,

'Oh, alright then. I'll go. Archie give me a ring if you need to be picked up. And good luck.' And Jo swung the car round and drove away as directed by the policeman.

Distracted by what I could see, I dumbly turned and made my way along the street, pausing to stare in astonishment at what was left of our home.

It looked as though a giant hammer had come down through the roof. The neighbouring houses appeared intact apart from some cracked window panes, but my landlady's house lay spilled across the pavement. I stared in disbelief. How could Mrs White possibly be inside there and unhurt. And what about Peter, our fellow tenant? As I approached a fireman stopped me. 'Can't come any closer, sir. There's nothing more to see anyway.'

'Mrs White is inside, my landlady. The police asked me to come. But how the fuck do I get in? And what about Peter Watson? He lives there too.'

'Ah. You're Mr Smith then. She said he's gone down to his club, No one else was in there when it happened. You have to go round the back. They said the back rooms downstairs are pretty much as they were.'

'Christ! What a relief.' I turned and made my way to the narrow alley which ran past the rear of the houses. Another fireman was standing by the open door into the small walled garden and once again I identified myself, this time having to use my office pass for confirmation.

'Right Mr Smith. She's in there - you'll know the way. Try and persuade her to leave pronto. There's a policewoman just gone in to be with her. If that lot of rubble upstairs decides to move, they won't stand a monkey's'.

I looked at the menacing pile of stone heaped above the two cracked windows on the ground floor and shuddered. 'I'll do what I can.'

I gingerly opened the back door and let myself in. The passageway leading to the front door was blocked by a pile of rubble and the air was full of dust. I could hear voices from the small sitting room at the back and I crossed to the open door, tapped and walked in. My landlady, with tears tracking down her dusty cheeks, sat on the couch with a young policewoman at her side. The normally spotless parlour was blanketed with powder. I couldn't help glancing up at the ceiling through the dusty air and was surprised that not a crack marred the smooth face of the plaster.

'Oh Archie! There you are. They said you would come!' My name for once was effortless and natural and Mrs White again burst into tears and held out her arms to me in childlike appeal. I sat down and wrapped my arms round her. 'Oh! Oh!' she wailed into my shoulder and I patted her thin back helplessly, looking over her head to the young policewoman who sat on the other side.

'Come on Mrs Double-u. I know it's bad. But you're OK. And so's Pete Watson they said. Come on. No one's hurt. That looks like a miracle to me.' I spoke quietly and her sobbing lessened. I could see the urgent appeal in the policewoman's eyes and gave the smallest of shrugs.

'It's like the blitz again Archie, when I was a child.' She kept coughing from the dust hanging in the air. 'I never left the house then, except to go to the shelters of course. And I'm not leaving now. It's alright here, isn't it?' She looked up at me for reassurance.

'Have you been outside yet?' I asked.

She stared at me suspiciously. 'No. Why?'

'Because I think if you saw what's resting on that,' and I pointed to the ceiling over our heads, 'I don't think you'd want to stay here much longer.'

A look of terror crossed her face. 'But this is my home! All my things. Mother's china and all. And where could I go? Not into an old people's home. No, I won't go! I can't!' And she began to rock to and fro in misery.

I suddenly remembered her weekly visitor. 'What about your sister? Couldn't you stay with her until they fix this place up again?'

'My sister?' She straightened and looked at me, her tear-stained face brightening. 'Well, yes, I suppose Dolly would take me.'

The policewoman chimed in. 'That sounds a splendid idea Mrs White. You said everything is insured, so they'll sort things out for you until you can come back home. Why don't we go outside and phone your sister now?'

We lifted her to her feet and once at the end of the garden, she turned round and almost collapsed when she saw the damage. We helped her to a waiting police car and I called my landlady's sister right away. She was shocked when I told her what had happened, and demanded to speak to her sister to prove she wasn't hurt. Mrs White wept as she spoke, and very soon nodded her head to us. 'Yes, Dolly wants me to come right away. But how will I get there?' The

35

policewoman said she'd drive her and I thanked that very brave young woman for what she'd done. Leaning into the car I gave my landlady a hug and told her I'd keep in touch as I now had her sister's number.

'God, that's a bloody relief,' the fire officer exclaimed as the car drove away. 'Can't be soon enough for me. I've seen these things too often, sitting there quite stable for an hour or two, then wham! Bloody lot comes crashing down with no warning.'

I looked back towards the house. 'What the fuck happened? Was it a gas explosion or something?'

'The old lady said someone came yesterday to fix the gas boiler upstairs and this afternoon there was a big bang. Some big bang eh?'

I stared again at the ruin of our home and started to brush some of the powder from my clothes.

''fraid you won't salvage much from that lot.' A second fireman nodded towards the rubble. 'We'll do what we can, mind. Photos and things. Sometimes albums can survive. But clothes, well, you won't get much that'll still be wearable. Full of dust and soaked with water.'

'Was there a fire as well?' I asked.

'Only for a few minutes - the roof falling in put it out. But we have to be sure nothing is smouldering so we use the hoses.'

I heaved a sigh. 'Oh well. Stuff's insured. Bloody nuisance though. Jesus, just think of all the shopping.' I paused, taking in the extent of my losses. 'Thanks anyway for all your help with Mrs White. I'd better get back to work. No point hanging round here.'

'Yeah. Well, like I said, we'll save anything we can. Thank Christ you got the old dear to move. Worst combination I know, two old ruins in the same place!' And he laughed wheezily at his joke.

I walked slowly back to the office, needing time to assemble my thoughts. I'd have to organise somewhere else to live. Get some clothes. Toilet stuff. The list bubbled up in my mind, unending. Insurance. I'd better get on to that presently. I looked at my watch, noticing the caked grime on my hands. Ten to five. Maybe Jo had already left the office for home. Then I remembered I had her number and a minute later I was speaking to her.

CHAPTER EIGHT

Several of our colleagues had waited with Jo to find out what had happened. Now they all gathered round me in concern. Offers of a piece of floor to sleep on came from one or two. Then Jo said, 'We've got a spare room you could use until you get fixed up. My flat-mate won't mind,' she added amid wolf-whistles and ribald remarks.

I felt my face clear with relief. 'Well, that'd be great. And thanks boys. I may need to take up your offers too when Jo kicks me out.' I looked down at my dusty clothes. 'Jeez, this is all I now possess! What time do the shops shut?'

'Archie! Don't you live in the real world! There's late night shopping all over the place. But you'd better try and clean yourself up a bit first!'

Someone found a clothes brush and there was a lot of exaggerated coughing as they beat clouds of plaster dust from my trousers, cracking my shins without mercy. I pulled off my sweater and Jo shook it vigorously through an open window and presently we all left the office together.

In her mini, Jo handed me a notebook and pencil. 'Make a list of essentials, Archie. I don't think you're up to a big shopping session this evening!'

I grinned a rueful agreement, my mouth dry with more than dust. 'Thank God I had my own laptop and those certificates in this bag at the office,' and I patted my briefcase as I spoke 'I must go and see old Watson. He's my landlady's other tenant. He's at the Sailor's Rest Club. Goes there every Thursday. What a piece of luck, eh?'

'Right. As soon as we've done your shopping, I'll drop you there and then I'll go along to the deli to get something for supper, and come back to the Club to wait for you. OK?'

I slumped back in the seat and closed my eyes while she slowly filtered the car through the rush hour traffic.

The shopping didn't take long. I bought some boxers, a couple of shirts and some socks. The sweater and trousers I was wearing would do for the moment. Then to the toiletry section for essentials; toothbrush, deodorant and shaving gel. And with the shopping done, off we went to the Sailor's Rest Club. Jo dropped me there and I went inside and asked to see Peter Watson. The receptionist was pleasant and led me to the lounge where Pete was sitting with some of his friends.

He seemed very glad I'd come and after quickly introducing me to his companions, he stood up and took me across to some empty chairs in the bay window. 'Now, tell me exactly what's happened, Archie. I told the police about that chap who came yesterday to fix your boiler. And I'm surprised you didn't tell Mrs White you had a problem. But there… Have you been round our place to see the damage?'

'Oh yes. It's in one hell of a mess. It'll be weeks before it gets fixed. The roof has come down and squashed yours and my rooms dead flat. Just thank Christ you weren't in there Pete. You wouldn't have stood a chance. And I didn't have a problem with my boiler. So I don't understand why a gas bloke called.'

He shook his head. 'Just what I've been wondering about. Anyway, I'll be able to stay here until our place is repaired. But what about Mrs White? Where's she going to stay?'

I told him about Mrs Double-u going off to her sister's and we both grinned at each other, remembering how often they quarrelled. We chatted for about half an hour and then I stood up to leave, holding out my hand to shake his. 'I'll keep in touch with you Pete. And Mrs White will as well, I'm sure.'

He held on to my hand for a moment and as I left, he gave me a watery sort of smile. I ran down the steps from the door of the Club and into the car park and found Jo sitting waiting in the mini.

I was glad to see her and said I was sorry to have been so long.

She shook her head. 'I've only been back here about ten minutes. Queues at the deli checkout were about a mile long. How is the old man?'

'Fine. He's been talking to the police of course and he told them some bloke came yesterday to fix my gas boiler. My boiler! Thing is, there's been nothing wrong with it. What the hell can it mean?'

'Wow! Did the police ask you about it?'

'No. I think they were most concerned with getting Mrs White out.' I frowned. 'They won't know how to get in touch with me this evening.' I gave a little smile. 'I'm glad. I want to try and forget about it for a bit. I'll go and see them tomorrow of course. But why on earth would anyone want to mess with my gas boiler? It doesn't make sense.'

'Wait and see what the fire people come up with. There may be a perfectly simple explanation. Well, here we are, nearly home.' She was turning the car down a leafy cul de sac. 'I'd better warn you about my flat-mate, Gloria. She's a bit of a man-eater. But there, you may like that sort of thing.' Her voice was flat. 'We park round at the back,' and as she spoke she drove round the side of a large Georgian house.

We gathered up all my bags and Jo's groceries and walked into the house. 'Upstairs, first right.' Jo seemed suddenly shy and awkward and I thought perhaps this Gloria might object to my staying and wondered how soon I could raise the matter of paying my way, for however short a stay it might be.

There was a wide hall, an old Persian rug on polished floor boards and an aspidistra on a Victorian stand. As we climbed the stairs, Jo waved her hand at the faded grandeur. 'This all belongs to my mother's aunt. She lives downstairs. The house has been two flats for ages. But she likes having 'family' in the house. Come on. Put all your bags on the bed for the moment.' And she showed me into a small neat room which overlooked the back garden. 'Bathroom's second door along. I'll be in the kitchen.' And she whisked off along the landing.

I took her at her word, dumped the various carrier bags and followed the rattle of pots to the kitchen. This too was old fashioned. A huge ceramic sink stood between wooden draining boards and an old dresser crowded with china took up most of one wall.

'Now, this is what I call a kitchen!' I exclaimed. 'I'm a pretty good cook, you know. If you give me the run of the place, I'll make the dinner.'

She flashed me a smile. 'Great! But come and see the rest of the place first. Get orientated.' And she led me to a large bright sitting room at the rear of the house. There was a motley collection of furniture, big chairs, a chesterfield and a huge sideboard and polished mahogany table.

'This is nice,' I smiled my appreciation.

She walked over to the window. 'The bottom part of the garden gets the sun until late in the summer. Aunt Edie eats out there all the time when it's shining.' The long garden was walled on either side, the grass roughly mown with clumps of fruit bushes and a couple of apple trees. 'That bed by the wall will be a mass of colour in a few weeks time.' Jo's voice was cheerful. 'So nice to look forward to weeks of sunshine.'

'I agree,' I turned from the window and found I was standing near her and wanted to reach out and touch those Titian locks of hers.

'Oh, there's Gloria! She's early.' And Jo ran to open the door for her flatmate. I was disappointed, regretting this sudden invasion of our privacy by a stranger. A tall blonde came into the room, Jo telling her about the explosion and introducing me.

'Oh no! How awful! Let's have a drink then. Not to celebrate of course,' she smiled a wide and practised smile. 'A sympathy toast if you like.' Swiftly she moved to the sideboard and poured two whiskies. 'Wine for you, Jo?'

Jo nodded, smiling and I crossed to her side and clinked my glass against hers and we sipped our drinks while Gloria prattled animatedly from the sofa. Jo told her that I'd offered to cook their meal and Gloria instantly leapt to her feet and insisted on showing me the layout of the kitchen, opening and closing the cupboards busily while Jo remained, silent, in one of the big armchairs in the sitting room.

Gloria lowered her voice. 'She's in one of her quiet moods. She'll be fine again later. It's just over two years since her husband was killed in a crash on the motorway. They hadn't been married long. Most of the time she's OK but every now and then she gets a bit withdrawn.'

I nodded. 'So I've heard. How long have you know her?'

'About six months. She advertised for a flatmate when she came back from Germany. Her family were worried about her being on her own out there when her sister's husband and family were posted to Ireland.'

I muttered a reply and started preparing the vegetables. Gloria kept up her constant chatter with a total disregard to my lack of response. Perhaps she thought I was concentrating on the cooking, but I was once again moved by Jo's story. She seemed so young and vulnerable to be left on her own. I wondered briefly how I'd feel when she went from my life and was startled by the pang which shot through me at the thought.

Soon the stir-fry was ready, and I piled the egg noodles onto hot plates. 'Damn! I forgot to set the table! That's what comes of living alone!' I gave a rueful grin.

'It's alright, the table's laid.' Jo stood in the doorway smiling at us both. 'I gathered everything was ready from the smell. Come on, I've already uncorked the wine.'

We sat at the oval table where the glasses were reflected in the gleam of the polished surface. I was glad my cooking had come up to scratch and Gloria's prattle was silenced for a while as we ate. Presently Jo fetched fruit from the sideboard and cheese from the pantry and Gloria made coffee and we sat for a long time over the remains of the meal. By mutual consent none of us mentioned the explosion and the reason for my presence in the flat, but I kept getting flash-backs to the dust and rubble of my landlady's shattered home. And wondered about the mysterious gas fitter who'd come un-summoned to fix that boiler...

'Hm?' Gloria had repeated a question.

'I'm sorry. I'm not a good guest. I was wondering about all the things I have to do, flat-hunting and shopping and so on,' I finished lamely.

'Jo said you're taking some time off next week. I'll come and help with your shopping one day if you like. Steer you to all the best shops. I know just the sort of shirts you should wear,' and she gave me a hundred watt smile. I wondered how she'd managed to keep that bright lipstick on throughout the meal. Jo's lips were pale.

I frowned. 'That's part of the problem. I have business in St. Hayes next week.' I saw Jo's head come up, her eyes bright with interest. 'And meantime I must arrange somewhere to live until my landlady's place is fixed.'

'Don't worry about that, Archie. You can stay here for as long as it takes to find somewhere. Can't he Gloria?' She turned to her flatmate.

'Oh yes!' There was no mistaking Gloria's enthusiasm and I knew my dream of a brief idyll with Jo was not to be.

But I had a sudden idea, a way to get Gloria off my back. As the three of us rose to clear the table, I crossed to Jo's side and put my arms round her. 'Jo, sweetheart, sit down. I'll do this.' I felt her stiffen in my arms and as I smiled down at her, I gave her the slightest of winks and bent my head to kiss her cheek. I was rewarded by the look of disappointment on Gloria's face as I turned, but I'd also seen a warm flush rise in Jo's cheeks and found the brief embrace had set my own pulses racing.

I released her and went to the table to stack the plates methodically. Gloria had got the message and I was left alone in the kitchen where I cleaned up with practised thoroughness, thinking all the while. I was dangerously close to falling in love. It had never happened before. I'd had brief liaisons of course; but always with the knowledge there was no commitment on either side, and always with the sort of girls who were looking for nothing more than a brief fling, an expensive holiday, an amusing interlude. Never had I allowed myself to become emotionally involved.

I stacked the dried dishes neatly. I had no family, no past. No plans to go into the future other than alone. As a child I'd found that if I cared for someone I'd end up being hurt; friends vanished overnight, staff changed, surroundings altered. It was safer to be alone, unattached, inside a carapace of indifference. But now... This girl had got behind my defences. And the other fear rose in my mind; the fear of my unknown origins. I remembered a woman at Wilton Hall talking to someone else, oblivious of me, the child sitting beside the door. 'Of course, you never know where they've come from, do you, these kids? Fathers and mothers could be murderers, madmen, crooks, anything. 'Cos they'd never have abandoned them in the first place, would they, if they'd been normal, like?'

They were old remarks, old questions and I knew that until now they'd served to keep me in my solitary state. And I could see how cold and cheerless they'd made my childhood. Merciless. But even now they were valid in a way. If only finding out about my namesake could change my whole outlook on life...

CHAPTER NINE

Gloria had switched the television to her favourite TV comedy and it served to cover my silence though I did try to join in now and then with the canned studio audience laughter. Then there was the news. When I glanced at Jo I had the feeling that she too welcomed the neutral territory of the programmes we were half-heartedly watching.

Soon after eleven I pleaded fatigue and went to the room Jo had prepared for me. Presently I lay in the bed, hands behind my head, glancing at my surroundings. A pleasant room, cell-like in its smallness but feminine touches showed in the flowered curtains and the prints which broke the bareness of the walls. A room like many others I'd known; a room where deliberate effort had been made to welcome a transient passing guest.

I read for a while, one of the paperbacks that had thoughtfully been left on the bedside table, and at last felt behind my eyes the prickle of tiredness that heralded sleep. I put out the light and let the hum of distant traffic lull me to oblivion.

It was the dream again. I woke sweating and rigid with terror. I forced my tense muscles to relax but still could not dispel the desolation that steeped my body. I listened. No sounds from either of the girls' rooms, only the occasional purr of a motor along a distant street. I strained to hear - dreaded to hear - the echo of the question that had screamed through the nightmare of my sleep. But there was nothing, nothing in the silence but my heartbeat and the in-drawing of my breath.

When I was eleven, this same dream had driven me from my bed, from the Hall, sent me running, falling, down the gravelled drive, down to the main road. That time I'd been brought back by a worried taxi driver; a small, muddy, bloodstained and bewildered kid with gravel rash on my hands and knees. That was the second time, after the episode on the balcony. That was why they'd got the doctor - psychiatrist - I now supposed. It didn't help of course. I could tell them nothing. Just this awful empty dream and the words I couldn't catch, the desperate search for something undisclosed.

To hell with this. I reached for the light switch. I was not eleven now. The lampshade cast a dark shadow on the ceiling, a swathe of light across the unfamiliar room. I clasped my hands behind my head again and stared at the flowered curtains.

They'd put me on tranquillisers after that. Until my friend, Edith the cook, made them get me a bike. 'Chuck those tablets away,' she'd told me. 'They won't know. What you need is plenty of exercise. Cycle to school. Do you good.' And the dream hadn't recurred so much then, and never so intensely except for a spell in my late teens. And now tonight.

I found my body was tense again, taut with suppressed fear. Once more I consciously relaxed my muscles. This was the worst part of the dream, this awful hangover of emptiness and loss.

What could have triggered it? Not the girl. Surely not Jo. Perhaps the destruction of the flat? But I'd no great attachment to anything I'd lost; my music perhaps and books. But they could be replaced. And there'd been plenty of other times I'd experienced sudden drama and stress and had no nightmares then.

I sat up and thumped the pillow, turned on my side

and lay down again. I kept the light on. Lying there I thought with longing of the days when I'd smoked; to focus on a familiar ritual, the removal of the cigarette from the packet. The satisfying click of the lighter, the smell of freshly burning tobacco, the first inhaling of smoke... My mouth felt dry.

A cup of tea. That too would be an old ritual, comforting in its familiarity. Why not? Jo's kitchen was just along the landing from my room. I swung out of the narrow bed and padded off on bare feet.

The switch in the kitchen clicked loudly and I closed the door to contain the light. I looked at my watch. Two thirty. I must be careful not to wake the girls, particularly the voracious Gloria.

Quietly I held the kettle under the tap, filled it and plugged it in. The hollow roar began and I could feel the kettle's busy vibration through my hands as I leaned on the worktop. I tried consciously to concentrate on the present, to push away from myself the horror, those lonely caverns of darkness and fog, the essence of the dream from which I'd just escaped.

There was a movement at the door and startled, I turned. Jo stood there, blinking at the light, her hair a tangled mop, cream satin dressing gown carelessly drawn together at her waist. She looked at me with concern. 'Are you OK? I heard you come in here.' She noticed the kettle beginning to steam, 'Oh, good idea. I'll have a cup too.'

I forced a grin. 'Sorry if I woke you. I tried to be quiet but I woke up with a raging thirst.' I certainly wasn't going to talk about my recurring bloody nightmare.

'No problem. I wasn't asleep anyway.' She ladled tea into a small brown pot and poured in the boiling water, took two mugs from the shelf and set them on the table with the teapot alongside and pulled out two chairs.

48

'D'you want a biscuit?'

'No thanks,' I shook my head. 'Late to be still awake isn't it?' and I nodded to the clock on the wall.

She didn't look up, staring at the spoon with which she stirred her tea. 'I don't sleep very well. Haven't since Richard... since I lost Richard.'

I felt a wave of compassion sweep over me, noticing how she avoided the finality of 'since Richard died'. 'You didn't live here then, did you?'

'No. After the accident I went home for a while but I couldn't take it. His parents live in the village. He was their only son. They clung to me. We'd always been friends, you see. From toddlers. In and out of each other's houses. I've got two brothers and a sister and Richard was an extra - a special playmate even as a child. When we fell in love...' She stopped and held her mug carefully in both hands, elbows on the table, head bent. 'So I just had to get away. To a place where people didn't keep looking at me like they did at home. To escape from seeing his grieving parents...' She sipped her tea.

'You went to Germany?' I kept the question quiet and impersonal.

'Yes. My sister was there with her family. Rupert, her husband is in the army. She made me find some work. Which is easy when you have languages.'

'Must be interesting, working in several places like you do.' Still on safe ground.

'I like it. Like the variety. And free-lancing gives you freedom too, the chance to take a quick holiday or something.' She looked at me directly. 'David Phillips let everyone at the office know I'm a widow. At other places I just let them think my husband is away.'

'How long is it now?'

'Two years and three months. We were both twenty-four. We'd been married just over a year.' I could hear the bruise in her voice.

'Poor kids,' I muttered slowly.

She looked up, noticing the plural. 'At least you didn't make some trite remark like a lot of people do when they find out.' We shared a weak grin.

'Do you still see his parents?'

'Oh yes. Whenever I go home. Thank God his sister has just had a baby. It keeps them busy. That and raising money for charity.'

I sat quietly drinking the tea. Her story touched me deeply. Presently I spoke. 'At least you've had something real and good in your life.' She looked up at me, puzzled. 'A bond, if you like,' I went on. 'I've never known that. Of course it has two sides - you're paying the price now. Paying for the loss.'

She sipped her tea, swallowing hard. Perhaps it was the hour, the night hour, the pair of us encapsulated in a sleeping world, but I was swept by compassion for her. I wanted to put my arms round her, hold her like I'd held my old landlady, to hold her close for comfort.

She put down her cup and raised her head to look at me. 'We shouldn't be talking of this.' She made a visible effort. 'You've got problems enough of your own.'

Then I did reach out and put my hand on hers. 'Jo. There's no comparison'. The hand beneath mine moved and I released her. She stood up, not looking at me as she picked up the mugs and took them to the sink. I followed her, teapot in hand and placed it on the work surface. The soft shiny material of her gown followed the lines of her body as she moved and with a suddenness that took me by surprise, I was ablaze with desire. I watched her move about the kitchen, here and there as if loathe to leave.

At last, as she came towards me, towards the door, I said, 'Thank you so much for all you've done for me, Jo' and I put my arm round her shoulder and bent my head to give her a chaste kiss. But she'd turned her head and our lips met. And met again. As we drew away, her eyes met mine and I saw recognition in their smoky grey depths, and surprise, and something else. Her gown revealed the flimsy nightdress clinging to the generous curve of her breast and with a catch of my breath my hand enfolded the silken curve and as I drew her towards me, her arms crept round me too. We clung together and after a while, she whispered, 'Gloria might come.'

In response I moved with her to the door and clicked off the noisy light switch. Holding her close, I whispered, 'Can I... Can you?' and her head against my shoulder nodded. In close embrace we slowly made our way to her room at the front of the house. Soft light from the street below illumined the room, the shape of the furniture, the expanse of the turned-down bed.

'I have to fetch...' I murmured into her neck and reluctantly pulled myself away. I went swiftly to my bedroom and fumbled around for the packet I'd bought along with my toilet things, bought on a sudden impulse of wishful thought. But I cursed the delay, desperate lest she should have changed her mind by the time I reached her again.

But she had not. She was lying on the bed, nightdress and gown in a silken heap on the carpet. She stretched out her pale arms and I sent my pyjamas, new-smelling and crisp, to join hers and let myself down into that eager embrace. There was the exquisite shock of her skin against mine, the fierce merging of our mouths and presently, the slow fusing of our bodies.

Then there was no outside world, no past griefs or

enigmas, no future uncertainty; there was only here, only now, only the two of us, only the one of us.

When at last we separated, barely moving, I held her against my shoulder and we didn't speak. But later I felt her tears on my skin and I said nothing but stroked her hair and moved my face against her wet cheek.

We slept. And later, when the early morning traffic preceded the dawn, we woke and we were more fierce, more controlled and when we fell back in mutual exhaustion, a look of startled wonder on Jo's face replaced the tears of the night.

Curled together like a pair of contented puppies we dozed until the ringing of Jo's alarm clock brought us reluctantly once more into the world of the present.

All three of us breakfasted on the hoof as we hurriedly got ready for work, Gloria seeming oblivious to the feeling between Jo and me. There was a stolen moment while she was in the bathroom when I took Jo into my arms and held her close. Neither of us spoke, both somehow shy, uncertain about this fierce new emotion. And I felt Jo was relieved when we heard Gloria unlock the bathroom door and I reluctantly released her.

We all left the house together and set off for work, Gloria in her sports car, and Jo in her mini. I was to catch the bus at the top of the cul de sac. Jo was on a different contract today and once again I felt she was glad, in a way, because she needed to put distance between us. But her spare key nestled in my pocket and there was the evening to look forward to. And perhaps, the night. And I walked briskly up the road to the bus stop.

CHAPTER TEN

As I walked into the office, Tim, the firm's newest recruit greeted me. 'Ah, there you are at last. The phone was ringing when I got here half an hour ago. It was the police. They want you down at the station ASAP.'

I expected that so I opened my briefcase and took out a sheaf of papers. 'Right. I'd better find out what's happening. Take a look through these papers, Tim. Specially the ones on French Guyana. You'll need to be up to the minute on their regulations. I shouldn't be long.'

'Don't worry Archie. We'll get you a good lawyer and bail you out,' Tim yelled at my retreating back and I gave him a two-fingered salute as I entered the lift.

'I'm Detective Inspector Green and this is Detective Sergeant French. Sit down, Mr Smith.' The middle-aged officer extended his hand, a burly man and happy with his bulk, heavy lidded eyes half closed. The other officer was young, straining at the leash in his enthusiasm as the three of us settled down in the tiny office.

'We've had a word with the Fire Department and they brought us a few interesting bits and pieces.' As he spoke, Green opened a plastic bag and produced some scraps of twisted metal. 'Recognise any of this, Mr Smith?'

I could see at once that there on the desk were the remains of a timing mechanism. 'Christ!' The exclamation was involuntary.

'Exactly! An incendiary device Mr Smith. Now who could want to do this to you?' The heavy-lidded eyes bored into me.

I shook my head. The idea that the explosion might not be an accident had been niggling at me ever since Mrs White's remark about the gas fitter, but the confirmation winded me. Who would do this? And why?

'I believe you are an engineer, Mr Smith,' the younger man leaned back in his chair, elbows on the arm rests, fingers steepled. 'Do you handle explosives in the course of your work?'

'From time to time, yes. Not personally, but I know the procedures.'

The young detective rocked farther back on his chair and I willed it to tip. There was a wobble and then the crash of the chair legs hitting the floor. The older man's eyes gleamed but he said nothing.

'Ah. You "know the procedure".' I couldn't place which TV cop's mannerisms this young one was imitating; whoever, it needled me.

'I'm thirty, Sergeant. I imagine most fourteen year old boys will also know the procedure.'

'Ah.'

The implication was too much. 'Listen! Why the fuck should I blow up my home! Everything I own has gone. Not to mention old Watson downstairs could have been killed as well as my landlady. I've lived there with them for years. Just you tell me why you think I'd go out one day, buy the gear and blast the bloody place to hell and back!'

'Suppose you were the target, Mr Smith.' Inspector Green's voice was quiet.

'Me!' I shook my head. 'And anyway, I'm never there in the daytime.'

The senior officer picked up one of the scraps of metal. 'Forensics say it was a digital timer. And we

54

know it went off at fifteen hundred hours. Three o'clock in the afternoon. Now suppose whoever set it up meant it to go off at o-three hundred hours, the middle of the night. Suppose they got muddled over this twenty-four hour clock.'

I blew out my cheeks. 'Long shot that, surely?'

Green's smile creased his chubby cheeks. 'Wouldn't be the first time in my experience.'

A signal must have passed between the two officers because the young one now spoke, leaning forward earnestly. 'Think very carefully before you answer, Mr Smith. Can you think of anyone who might bear you a grudge. You hire and fire, I believe, in the course of your work. Anyone you sacked lately? Cast your mind back. Think.'

I stared at my hands. Presently I spoke. 'Last ones I sacked were a couple of non-English-speaking natives in the Brazilian jungle. They had rings in their noses.' I aimed my flippancy to the younger man. 'Oh yes, and there's a little shit of an excise officer at Heathrow. I had a go at him too when I got back last week from Africa.'

'What about insurance?' It was the comeback kid again, sarcasm bouncing off his hide.

'Insurance? Yes. My things were insured. But nothing of any real value.'

'What about life insurance? On yourself.'

I spoke slowly. 'Well yes, all of us engineers are well covered. In case of accidents. But…'

'And who would benefit from your death?' the young officer flourished a pen in anticipation.

'Hm. There's the NSPCC. And Barnardo's Homes. And a couple of others I can't remember offhand.' I enjoyed the young policeman's discomfiture. I'd no intention of mentioning my dear friend Edith.

The senior detective suddenly grinned. 'This isn't getting us very far. Let us know what your movements will be over the next couple of weeks so we can get in touch.' And he too reached for a biro.

I frowned. 'I'm not too sure. I shall be going to St. Hayes in Cornwall sometime soon. And possibly to Glynwood.' And in reply to the unasked question, I went on, 'I'm doing some research into my background.'

Detective Inspector Green used his silence as a probe. The slight warning gesture of his hand had stilled the other officer's tongue. After a lengthy pause, I went on. 'There was this advert in the paper. Strange co-incidence. I want to follow it up.' And I pulled out my wallet and unfolded the cutting.

Both officers looked at it and compared the names. The older one spoke. 'What have you done about it so far?'

I shrugged. 'Got in touch with the Treasury Solicitor. No help there. And I went to St. Hayes and got a copy of the death certificate. Phoned his housekeeper and spoke to her.'

Those hooded eyes searched mine. 'What did she tell you, the housekeeper.'

I shook my head. 'Said she would pass on my enquiry, something like that.'

'And when was this?'

I thought back. 'About three weeks ago. I had to come right back from the town to go on an emergency trip to Africa. I've still got a few bits and pieces to sort out at the office, but when I've done that I'm going off to St. Hayes again to ferret around the place a bit.' I frowned again. 'This bloody explosion has buggered things up completely. But I still intend to go.'

'You've heard nothing since from this housekeeper?'

I shook my head. 'I didn't think I would. She wasn't exactly forthcoming.'

'Do you know the size of this man's estate?'

Once more I shook my head. 'I can't imagine anyone telling me that, can you? Me with nothing to go on except the co-incidence of a name.'

Inspector Green nodded. 'Fine. Let's write down the address of this place you're going to in Cornwall; St. Hayes, Keyes Lane House. And now you may as well be off. I don't have to remind you to get in touch with us if you think of anything. Here, take my card.'

He came with me to the door and held out his hand while the younger policeman remained at the desk. 'Good luck with your search.'

But as I ran down the steps to the street, I could feel those gimlet eyes on my back and wondered just what was going through the officer's head.

Walking back along the street, I suddenly stopped and gave a quick laugh. I'd just remembered the big bag of washing I'd taken to the local laundrette a couple of days ago. My heart lifted; a pair of chinos, some shirts and tee shirts and shorts from my African trip, and a sweatshirt. Plus underwear of course. Great. What a relief. I swung round and made a detour and collected the bag of laundry on my way back to the office.

I was greeted with jeers and teasing about escaping from the police station, but my colleagues were all keen to know exactly what had happened and they were every bit as mystified as I was about who could have blown up my flat. The bosses were also concerned and when I told them I'd need a couple of days off soon, they swiftly agreed.

I remembered Jo saying she was going home to her parents after work on Thursday and I'd no intention of staying in the flat with Gloria on the prowl. So I said

I'd like to take Thursday and Friday off and would probably be back by Monday. How would that fit in with things? Plenty of reassurance from everyone, so I quickly settled down to get on with my work but my thoughts of Jo and of our night together kept overwhelming me and I had to pull myself together to concentrate once more.

When I left work I took a taxi to the Seaman's Club to see my old neighbour again. Peter Watson was cheerful, the centre of attention and apparently enjoying every minute of his stay. But as I left, the old man asked if the police had solved anything yet. And could he have Mrs White's sister's number so he could talk to Mrs W. I gave him the number from my phone and he looked quite cheerful as I left.

As soon as I could I made my way back to Jo's flat. Neither of the girls was back yet, so after I'd dumped my laundry bag in the kitchen I phoned Mrs White, my landlady. I gave her an update on Peter Watson and on the insurance people and during our chat, I told her I'd be going away for a few days but would get in touch with her again as soon as I got back. She seemed loathe to end our conversation but told me she was determined to get the house rebuilt as soon as she could make them settle everything. She did add it might be nice to have a more modern kitchen and I could give her any ideas I might have about my attic flat. When I hung up, I was smiling because she was no longer that terrified old lady I'd helped into the police car.

I hunted for Jo's ironing board and found the iron and set about sorting through the laundry bag. Gloria arrived before Jo which made my heart sink, but as soon as I finished my ironing, I'd a good excuse to put away my clothes. Back in my bedroom I changed into an old familiar sweatshirt and the pair of chinos. I looked at the time and wondered how long it would be before Jo came home. I was very glad I'd arranged to leave on Thursday morning and not have to cope with more time alone with Gloria. Remembering I'd need to hire a car again, I phoned the firm me and my colleagues used, and arranged to pick up the car on Wednesday evening. Tomorrow evening, I reminded myself.

Ten minutes later I heard Jo come up the stairs and I quickly left my bedroom and met her on the landing. We met with a brief kiss and then joined Gloria in the kitchen. It was her turn to cook this evening so Jo and I sat together on the sofa and I brought her up to date with the day's events.

'So you're going off on Thursday morning, just as I set off for work?' she laughed. 'Good. I'm glad you're going to track things down. That housekeeper woman has obviously done nothing. They're OK at the office about you taking time off?'

I nodded. 'I'm due leave anyway. And it might be a month or so before a job comes up that I want.' I smiled. 'I've been with them long enough to be able to pick and choose. Unless it's an emergency of course.' And I suddenly wondered how I'd feel about being away from Jo for several months at a time. Wondered how she would feel. And felt the old taboos crowding in from the shadow.

Gloria called out from the kitchen that the meal was ready and it was a relief to be snapped out of my musing. Thankfully, as soon as the meal was over, Gloria announced that she had a date and would be late back and probably a bit late getting up in the morning. 'And as you're going to be leaving early on Thursday, you'd better kiss me goodbye now, Archie.' She pressed her sinuous body against me while Jo retreated into the kitchen.

'Bye then Gloria. See you when I get back,' and I disengaged myself and waved her down the stairs. 'Phew! What does she do for a living, Jo? No. Don't tell me,' I interrupted as she opened her mouth to speak.

Jo laughed, then. 'Right, what shall we do this evening?'

I couldn't help myself. I put my arms round her and held her. Such a different embrace from Gloria's suggestive squeeze. But I felt Jo's reluctance and held her away. 'Something wrong, Jo?'

Tawny eyelashes masked her eyes. 'It's just... Oh, I don't know. I feel so... guilty.'

I said nothing, my hands still on her shoulders.

'I hardly know you. It's only been a few weeks. And then, last night...'

'You're thinking about your Richard, aren't you?'

She nodded and a tear trickled down the freckled cheeks. 'I loved him so much. I still do. So how can I...?'

This time she didn't resist when I drew her to me. 'Of course you love him. You always will. Any man who comes into your life will have to get used to that.' And as I spoke I knew I easily could; that the young man who'd shared her childhood would pose no threat to me.

She pulled a tissue from the sleeve of her shirt and blew her nose. 'I still feel it's all too...fast.'

I nodded. 'Plenty of time, Jo. And we're both going away on Thursday. Time for us both to sort things out. Yes?'

Now she too nodded and straightened her slim shoulders. 'Come on. Let's go out.'

And though I'd have preferred to stay in the flat, I

went along with her and couldn't fault the small pub where she took me. We talked a lot; about her parents who ran a small post office, about her brothers and her sister's family. She asked me how my neighbours were coping and together we listed the places I should call at, in St. Hayes. I was grateful for a suggestion she made to find the solicitors who were dealing with my namesake's estate. And to call at the iron foundry of course. Time flew, and when we unlocked the door of her flat, Jo's kiss was the invitation I'd hoped for; an invitation to her room, to her bed, and to her slender infinitely desirable body.

CHAPTER ELEVEN

Next day I was kept busy in the office. I was glad to see Gordon back at work, his wife and baby at home now, and thriving. Everyone still wanted to hear anything new I could tell them about the explosion, and I could see they also wanted to know why I was going away for a couple of days. I simply told them I was doing some research into my family background and changed the subject and we all settled back to our work.

When I left, I collected my hire car from the garage, this time a red Fiat 500 with a black stripe. I parked it round the back of Jo's aunt's house and saw that neither she nor Gloria were there yet. Upstairs, I took out my phone and had a long chat with my old friend Edith. As I said goodbye to her I felt that familiar lump in my throat remembering how much she'd done for me when I was a child. She'd been the only adult I felt I could trust, and she too, who seemed not to want close contact with many of the children who passed through The Hall, put herself out for me alone. She had made sure I took my place at the best comprehensive school in the next town. The manager wasn't prepared to give me a lift, although he drove into that town each day to drop his son at the private school around the corner from where I needed to go. Edith had insisted I was given a new bicycle to ride in; only five miles, she'd said. You can do it. And so I did, never getting a lift from the manager, regardless of the weather. And as soon as I was sixteen and about to study for my A levels, I was told my time was up at the Hall. Once more Edith came to the rescue. She asked an old friend of hers to take me in as a lodger, and was pleased when

I got an engineering apprenticeship in a nearby factory. Because I was such a loner, I spent much of my spare time studying and by the time my apprenticeship was up I also had an open university degree which made it much easier to get a well paid job.

I shook myself out of my reverie and when Jo came home we had time for a close embrace before setting about cooking the evening meal. When I saw Jo standing in front of the sink, I couldn't resist crossing the room and wrapping my arms round her waist and pressing her against my chest. She too, enjoyed leaning back in my arms and pulled my head down for a kiss. Gloria's arrival however, made us get on with our work though we kept exchanging smiling glances. Luckily, Gloria had another date and went off and we made our meal together and spent the rest of the evening snuggled together on the couch.

Before we went off to bed, I set about packing my new holdall ready for the trip to St. Hayes and suddenly remembered the charger of my mobile phone had been lost in the explosion of my flat. I'd have to get a new one but in case the mobile ran out before I got one, I made a list of some of the numbers I had on my phone. Jo gave me her home number as well, and I jotted down Mrs White's sister's number as well as Peter Watson's.

Another evening. Another night together. And then the next day arrived.

At seven o'clock in the morning, Jo came down with me to the car. She was in a scarlet fleece robe, and stood shivering slightly in the coolness of the spring morning as I threw my holdall on to the back seat. She handed me her AA book. 'You may need this, Archie, you haven't got a sat nav in this car.'

'Thanks Jo.' I could find nothing else to say. I'd never

known a parting like this. I reached out.

'You have to go,' she spoke against my chest.

'I know.' My own voice was curiously taut. 'I... I just hate having to leave you.' There was such surprise in my voice that Jo gave a shaky laugh. 'I wish you were coming too,' I muttered.

She disentangled herself. 'I'll join you next week if you're still away from work. As long as you give me time to arrange things.'

'Would you? D'you mean it?' I released her, suddenly cheerful. 'I'll hold you to that. And now I'd better be off. A wild goose chase if ever there was, but wish me luck anyway, Josephine Laura.'

'I do, Archie. I really do wish you luck.' She was nodding her red mane sagely. 'And I've a feeling you're going to get somewhere too. And don't forget you've got my home number in case you need to call me and your mobile isn't working.'

Now it was easy to climb into the car and wave casually and drive off, while the bright figure standing on the sunny pavement grew smaller and smaller in the wing mirror until I'd turned the corner and was alone once more.

The morning sun had vanished by the time I reached St. Hayes. It was twelve o'clock. I pulled into the large car park where I'd stopped last time and as soon as I'd paid and displayed the parking ticket, I set off.

I hardly glanced at my surrounding as I strode along the main street. The ancient buildings and carefully kept pavements passed in a blur. I was looking for a solicitor's office. Any solicitors. In an old town like this there were probably several. I'd try them all in turn. Someone must be able to tell me something.

And at the third attempt I struck gold. The usual spiel

64

to the receptionist, 'Can I see the person who is dealing with the affairs of the late Archibald Ensor Gregory Smith?'

And this time the young girl simply said, 'Just a moment. I'll see if Mr Evelyn is free. Who shall I say wishes to see him?'

'Smith,' I replied. 'Same name.'

She was soon back. 'Mr Evelyn is with a client at the moment. If you like to wait, he shouldn't be very long,' and she waved me to a chair in the waiting room.

It was a long fifteen minutes. And with every passing second I felt more foolish. What on earth could I say?

A buzzer sounded and the girl came towards me. 'This way please, Mr Smith.' She took me up a flight of wide, shallow stairs, opened a door and introduced me to the man seated at the huge oak desk. He stood up, a tall thin man, and stretched out his hand, peering through thick glasses. 'And what may I do for you, Mr Smith?'

I grinned wryly. 'I'm not sure you can do anything, Mr Evelyn. But this is what I've come about.' I took the newspaper cutting from my wallet and laid it on his desk, then placed my birth certificate alongside, still thankful that it had been with the other papers in my briefcase at the office and not blown to shreds by the explosion.

The solicitor glanced from one piece of paper to the other. His gaze sharpened as he read the birth certificate and then he looked up. 'Good Lord!' He picked up the certificate and read it again. 'Parents unknown?'

I nodded. 'All I know is that I was left in a hospital foyer; Glynwood Hospital, in Devon, on the day I was born. Or so they assumed.'

'Glynwood. That's about a hundred miles from here, in Cornwall.' He looked at the date on the birth certificate. 'You're thirty. I expect you are thinking you're an illegitimate son, or something.'

'Something like that. How else would I have been given such a name?' I explained the note pinned to the infant's shawl. Then I produced the other baby's birth certificate. 'It was even more of a coincidence that another child should have been born the same day to my namesake.'

The solicitor exclaimed in astonishment. 'Good God! I remember something about that now. Before I joined the firm of course.' He frowned. 'But what I can't understand is why they didn't advertise about the baby from the hospital. Gregory Smith is a well-known name in this area. I should have thought someone would have picked up on it. At least made some enquiries.'

'I contacted the hospital years ago, looking for clues,' I replied. 'I asked them if they'd made any attempt to trace my mother. They said of course they'd put a piece in the local paper at the time. But unfortunately, the night I was found there was a bus crash locally. It had gone over a bridge. Lots of people died and were injured. They were rushed off their feet at the hospital for days. And I suppose one small paragraph in a paper full of tragic stories didn't stand that much of a chance.

The solicitor reached for his telephone. 'Look, I'm going to ring my father. It was he who dealt with the Gregory Smith affairs. He's had to retire due to ill health, but as he's no longer practising, he may be able to help you. Unfortunately, I can't tell you anything. Client confidentiality you know. But Dad, well, he may be able to give you a few pointers; he'd be able to tell you any bits of gossip or such that he's heard. I find this intriguing. He will too. His name is Geoffery Evelyn.' He spoke briefly, affectionately, into the receiver and then turned to me as he replaced the phone. 'Dad will be glad to see you. Here, I'll draw you a map. Quite easy to find. You've got a car?'

And twenty minutes later I parked the car on a sweep of gravel before a large mock Tudor house. The housekeeper showed me into a conservatory where bougainvillaea flourished in the warm humidity and it took me a moment or two to see the old man seated in a chair behind a huge palm.

'Sit down, young man and tell me this strange story my son said was coming my way. Then I'll tell you all I legally may.' Keen eyes inspected me as I told my tale and fished out the papers and handed them across to be examined. Presently the old man looked up. 'Now, young sir. I can't pretend to understand what this is all about. But if you're thinking you're Greg Smith's illegitimate son, you're barking up the wrong tree. Greg was never interested in women until he fell in love with Sylvia. She was his secretary. A lovely girl, much younger than him. But he was the most honourable of men. If he had started an affair, which I very much doubt, he would never have let the girl down. Never let anyone down.'

'You don't think I could have been a twin of the baby who died?'

'No, no. That child was born in the nursing home in Conborough. And you were found many miles away. And why on earth would that have been?'

I smiled ruefully. 'Of course. It's just a long shot I know.'

The old man looked very grave. 'I can see why you want to ask around. I would too if I were in your shoes.'

I got to my feet and held out my hand. 'Thanks, Mr Evelyn for seeing me. At least you've explained why I can't be Greg Smith's child.'

The old man held on to my hand. 'I certainly don't think you could be, but there, I don't know everything. You could try calling at Greg's foundry, though I can't for the life of me see what they can tell you. If you do go there, ask for Barrymore, he's the work's manager.'

'Thanks for that. I thought I'd call there when I heard about the place. As you say, it's not very likely they can help, but I will drop in there. Someone said it's not far from the town car park?'

'Just a couple of hundred yards. But don't forget to put a ticket in your car. They don't miss much there. And I wish you all the luck you are going to need, young man.'

CHAPTER TWELVE

Back in the car, my thoughts were confused. Two babies born the same day! One dead. One abandoned. Linked only by a name. Twin! What a daft bloody thing to say when I was found about a hundred miles away from the place where the other child was born.

I drove back towards the town. If only I could get it out of my head, the feeling that I was the dead man's son. Wishful thinking of course. The old need for an identity.

I parked the car and made my way up the street until I reached the foundry. I stood for a minute, staring up at the name over the doorway. My name...GREGORY. It was an old building, a Victorian relic but it gave me a funny feeling. One of my names on a foundry! I found a door which opened on to a passageway and went inside, the engineer in me interested in having a look round despite my preoccupation.

The passageway took me into a large high-roofed space. There was a flimsy looking staircase at one end leading to a set of wooden offices which overlooked the working area where I stood. Several men were busy, one stoking a great furnace, others pouring molten metal into moulds. Marked areas in the floor were covered with sand and I knew that under them would lie cooling metal in large moulds. The men ignored me, intent on their work.

I headed for the stairs where I could see an 'Enquiries' sign in one of the windows. On the way I paused once or twice, intrigued by the work in hand. I stopped to look at a large empty mould, stooping forward, thumbs in my trouser pockets. Then I turned.

A man was standing on the stairs, on his way down, but now standing very still and staring hard at me. An elderly man with a thin lined face.

I straightened up and went up the steps towards him. 'Are you Mr Barrymore, the manager, sir?'

The man nodded impatiently. 'Reg Barrymore. Yes. And who might you be?'

He'd come down the last steps and we stood face to face. I looked into a pair of sunken eyes which stared back, sharp and unflinching. Suddenly a twinkle appeared and a slight smile. 'Better come up above. Can't talk here, too many distractions.' His gaze passed over the working men, missing nothing. 'Come on.' He turned and climbed back up the stairs, pulling on the handrail for assistance.

I followed. The staircase was firmer than it looked. At the top we went into a shabby office. Invoices and papers hung on hooks from the ceiling and box files were stacked on shelves along the walls. I felt it was an orderly and efficient place and this man would be able to put his hand on anything he needed. 'Well then, who might you be?' the manager repeated.

The sense of hopelessness swept over me again, unexpected and unwelcome. I spread my hands emptily. 'I wish I knew.' I gave a twisted grin.

'Sit down.' The manager's eyes never left my face as he fumbled in his pocket and pulled out a tube of peppermints. He offered me one and took one himself.

I popped the sweet into my mouth and pulled out my driving licence. 'There. That's what they call me.'

Barrymore read it with some interest and handed it back. 'You're a relation then? Something to do with Mr Duncan?'

'I don't know. I've only just recently heard of Mr Duncan and I was told he died before I was born. I was

70

found, abandoned as a baby. With that name pinned on a label.'

'What!' There was concern and sympathy in the man's voice. 'Where was that?'

'A hospital. Glynwood Hospital. It's way north of here, in Devon, they tell me.'

'Yes. Yes. I know that. Go on.'

Once again I took out the crumpled newspaper cutting. 'When I saw this,' I handed it to the manager, 'I started making enquiries. And now I just want to find out a bit more. See if there is some connection. Some reason for my name.'

'I should think you would be curious.' The older man spoke slowly and thoughtfully. 'I'll tell you straight, I'm not in the habit of passing information - ask any of the men. But when I saw you down there looking at that Turner mould, I thought I was seeing things.' He shook his head. 'You had the stance of Mr Gregory, the very stance. There's got to be some connection. I'd believe it if you were Mr Duncan's son. He was that sort. Different as chalk and cheese from Mr Gregory. But there, you found out he died before you were born. How old are you then?'

'Thirty. I was born in 1986.'

'What!' he exclaimed. 'That was the year *their* baby was born. The year I started work here. So you're right, you couldn't be Mr Duncan's.' He shook his head regretfully. 'He died a couple of years before that. We always felt that's what made Mr Gregory decide to get married. So he could have someone to pass the business on to. But there's no more family that I know of. And the solicitors have been advertising for quite a while with no response. Apart from a couple of triers, like.'

I sighed. 'I've got absolutely nothing to go on. Apart from the name.'

The other man gave me a sharp glance. 'I'd say from the look of you that you have a strong claim. But for the life of me, I can't see where you've sprung from, if you get my meaning. Mr Gregory wasn't one for playing fast and loose. Especially when he'd got a young wife he thought the world of.' He shook his head

I sat quietly, the feeling of having found an ally was strong. Presently the work's manager looked up. 'Look. I'll have to think on this. But right now there's things I should be doing. You call back here about five o'clock. That's when we close. There's maybe something I could tell you but I don't know as I should. I'll think on it.' He stood up and we left the office together. 'Are you staying up here somewhere?'

'I think I will stay for a day or two. Find a room somewhere.'

'My sister has a small guesthouse. Or would you be wanting somewhere grander?'

'No. That'd be fine. Can you give me her address? That'll save me having to search around,' and I pulled out my biro and notepad.

'Give it to me. I'll write out directions for you,' And while he wrote he went on talking. 'A a matter of fact, my sister might be able to tell you a bit about the family. She was housemaid there years ago. And there's old Mrs Timmins too. She worked there after my sister. I'll give you her address as well.' And my spirits lifted as I took back my notebook and thanked Mr Barrymore for his helpful suggestions.

'I'll be here at five,' I said.

Outside the office on the narrow railed balcony overlooking the works, I paused, once more fascinated by the scene. The older man looked at me. 'And what might your line of business be?'

I grinned. 'I'm a mechanical engineer. All this is

72

home territory to me.'

'Never! Well I'll be blowed!' He shook his head. 'Look, mind you're here by five. Missus worries if I'm late home.'

'I'll be here,' I promised and set off down the stairs. I put the notebook into my pocket and with some reluctance left the building.

As I walked back to the car park I thought about the manager's remark that I looked like his late boss. He didn't seem to be a fanciful man, Reg Barrymore, and yet he'd been genuinely struck by some resemblance. And that was before he knew my name. I remembered that rigid body on the stairs above me, hands white-knuckled on the rail as the deep set eyes stared down at me. There must be a connection. But how the hell do I find it?

With a sudden sense of urgency I decided to visit the old lady before I booked in at the guesthouse. I drove out of the car park, following the manager's directions and turned down a narrow street of turn-of-the-century houses. There was a parking space in front of a general stores and as I climbed from the car, I had an idea and went into the shop and bought a box of chocolates before walking along the street until I came to number twenty-nine.

The door was in need of paint and the step failed to match the dazzling whiteness of the neighbouring houses. I pressed the doorbell. Several moments went by until I heard slow dragging footsteps and the door opened as far as the safety catch allowed. An old lady peered through the gap.

I gave what I hoped was a reassuring smile. 'Mr Barrymore from the foundry sent me to see you, Mrs Timmins.'

'Reg? What does he want then? Wait. You'd better

come in.' Arthritic fingers fumbled with the door catch. 'Come into the front room,' and she turned and led the way.

The house smelt stale and fusty, but the small parlour was spotless. There was a three piece suite and several small tables draped in lace cloths and laden with ornaments and photographs in frames. A scarf with bright orange medallion patterns was draped across the back of the couch. She waved me to an armchair and lowered herself slowly on to an upright chair. 'Well?' she said.

'I'm trying to find out a bit about some relations of mine. The Gregory Smiths. Mr Barrymore thought you might be able to help.'

She peered at me. 'The Gregory Smiths. Relations. Well, that's news to me. Never knew they had any relations, not after Mr Duncan died. Are you something to do with him then?'

Once again I went through my story. Her eyes brightened with interest as I told her all I knew. But there was a preoccupation about her; I was sure I would get nothing here.

However, she began to talk. 'Fancy a little baby left like that. I wonder what the young mother thought. She must have been afraid for her family to find out I suppose. Some girls were like that even though times have changed since I grew up.' And she sighed deeply. 'Mrs Gregory lost hers too. Died in the night. And her so happy and proud that afternoon. My Ruby worked there, at the Nursing Home. Said Sylvia had a bit of a temperature but was happy as a lark over the baby. Ruby was friends with Mrs Gregory. Sylvia, she called her. They met through me working up at the big house. Got on grand together. They used to go to the pictures when Mr Gregory was away. Ruby said it was all that kept Sylvia going, stuck there in that great house with Iris Julian.'

'What did your daughter do, Mrs Timmins,' I was hoping to keep the conversation going.

'She was a nurse. Best nurse Dr Staton ever had, he told me. She helped to deliver Mrs Gregory's baby, she did.'

Thinking that this might be another lead, I asked 'Is there any chance I could talk to your daughter?'

She looked at me, eyes re-focussing from the past where she'd gazed. 'No young man. You cannot. She's dead, my poor Ruby. Dead.'

'I'm so sorry.' And I meant it, feeling a wave of pity for the old lady seated before me. I stood up and picked up a photograph in a silver frame and looked at the girl in the picture. A girl in nurse's uniform, a dark belt round the slender waist. An attractive intelligent face. 'She was beautiful.' I spoke quietly, almost to myself.

'She was. That she was. My lovely girl. She was all I had.'

'I'm so sorry,' I said again quietly.

She held out her hand for the photograph. 'She was killed. She died the very day the little baby died, Mrs Gregory's baby.'

I sat down again. 'What happened?'

'The bus crashed. Went over a bridge. Up at Glynwood, it was. In the night.'

'Glynwood!' I felt winded. A bus. A bridge. *At Glynwood*. What could it all mean? What on earth...

Mrs Timmins was carefully replacing the picture on one of the little tables.

'Awful!' my voice rasped through my dry throat. 'Did she have work at that Glynwood Hospital as well?'

She shook her head. 'I don't know why she went up there. All that way. She just came home from work

75

early and told me about Sylvia's baby and how she had to work that night. So when the police came, I told them they were wrong, she was doing night shift at Conborough Nursing Home. But in the end I had to believe it. When they took me up there to see her.' She drew the scarf off the back of the sofa and held it to her face. 'This is all I've got now to remind me.'

I leaned forward and looked at the photo again. Looked at the frank face, the open smile. I didn't want to believe this girl was involved. But involved in what? 'This nursing home, is it still there?'

She shook her head. 'No. No. Dr Staton sold up and went to Canada. Not that long after Ruby's funeral. Some sort of breakdown, they said. And there was talk. You know, about his man friend.'

Suddenly the musty room and the sad old woman were too much. I remembered the box of chocolates in my pocket and got to my feet and handed her the box with its bright ribbon. 'Thank you, Mrs Timmins for talking to me.'

She brightened at once as she took the chocolates. 'Ooh. That's nice. Don't get many presents nowadays. Except from Dr Staton of course. He still remembers me. Sends me a hundred pounds every Christmas.' There was pride and satisfaction in her voice. 'And all because of my girl.' She fell once more into a reverie, eyes gazing past me into space.

'You don't have his address, I suppose?' It was too much to hope, but I had to ask.

She shook her head. 'Can't write with these,' and she held up her twisted hands.

I took them gently in mine. 'I have to go. It has been very good talking to you.' And I left her sitting there and made my own way out.

CHAPTER THIRTEEN

Once again I sat in the car for a while puzzling at what I'd learned. A direct lead from the nursing home where one baby died, to the hospital where I'd been left a few hours later. What the hell could it mean?

I looked at my watch. Time to get booked in at that guesthouse, then back to the foundry to see what else Reg Barrymore might tell me. I put the car into gear and

drove off to the other address I'd been given.

Mrs Hawkins, the manager's sister, showed me to a well-furnished room at the back of the house. 'Quieter back here, dear. No traffic.' She beamed at me. 'Would you like a cup of tea, then?'

'That'd be great, Mrs Hawkins.' And when she brought the tray to the comfortable lounge, I was glad to see she was ready for a chat. I told her I'd just been to see Mrs Timmins.

'Ah, poor Ada. She's never been the same since she lost Ruby.' The landlady shook her head. 'A terrible tragedy that was.'

'She seems to have no idea why her daughter was in Glynwood that night,'

'Huh! Everyone else knows why she was there.' There was disapproval in her voice.

'Oh?' It was enough to set her off again.

'Ruby was having an affair. With a long distance lorry driver. I think, well, all of us that knew about it, think she'd planned to run off with him. I mean, that's the only way she could have got to Glynwood in time. In his lorry. We think they must have had a tiff and when he stopped in Glynwood, she spotted the Express bus at the terminal and ran over to catch it. Poor girl.'

My heart sank. Whatever I'd expected to hear, it wasn't this.

But my hostess was in full spate. 'Changed him, it did. Sid Chambers. He went to look like an old man after she died. Guilty conscience of course. Still, it kept his family together. Better than leaving his wife and children, wasn't it?'

I agreed. Then I looked up. 'Does he still live locally, this driver?' It was another long shot.

'Sid Chambers? Oh yes. He lives on a council estate in Conborough. Not far from that nursing home where Ruby used to work. Of course, that place closed down and the doctor went off abroad.'

'Yes, to Canada, Mrs Timmins said. He still sends her a present at Christmas.'

She picked up my cup and the plate with biscuits she'd offered me. 'He came back again, mind. Started another nursing home up the country somewhere. I only heard about it last year.'

About to leave, I paused in the doorway, alert. 'You don't know where, I suppose, Mrs Hawkins?'

She shook her head. 'One of them seaside places. Bournemouth. Or Brighton. Will you be wanting dinner tonight, love?'

'Yes please. And thanks for the tea. I needed that.'

The landlady beamed again as I left and I did indeed feel refreshed, both by the drink and by the fact I now had two more leads to follow; the lorry driver and the doctor. But first there was the interview with Reg Barrymore. 'Something I could tell you,' he'd said. But would he...

The manager was waiting for me in his gallery office, his desk cleared at the end of the day. He looked sombre as he invited me to sit down.

'I've been thinking about your problem, young man. And much as I'd like to help you, the fact remains that I don't know you. You're a stranger. And what I had in mind to show you was personal to Mr Gregory. So I'm afraid I've brought you back here for nothing.'

I swallowed my disappointment. 'That's OK, Mr Barrymore. You've helped already. I went to see Mrs Timmins like you said and what I heard from her is very strange, but it does fit another piece into the puzzle.'

'Oh?' The older man was visibly relieved at my calm acceptance of his decision. He took out a pipe and began to pack it with tobacco, waiting to hear what I'd learned.

I told him about Ruby's late night visit to Glynwood, the town where I'd been left in the local hospital. 'There are too many co-incidences, Mr Barrymore. I was told years ago that the staff had seen a young woman in a bright headscarf in the foyer that night. We know Ruby caught that bus and her mother has Ruby's scarf in place of honour in the front room. And Ruby was assisting at the birth of the Gregory Smith baby that afternoon. And left there that evening. Too many co-incidences altogether.'

The manager's hands were stilled, matches poised and unstuck. I noticed his fingers were unsteady. 'Ruby! Never! Never in this world would she have done anything to upset Sylvia Gregory Smith. They were real good friends. I don't know why she went to Glynwood, but...' He shook his head again.

'Another strange thing,' I went on. 'Dr Staton still sends Mrs Timmins money every Christmas. One hundred pounds each year.'

'What!' The manager was astounded. Suddenly he

stood up. 'Now look, I've changed my mind. I'm going to show you Mr Gregory's letters. From what you've just told me and from your whole appearance, I feel you've a right to know.' And he turned and opened the ancient safe that stood in the corner of the office. He bent down and withdrew a package. 'Here you are. These are letters his wife wrote to him after she left him. Sent them here to the office because she never trusted that Iris Julian. They've been in that safe a lot of years, thirty or so. I never looked at them until after Mr Gregory died. I read them then, to see if I should give them to the solicitor. But I think they're too private. No good to them anyway.'

He handed me a large brown envelope, turned round and picked up a bunch of keys. 'I'll check the place over while you take a look.' And he made his way quickly out of the office.

I sat for a moment with the package in front of me, a feeling of distaste at the thought of reading the private and long-cherished letters of a dead man. Wondered too what exactly had made the manager share these documents with a total stranger. I sighed and picked up the packet.

Inside the envelope were half a dozen or so handwritten letters. I unfolded the topmost and began to read. The letter was dated July 1986, a couple of weeks after my birth date.

My dear Greg

By now you will have been told that our baby is dead. I didn't believe it when they told me. He was so strong and bonny. How could it be? They brought him to me in the end. Such a pale tiny scrap. You wouldn't think he could change so much just by stopping breathing.

Oh Greg. I don't know what to do. I can't go back to that house again. There's nothing there for me. I know you had to go on that expedition. There was no one else - it was your invention. I know all that.

But I've only had one letter in all these months. I collected it off the postman and read it on the bus into town. You were having a marvellous time. The challenge of the terrain, the way your ski-sled was standing up to the battering. The people in your team. And I was sitting on the bus with only that awful woman to go back to. Staring at me and following me on her silent feet.

If our baby had lived, it would have been alright. Cynthia invited me to come and stay for a few weeks. I would have stayed with her until you came home. She's always been my very good friend.

But now I'm not coming back, Greg. I should never have married you. You don't need a wife. You don't need anyone. Just your work. You were complete before you met me. And you only wrote to me the once.

You can reply to the box number above. I won't be living in that town though, so don't try to find me. Goodbye Greg.

I'm sorry about our baby. Sorry about everything.

Yours, Sylvia

The letter was smudged and tear stained. I put it down. Shakily. And picked up the next. This was obviously a draft, covered in crossings-out and corrections, written with intensity.

My darling, darling girl,

Why did I go and leave you? Why? Why? I keep asking myself these futile questions. You were my wife. Expecting my child. And I had to go off to the ends of the earth because of a bit of equipment I had the misfortune to make.

But I did write. Every day. Every single day. A sort of diary. Not just about what I was doing, but wondering what you had done that day -walked in the woods, perhaps. Or gone down by the river. Picked flowers. I thought of you. Your face drifted in front of my eyes before I slept and every spare moment of the day.

The mail went out every two weeks. Always a fat packet for you. And now and then I wrote on a flimsy as well. You must have got one of them. But what happened to the rest? No one else had problems with their mail.

Please, my darling. Give me another chance. I got back here today and found your letter waiting at the office. So it's nearly a month since we lost our little boy. And you alone all that time. I love you Sylvia. You're the only woman I've ever loved. You came into my life like a revelation. I can't put it into words how I feel. And such a dreadful time you have had. But please forgive me. Come back. Please.

Ever your husband,

Greg

I put down the letter into the pool of light on the desk and wondered if I could face reading any more. They were so private. So poignant. And such a long time ago. And how could it help? But despite myself, I reached for the next piece of paper. It was a brief note.

Dear Gregory

I can't come back to you. I've got a job now. It's helping me to get better. Cynthia is good to me. I've met a lot of new people. People of my own age. People with no commitments. I'm having the sort of life I never had before. All my teens were spent looking after my mother. Maybe that's why I turned to you when she died. For comfort and security. I don't know. You were so kind.

I hate to think of you unhappy. But you don't need me. You truly don't. I think Mrs Julian must have done something with those letters. The only one I got was the one the postman gave me down by the gate.

Goodbye Gregory. Please don't try and find me. There's nothing I can give you any more. It's all over between us.

Sylvia

There were no more drafts of letters from her husband, but obviously he'd written several times from the content of the next letter she'd sent him. It was dated six months later.

83

Gregory

Please. I've just collected five letters from the post office. It's no use. Believe me. You are only torturing yourself. I'm a different person now. I'm not a young girl any more although I'm free to act like one. I've had a child and lost it. I've grown up. I've made a choice, and it stands.

I will never come back to you. I might as well tell you. I've met someone else. I know that will hurt you, but it's better to tell you the truth. I would like a divorce. I'll send someone to collect from the post office at the end of the month. Depending on what you agree, I shall cancel the poste restante after that.

Goodbye Gregory. I hope you will do as I ask. And then forget me.

Sylvia

'I've met someone else.' That sentence had hit me in the stomach. How much worse for the man to whom it was written. There was a finality about it that made the rest of the letter irrelevant.

I heard Reg Barrymore's feet on the stairs and put down this last letter and replaced the papers in the envelope. The manager shot a glance at me as he came in and I was glad my face was in shadow, only my hands in the pool of light on the desk.

'D'you think the solicitors should have had these letters?' Barrymore's voice was worried.

I shook my head. 'As you said, nothing in there to help them. I suppose someone else knew about this friend, Cynthia?'

The manager nodded. 'Yes, they knew. Trouble was,

84

no one knew her surname. The only one who could have told them where she lived was Ruby. And she was dead.' He looked at his watch. 'Look, I have to go.'

'Right. I'm grateful to you for letting me read these.' I handed over the packet and watched Barrymore lock it back in the safe. 'And thank you for fixing me up at your sister's. Do you live near? Or need a lift?'

'Oh no. My place is just ten minutes walk away and I always like the walk.' We left the building together and the manager paused when we reached my car. 'Good luck now. If I can think of anything else, I'll give you a ring at my sister's place.' And he swung off, waving aside my thanks for what he had done for me.

Once I was settled in my room, I took out my laptop and googled Dr Staton's name, but to my disappointment, apart from a brief account of the last nursing home he ran near Brighton, there was nothing to say where he now lived. I switched off my laptop and called Jo. She'd just left work and was about to drive back to her parent's home.

'Archie!' Her voice was warm and affectionate and my pulse leapt.

'My mobile is getting low, Jo. So I'll make this as short as I can. First of all, when you're at home tomorrow, will you see if you can track down a Dr Staton somewhere in the Brighton area. Dr Ian Staton. He ran the nursing home in Conborough where the baby Jonathan was born.'

'Wow! Of course I will,' she said

'Trouble is, I've looked online but couldn't find anything.' As I spoke to Jo I found I was cuddling the phone against my face, thinking of her smooth skin…

'What have you found out, Archie? And where will you be so I can reach you if your phone packs up?'

I quickly gave her the landlady's phone number. 'I meant to get a new charger when I lost mine in that explosion, but I forgot. When I get one tomorrow, you'll be the first person I phone. But right now I'll tell you what I've discovered.' And as briefly as I could, I told her how I'd spent the day and what I'd found out.

'But it's really amazing.' Jo exclaimed. 'Only none of the pieces seem to fit. What a sad story it is. I hope I will be able to track down this Doctor Staton. He must know something.'

'I'm going to try and find this lorry driver tomorrow morning. It seems he lives quite near. He's driving buses now they say.'

We talked for a couple more minutes. 'I'm missing you, Jo. I can't believe how much I'm missing you since this morning.'

'Good. Then I'm not the only one,' her voice was light and happy. She made sure I still had her parent's home number so I could phone her over the weekend and we finally said our goodbyes with much love.

CHAPTER FOURTEEN

Before I went upstairs to my room, I looked through the phone book on the hall table. There were four Chambers listed, and I found Sidney Chambers on my second attempt. A child answered the phone. 'Grandad's in the bath,' she said. 'He says if it's about the Scottish bus trip, you'd better come round tomorrow morning. Anytime, he says.'

Congratulating myself on this piece of luck, I went up to my room and made a few notes. I looked at the map in the AA book and found it was only a few miles from St. Hayes to Conborough. And eighty-five miles from Conborough to Glynwood. All those years ago it would probably have taken a lorry a couple of hours to cover the distance. But plenty of time for Ruby to catch that bus back to her home. Pointless to speculate but I lay on my back, staring at the ceiling for a long while doing just that, until I finally slipped into a dreamless sleep.

Sid Chambers lived on a council estate where most of the houses were now privately owned. His was one of those; as evident from the new double-glazing, the fresh paint and the immaculate paths. And a lovingly tended garden.

The man who opened the door was short and thickset. What hair remained was still black and large dark eyes inspected me with calm detachment.

''We'll go round the back,' he said as he stepped on to the path and led me round the side of the house to a wooden chalet at the end of the garden. 'This is my office,' he spoke over his shoulder as he opened the door. Inside there were a couple of chairs and a table in front of the window, box files on a shelf and other shelves crammed with books. 'Now then, Mr Smith, you said. From Samson's, or are you the new man at Packard's?' His voice was deep, a velvet baritone. As he spoke he sat down and waved me to the other chair.

Crunch time. I put my hand on the back of the chair but didn't sit. 'As a matter of fact, Mr Chambers, when your grandchild assumed I was phoning about your bus, I didn't correct her because I wanted to speak to you privately. It's very important to me.'

The man stared up at me with those dark unfathomable eyes. A sudden grin split his face. 'Well, that makes two of us lying. I was watching football and I always tell them to say I'm in the bath when there's a good match on.' He waved again at the chair and with relief I sat down. 'Private, eh? Well then, go ahead Mr Smith. If that really is your name.'

This time I was the one who grinned. 'Well that's exactly what I want to find out! I'll explain it all if you'll hear me out. But first,' I took a deep breath, 'I need to know about that lift you gave to Ruby Timmins. To Glynwood. The night she died.'

The smile in those lambent eyes died away. The calm face became a mask. I cursed my stupid outburst. I should have trodden cautiously, much more carefully.

'Are you police? Or a private detective?' The voice was hard; had lost its music.

'Neither.' But the response encouraged me. Why think 'police' if that last journey had been entirely innocent? 'I need to know why she took that trip, Mr Chambers. And about the baby.'

This time the eyes were guarded. He shook his head. 'Sid,' he said abruptly. 'Everyone calls me Sid.' I could see he was playing for time. 'I don't know why she took that trip. Or anything about a baby.' He shook his head. 'Sorry. Can't help you I'm afraid.' And he began to his feet.

Quickly I took out the familiar documents. My driving licence. The birth certificate. The newspaper cutting. 'Look,' I said. 'all I want to know is who I am. That's all. And I know you could help. If you would.'.

Reluctantly Sid Chambers sank back in his chair and picked up the papers. He read them. Put them down on the table and leaned back, staring into space, pulling on his bottom lip. I found I was holding my breath. The silence stretched. Encouraged, I began to speak, quietly, telling all I'd learned about how I was left at the Glynwood hospital that night. 'You remember the date, Sid. I know you do. Haven't you any idea what it was all about?' and this time I couldn't keep the despair out of my voice.

At last the man looked up. There were tears in his eyes. He pressed the backs of his hands against them. Sighed, and began to speak. 'Yes, I remember the date. But I don't know what it was all about. I'll tell you what I can.' He stood up and went across to a small sink in the corner and began to fill a kettle. He put teabags into a pot and placed two mugs on a tray. 'Sugar, Mr Smith?'

'Archie.' I shook my head. 'Tea will be great though.'

Sid Chambers began to speak before the kettle boiled, his deep voice breaking at times. And as he brought the tray to the table, once again there were tears in his eyes and this time he made no attempt to check them as they began to course down his cheeks. 'We were in love, you see. It was no good, of course. I met her when I broke my leg in a motor bike accident. I was in traction for weeks and Ruby was my nurse. They say everyone falls in love with their nurse. Only difference was, she fell in love with me too. And I was twenty-one. Already married with a twelve-month old baby and another on the way.' He sighed and picked up his mug. Aware of his tears he drew out a handkerchief, wiped his face and blew his nose.

'Ruby didn't know for ages that I was married because my wife Paulette never happened to visit when Ruby was on duty. And to begin with the question never arose. But then, we just clicked. Lots of laughs. Flat on your back for weeks in traction, you get bored. And she lent me books. The sort of books I'd never read before. We talked about them. About everything. She was magic. Full of light. They were all crazy about her, the rest of the blokes in the ward. And I never meant to fall in love with her. But it happened before I knew. To both of us...'

I sipped the hot drink. Perhaps it was the voice, that deep baritone. But the story, the tragic love story, unfolded like a libretto. 'Then one day I kissed her. I was trying to walk, to balance on my leg at last. And she was at my side. And I staggered. On purpose. So I could put my arms round her. And kiss her. And it was another week before I told her about my family; the wife and babe.' There was a long silence as he went over the memories of that week. That intoxicating week. And the dread of the inevitable.

'So I told her. About having to get married at nineteen. That Paulette and me, we'd got nothing in common. That I'd try for a divorce. Ruby wouldn't hear of it of course. But...' There was anguish in the word. 'We met from time to time when I was back at work. We both tried not to. But sometimes I'd see her on the road and I'd stop the lorry and pick her up. We couldn't help ourselves.'

And I knew that only a few weeks ago, I couldn't have understood. But now I did, and I intensely sympathised.

'Then one day she saw me in the park with the kids. Saw Jason run to me and she told me she's seen him hold on to my leg.' Sid Chamber's voice trailed off and presently he blew his nose again. 'That was the end of it. The very end, I thought.'

I held my empty mug, afraid if I set it down, the story would stop. But after a long pause, the man went on. 'One day I saw her at the bus-stop. And she waved me down and asked me if I would do one thing for her.' That sudden grin flashed again. 'I thought Christmas had come!' Then his face grew still. 'She wanted me to take her to Glynwood one evening. Only she couldn't tell me when. Said she would phone me and give me a few hours warning. I arranged my jobs so I'd be free every day by six. And that wasn't easy, I can tell you.' He paused and that grin came again. 'And then, about a week later, she told me she'd meet me at six that evening in the lay-by on the outskirts of town.' He closed his eyes and was silent for a stretched minute. 'I helped her up into the cab. We didn't speak for ages. Didn't need to. It was still there between us. Thousand volts.'

His eyes were open now and he turned to me. 'I've never told anyone this. Never talked to anyone about Ruby and me. All those years ago. And now it feels like it did then. God, how I miss her. I still think of her every day. She changed my life, see. Brought me into all this,' and he waved his hand at the packed bookshelves on the wall. 'The missus won't have books in the house. Clutters up the place, she says. I ask you...' Again there was a long drawn out pause. 'One of the things Ruby said that night was, use your mind, she said. For yourself and for your boys.' He raised his head. 'And I have done.' He gave another smile. 'I'm doing a degree course now. Open University. That's one of the troubles about my job, long distance driving. You can't go to evening classes on a regular basis. But it was the only way I could make good money then. Nowadays I do bus trips. As a matter of fact you're lucky to catch me. I just got back from Belgium on Wednesday and I'm off again next Monday on the Scottish Highlands trip.'

I made some comment. Some reflex remark. This wasn't what I wanted to hear, but I had to keep the man talking.

Sid Chambers put down the mug he'd cradled against his chest. 'Well. There it is. I took her to Glynwood.'

'Can you remember where you dropped her off?' It was worth a try.

Again the dark eyes filled with tears. 'Not far from the centre. She'd told me she had to get the Express bus at ten and her business wouldn't take more than a few minutes. So we sat in the cab in a car park for over an hour. It had been a dark day for July. And then it started to rain. But she wouldn't let me take her there, where she had to go. She said it was no place for a heavy lorry to be seen. So in the end I helped her down and I held her. Held her for the last time.' And the large face suddenly twisted with grief.

I was silent. I couldn't ask the man the things I needed to know. Not now. But my companion looked up and went on. 'Ruby never told me what it was all about or why she was doing it. She did say she would be glad when it was all over. All cleared up. But I know Ruby. So whatever it was, I know she wasn't doing anything wrong. I watched her walk away up the drive. She never turned back.'

'The hospital drive? With the baby in the bag?' I kept my voice casual.

The man nodded, staring into space. Then he collected

himself, his eyes sharp. 'A bag, yes. I don't know about any baby.'

I stood up. Another piece of the puzzle had slotted into place. But the pattern was as obscure as ever. 'Sid. Thank you for your help. I'm sorry I've brought all this sadness back to you.' I held out my hand.

The man too stood up and took my proffered hand. His eyes were still damp but he gave the grin that made me see him as Ruby must have done, when he was young and carefree. The voice had regained its music. 'Don't be sorry. It's been good to talk about her to someone else.' He released my hand. 'If you do find out, find out what it was all about…?'

'Of course I will. I'll phone you if I find out.' I walked back along the path and at the corner of the house I turned and raised my hand. Sid Chambers stood in the doorway, his bulky shoulders slumped against the frame, his forehead against the wood. Unseeing.

And as I walked back to the guesthouse I knew that this man was another victim of the tragedy that had been played out on the dark July day when I'd been born.

CHAPTER FIFTEEN

There was no point in staying any longer. There was nothing else to find out unless I could meet Iris Julian. But when I mentioned this to my landlady, she told me she'd phoned the woman the previous evening.

'I told her you were staying here and I felt she should meet you. There's something... I don't know how to explain it, but you do remind me of someone. Can't say who, mind you. Anyway, she was her usual rude self and hung up on me. So I don't think she'll answer the door if you call round there.'

I thanked her for trying and told her I was going up to Brighton to see if I could meet this Dr Staton she'd told me about. 'I'll pay for two nights of course. That's what I booked.' And after a weak protest, Mrs Hawkins gratefully accepted the payment.

'You must have a cup of coffee before you go.' At the door she turned. 'My Albert's out there with Betsy as usual. Give him a shout for me will you? If I go he'll get me cleaning the windscreen or something. Always does.'

'Yes, sure. My packing won't take a minute anyway.' And I strolled outside to the parking area at the back of the house. 'Betsy' was a 1922 Ford Roadster, bright yellow with gleaming lamps and lovingly polished chrome. Albert was only too happy to introduce me to the car and in the end, Mrs Hawkins herself came out and told us both sharply that the coffee was getting cold. By that time I had oil on my hands and she insisted on brushing the leaves off my trousers. 'Lying down on the damp ground like that! I don't know.' And Albert gave me a cautious wink behind her back.

When the three of us were sitting in the conservatory drinking the very good coffee, Mrs Hawkins determinedly changed the subject from cars. 'That friend of Mrs Gregory Smith's, I nearly had her name last night. Cynthia… Oh dear! My poor brain.'

Her husband looked up, his sparse hair ruffled by the wind. 'Cynthia Martindale? What d'you want to know her name for?'

Both of us listeners turned to him, astonished. 'Well I never! Fancy Albert knowing her name! That's it, of course. Cynthia Martindale!' his wife exclaimed.

Albert stirred his coffee and looked up. He leered at his wife. 'Course I remember her. Like a film star, she was. All blonde and curvy. Bit nervy, mind. Always dashing around. Never still.'

His wife stared at him open-mouthed. 'Well!' she said again. 'And how do you know all this, then?'

Albert smirked. 'Used to see her at the garage. Filled her car up lots of times when she was staying up at Sylvia Greg Smith's place. She only used to put in one gallon at a time.' He leered again. 'Not that I minded. She was quite a flirty little piece. There used to be a race with the other lads to see who could get to her car first.'

I smiled at the look on my landlady's face, then turned to Albert, my face serious. 'Cynthia Martindale. You're sure?'

'Course I'm sure. Mind you, that was her maiden name. She got married just after we were getting used to her calling in for petrol. Mrs Gregory went up to the wedding. Up at Sladesbridge.'

'Sladesbridge. How far away is that, Albert?'

'Not far. About forty miles I should think. You could get there by lunchtime if you want to,' and he looked at me inquisitively.

But I was not about to be drawn. I finished my coffee and stood up. 'Well, thanks for everything. But I really must be off. I'm planning to be in Brighton this afternoon.' Up in my room, I packed my holdall, which, I thought wryly, did just about hold my all. I checked to make sure I'd not left anything behind as I always did on my travels and made my way back downstairs where I thanked my hosts again. I promised to drop in if I was ever back in the area, and off I went.

Sladesbridge. Not far away, Albert had said. Plenty of time to make some enquiries there. And then I'd motor up to Brighton and see Jo and her family.

On the journey I drove fairly slowly as I mused again about my quest. I was ninety-nine per cent sure now that I'd had been the child - the baby Ruby Timmins had taken from the nursing home to Glynwood Hospital on the evening of the day I'd been born. But who then was the dead baby? And why? Above all, why should a child have been taken from Conborough to Glynwood? And was left there with a definite note of identification. It was no good. The pieces of the puzzle I'd assembled, made a frame. But the picture inside was missing. Totally missing.

Ah well. Sladesbridge Church. From the register I'd be able to find Cynthia Martindale's married name. And then track her down if possible and find out whatever she might have known.

Sladesbridge was a small ancient town. I drove slowly along the main street where granite houses with windows overlooked the busy pavements and found a car park near the town centre. When I'd locked the car, I looked about and spotted the slender steeple of a church over the roofs of the houses. There was a path

96

leading that way, a path which skirted a lake where ducks cavorted cheerily, regardless of the haughty sneers of the elegant swans.

Soon I came upon the church, lying somnolent in the pale sunshine, a great sleeping beast from the past, beached on a patch of twenty-first century grass. I stood for a while, just looking. Presently I shook myself and set off to find the verger, or someone who could give me access to the registers of thirty odd years ago.

But it's a Friday, of course, I was told. 'You'll have to wait until next Monday. Our vicar looks after three parishes, and he's never round here on a Friday. Not here.'

Blast! As I turned away I noticed a sign which read 'Lunches, twelve to two'. I looked at my watch. One thirty. A long time since that breakfast of toast and coffee which had so shocked Mrs Hawkins. 'What, no cereal! And no bacon and eggs or anything! I'll make you scrambled eggs if you like.' But now I was suddenly hungry and the smells which drifted along the passage from below were tantalising.

I descended the steps and entered a large room lit by tall leaded windows which seemed to be a twentieth century annexe. A rack of choir boy robes stood at one side and several trestle tables had been laid with fresh white cloths. From the counter across the room came a busy chatter. There were more helpers than customers just now, for only half a dozen people still sat at the tables and they were enjoying the flurry of service around them.

As I paused at the door, two white haired ladies detached themselves from the group behind the counter and bustled across to me and led me to one of the empty tables. 'Now my dear, just sit there and we'll bring your meal to you. Not much choice now, it's a bit late. But we'll see what we can do.' And a minute or two later they returned with a tray bearing a plate with a huge slice of home-made quiche buried with coleslaw and rice salad. 'Here's some beetroot and pickle. Jane, you get the bread rolls. He can have two. Pity for them to go to waste.'

And as Jane trotted off, I smiled, the sudden smile that Jo said brightened my somewhat impassive features. I stretched out my hand to the other woman who leaned on the back of a chair. 'Stay and talk to me. I feel a bit exposed here, all alone.'

She paused in surprise. She was small and birdlike with bright eyes and permed white hair. Flattered, she smoothed her apron and drew out the chair and sat down, inspecting me keenly. 'Well, I don't very often get an invitation like this. Alright. I could do with a bit of a sit-down. We've had a busy morning and Jane won't mind.'

And when her friend came back with a plate heaped with bread rolls, she too helped herself. 'I'll have one of these, Jane. I've been invited to keep this young man company for a bit. That'll give Lucinda something to talk about!' And the two women laughed at some shared joke.

'This looks good!' I began to tackle the mountain of food before me. 'And it tastes even better than it looks,' I grinned.

As I ate, we chatted. Her name was Marian and she gave me a potted history of the old church, its burning, its plague and the more recent trouble; the roof and the shortage of bell ringers. And, of course, all about the new vicar. I fed a few questions, enjoying both the food and the conversation. Twice a helper came over and piled more food on to my plate with the comment, 'We want to wash out the dishes'. And the moment I finally put down my fork, two more women appeared at my side. 'Russian cream, fruit jelly or strawberry mousse. Or you can have some of each if you like.'

Laughing, I watched as they arranged the food temptingly on a large plate. 'Yes, I know, you want to wash out the bowls! Well, I'll do my best, but after that huge meal... When do you close?'

'Oh, don't you worry about that my dear,' my table companion chimed in. 'I'm locking up today and I'm in no hurry.'

There were a few surprisingly ribald comments from the other women as they went off and then I turned back to Marian. 'My aunt asked me while I'm in the area to see if I could find out the address of an old friend. She used to live hereabouts. Got married in this church thirty-odd years ago. Cynthia Martindale.'

The old woman selected a piece of fruit from my dish. 'Martindale. That's an old Sladesbridge name. Plenty of them in the churchyard. But I'm a newcomer, I've only been here eighteen years. I'll ask Mollie.' she called across the room and another woman left the melee round the sink and strolled across.

'Do you want some more, dear? I'm afraid we've just scraped out the dishes.' Concern showed on her plump features.

'No, of course he doesn't want more, Millie. Look at his plate! He's asking after one of the Martindales. A Cynthia. Do you know a Cynthia?'

The woman's face lightened and she too pulled out a chair and sat down with evident relief. 'Oh yes, I remember Cynthia. She married George Dawson. They were overseas a lot with his job, but they kept their house over at Ivybridge. I can't tell you the address, but they'd know at the post office. It's only a small place, Ivybridge. It's about ten miles the other side of

Glynwood.

'Glynwood!' I echoed. I put down my spoon. Both women looked at me with curiosity. I tried to cover my shocked surprise by going through my pockets to find my diary and made a point of writing down the information, including the name of the town, Glynwood. As though it wasn't already branded on my memory. 'Mm. I've heard of Glynwood. Well that's marvellous. My aunt will be pleased to get in touch with Cynthia again.'

'Well dear, you'd better tell your aunt that Cynthia's not been too well. She suffers from her nerves, you know, though I did hear she's been a lot better lately. But even so, I think you'd better phone first if you're planning to visit. Now you'll be wanting some coffee.'

But coffee was already on the way. And though all I now wanted was to go and find this Cynthia Martindale, who'd become Mrs George Dawson, despite myself, my companions kept me amused with their stories of the trendy young vicar. The vision of the ancient sexton dancing to the sound of the guitar and cymbals, and the churchwarden's wife using her prayer book to slap away the 'hand of friendship', had me spluttering in my coffee.

But at last I stood up. 'You've been a great help.' I turned to Marian. 'And thanks for keeping me company. Who do I pay?'

Marian pulled herself up. 'Victoria will take the money. I must go and see if the girls need my help. And you're welcome to come again, young man.' She gave me a wide smile.

'I shall come again. And next time I'll bring my girlfriend. And you shall have lunch with us properly and not just eat off my plate.' I took her hand and smiled down at her.

'Now off you go my dear. I shall be the talk of the town if you're not gone soon!' she said with a laugh.

With a flurry of goodbyes and good wishes echoing in my ears, I finally left the building and made my way back to the car.

Ivybridge. Ten miles from Glynwood. Ten miles from the hospital where I'd been left. And Sylvia had planned to go and stay with Cynthia... What the hell did it all mean?

In the car park I leaned for a while against the roof of the car, the mellow sun warm on my back. Presently I unlocked the door and reached inside for Jo's AA book. When I reached Ivybridge, I'd have driven two sides of a triangle from St.Hayes; to Cynthia's home town before she married, and then to her house only a few miles from Glynwood hospital. I slipped behind the steering wheel and inched the car through the cluttered streets where every shop seemed to be taking deliveries. But at last I found the road I needed, and leaving the delights of Sladesbridge behind, I headed for Ivybridge, to find the home of Sylvia Gregory Smith's best friend.

CHAPTER SIXTEEN

I bypassed Glynwood and found the road leading to Ivybridge. The countryside here was hilly, with narrow twisting roads winding through dense woods where fallen leaves strewed the road. Dangerous if it rained.

I came upon the village suddenly as I rounded a curve. Ancient thatched cottages nestled together in a small group, surrounded by the sprawl of modern development which flowed up the hill on the other side of the valley.

The post office was already closed, which gave me a good excuse not to be able to phone the house. I leaned on my car and went online with my phone, Googling 'George Dawson' to try and find that name with an Ivybridge address. Ah. At last, the address listed said Wedgewood, Tasmania Close, Ivybridge. As I replaced my phone, I noticed a woman with a shopping bag just passing, and asked her if she could tell me how to get to Tasmania Close. She paused and put down her bag. 'Well now, it's up that hill, young man. On one of those roads up there. But I couldn't tell you which one to take. They're all of a muddle up there.' I thanked her and climbed back into the car and threaded my way up the winding road that led to the houses visible from the village post office.

I found Perth Avenue and Melbourne Way. But no Tasmania Close. The woman was right; it was all a muddle. I was about to turn the car around, when I spotted an elderly man standing on the corner. I pulled across and wound down my window and asked if this man could help me find Tasmania Close.

'Hm.' He peered into the car. 'T'would be a lot easier

102

to take you there than try and explain. But then I'd miss my bus. How long are you going to be there?'

I shrugged. 'Ten minutes or so. But I could give you a lift afterwards. Where are you heading?'

'I'm going over to my son's place for the evening. At Glynwood.'

'Oh that's OK then. That's where I'll be heading too. Hop in if you like.' I reached over and opened the passenger door and the old man got in stiffly, muttering about his arthritis. However, his directions were clear and soon he pointed out the sign which read Tasmania Close, the sign I'd been unable to find. It was almost hidden by overhanging laurels. 'All the new postmen complain they can't find the name, but the residents say it keeps away unwanted salesmen.'

The houses and bungalows in the locality were large and detached, standing in spacious gardens, with none in need of double-glazing reps. I soon found Wedgewood, the house I was looking for and I parked near the curb. 'I think this is the one. D'you want the radio on?'

'I wouldn't mind hearing the sports channel, Radio Five Live,' the old man smiled. I adjusted the set and as I walked away I could hear a familiar voice bemoaning the fate of the English team.

Wedgewood was a large bungalow set well back from the road. I climbed three wide curved steps and pressed the doorbell. As I waited, I turned and admired the view of the wooded valley below, the glimpse of thatched roofs through a gap in the trees. Then I heard someone opening the door and turned. A thin grey-haired woman in her fifties was looking through the narrow gap. I could see the guard chain. Summoning up all my hopeful charm, I launched into the speech I'd rehearsed. 'Mrs Dawson? I believe you had a friend called Sylvia Gregory Smith?'

'Sylvia! Oh my God!' she released the chain and opened the door a little wider, one hand at her throat. 'What's happened to Sylvia?'

'Nothing! She's alright! At least I suppose she is.' Shit, I thought. This wasn't what I'd planned. I'd blown it now.

'What do you mean? What are you talking about? Who are you anyway?' The door began to close and the chain went on with a click, the woman's eyes wide with fright.

'My name is also Gregory Smith.' I spoke rapidly, willing the door not to close. 'I'm trying to trace my family tree and I'd like to contact Sylvia. I daresay she remarried long ago?'

'What's that to you? I'm not telling you anything.' Her eyes went past me to the car where my white-haired passenger sat contentedly listening to the radio. I saw her start and her hand went to her mouth. 'Who's that in the car?' And without waiting for a reply, she began to close the door.

Despairingly I put my foot in the gap. 'Please, Mrs Dawson. If you give her my name and phone number, she can get in touch with me if she wants. Here's my work's card.'

'Get your foot out. I'll call the police!' Her agitation seemed chronic, set in all the lines and hollows of her tense face, down to the twitching hands on the chain.

'Look, it's alright. I'm going. I'm sorry to have startled you. But will you take my card and ask her if she'll contact me? It gives my place of work. She can check me out.'

'Get out. Now. Or I'll call the police'. She spoke like a robot.

I tried once more. 'But will you please tell her about

me. It's in her own interest that you should.'

The wild look in her eyes became suddenly wary. She seemed to freeze. 'Take your foot out. Put the card in the letterbox.' And as I withdrew my foot the door slammed in my face.

'Fuck!' I muttered under my breath. But I posted the card through the flap and turned despondently away. So this was her illness. Her 'nerves'. A wave of despair swept over me and I thrust my clenched fists into my pockets. I knew she wouldn't contact Sylvia. Oh well, back to the drawing board.

In the car my passenger was placidly taking in the latest score. 'What, finished already? Well, that's grand. I'll be at Jack's place long before the bus.'

But my passenger was wrong. Not a mile farther on, I turned down a steep hill and halfway down, as I changed gear, my foot touched the brake but nothing happened. Nothing. I yelled to my passenger, 'Christ! Curl up. The brakes have gone!' and I wrenched up the hand brake. The car slowed a little, but the speed was increasing on the steep gradient and there was traffic ahead which had slowed down for some reason. I pressed the hazard warning and blew the horn and faces turned to look out of the back window of the car ahead. Children's faces. 'Bloody hell.' It all seemed to happen in slow motion. There was a high wall on the right hand side of the road, and though there was traffic coming up the hill I knew they could avoid me. I wrenched the wheel, swung the car across the road and scraped along the wall, hoping it would bring us to a halt. There was a series of ear-splitting screeches of tearing metal as we bounced along. A gap in the wall appeared and I swung the wheel again this time into a driveway entrance. The car tilted into a ditch and the next moment there was a violent impact, the airbags exploded, the car folded round me and I hurtled into darkness.

CHAPTER SEVENTEEN

In one of the home-going cars, his newish Jaguar, George Dawson froze in horror as he saw the accident happening A car laden with children passed by, the occupants seemingly unaware of their narrow escape though they must have heard the blare of the driver's horn and seen the flash of the hazard lights. The air was filled with the sound of tearing metal as the car scraped along the wall. Then it swerved into an opening and crashed.

George was the first to get there. He leapt out of his car and rushed into the drive where the car lay tilted. He could see the passenger dangling in his seat belt and yelled to the man, 'Don't undo your belt!' The driver's side of the car was badly smashed and he took one look at the unconscious driver and pulled out his phone. But just as he was about to dial, an authoritative voice said, 'Stand aside. I'm a doctor.' With relief George stood back and watched the doctor look into the car to make a swift assessment. After a moment he nodded. 'Go ahead. Call for an ambulance. And the police. Quick as they can.' And he turned his attention to the occupants of the car. Already more help was arriving and a couple of eager young men hauled the car back on to its wheels and soon Archie's passenger was helped out; able to stand unsupported and seemingly uninjured.

George went over to him. 'Come on. Come and sit in my car until the ambulance gets here.' And he helped the old man over to the Jaguar and into the comfort of the leather seats.

'He told me to curl up. Curl up, he said. The brakes have gone. And he swung across the road to miss hitting the car in front. I saw that as I curled myself up. If I hadn't pulled up my feet...' The old man's outburst stopped abruptly and he slumped back with his eyes closed.

A minute later the police arrived with the ambulance in their wake. It took some time to extricate the unconscious man's body from the mangled wreck, and then, pale and still, he was placed in the ambulance. George went over to the medics and told them the passenger from the wrecked car was sitting in his Jaguar and they went across to take a look at him and see how he was. When he spoke they could see he was badly shocked and helped him out. They took him across to the ambulance and persuaded him to lie down inside and the vehicle soon sped off with sirens wailing. To the County Hospital. At Glynwood.

George Dawson told the police what he could and left his name and address and then continued his journey home. But first he phoned his wife from the car to say he'd be a little late - traffic problems, he said. For once she didn't complain. At least, he thought, when he told her about the accident it would give her something to talk about. Something other that her health. He sighed.

However, far from accusing him of uncaring neglect by being late, she flung herself at him as soon as he let himself through the door. She was shaking and tears streamed down her face. 'My dear. My dear. What is it? What's the matter?' When she was so distraught, it never failed to touch him deeply. Always he remembered the old laughing Cynthia, now reduced to this uncontrollable mass of complexes. He led her gently into the large sitting room, bright with the light of the sun setting over the hill across the valley, and sat her on the velvet couch. 'Now, my darling, what is it? '

Haltingly she spilled out the story of Archie's visit. 'I

thought for a minute that Sylvia had passed on. He said, "You had a friend called Sylvia…" And then,' her tears flowed again, 'As he left, he made a threat! A threat!'

He stroked her hair. 'What exactly did he say, darling?'

She wrinkled her already furrowed brow. 'I can't remember the exact words. Something like " she'd be wise to contact him". Something like that.'

'Where's the card you said he left?'

She shook her head. 'I don't know. By the door I suppose. I couldn't bring myself to look.'

George made his way to the hall. A small white card lay on the carpet behind the front door. He picked it up and turned it over. 'Archibald E G Smith. Chartered Engineer'. And the name and address of the firm. Although he'd never dealt with them himself, he recognised the familiar name of a well-known firm. A firm of repute. He walked slowly back to the lounge.

'You said he called himself Gregory Smith. Maybe he is connected with Sylvia's first husband, something to do with Greg.'

Cynthia blew her nose. 'I don't know. Sylvia hasn't mentioned Gregory to me for years. But that young man. He was trying to track her down. I know. And there was an old man in the car. I think it must have been Gregory himself. Whatever will Sylvia say if he finds her after all this time! Oh George! She'll blame me! I know she will!'

'Cynthia sweetheart. Now stop this. You have done nothing. You didn't say a word. I'm going to make you a cup of tea. And later, I think the best thing we can do is tell Sylvia about the visit. And give her the name of this young chap. Let her decide what to do. Because I don't believe for a minute that Greg Smith would want to cause her any distress. And after all this time. He seemed such a decent chap from all I heard.'

'Oh George. You always took his side. You thought Sylvia should go back to him. I know you did though you never said so.'

'It's all years ago, darling. So many years'. He stood up and held out his hand to his wife. 'Come on. Let's go and get that tea. And a strong drink for me. I've just seen a nasty accident on Bluff Hill.'

The distraction worked. 'I won't have tea just now, George.' She went ahead of him to the kitchen. 'Dinner is warming in the oven. You pour yourself a drink while I dish up. And a tiny drop of gin for me.'

The kitchen floor gleamed. Nothing stood on the bare work tops. It might have been a show kitchen; not a pot of flowers, not a discarded milk jug nor casually draped tea towel. Nothing to show this was a working kitchen. He reflected grimly on the daily washing of the walls. The ritual floor cleaning. And he longed for a little of the human disorder which had marked their home until the onset of Cynthia's obsessive illness.

At least there was the good smell of the casserole, and as they ate, he told her about the accident. 'I hope that young driver is going to be alright. His brakes failed on the hill, so his passenger told me. And I saw him swing the car side-on against the opposite wall. It was either that or plough into the back of a car full of kids. I saw him swing the wheel.'

She warmed a little to that. And George gave an inward sigh of relief that she was now calm. 'Come on. Coffee in the sitting room.' He stacked the dishes while he spoke and presently with their coffee on a silver tray, they returned to the comfort of the velvet couch.

'So there were just the two of them in the car?'

George cradled the delicate bone china cup in his hands. 'Yes. The driver and the old man. The passenger wasn't much hurt, but badly shocked of course. They took him off in the ambulance too and I expect he'll be kept in overnight.'

'What make of car was it?'

Responding to her passion for detail, he told her. 'It was a red Fiat 500. The same as the one we bought for Minty when she passed her test. Remember? Hers had a white stripe along the side.'

Her cup rattled in the saucer as she put it down. 'That red Fiat! Did it have a black stripe? Along the sides?'

Puzzled, he frowned in an effort to remember. 'Yes, I think it did. Yes, I remember seeing it as I reached in to switch off the ignition. Why?'

'It was them! Them! The old man in the car. It must have been him. Gregory Smith. And the young man was the one who called here and left the card. That's who it was.' And she stared at him, wild-eyed.

George took her shaking hand in his. 'Cynthia, sweet. You can't possibly know that. And whoever it was, that young man undoubtedly saved several lives by his action today.' He stared moodily into space. 'We had better tell Sylvia though. If you are right, and if that old man is Greg, then she should be told he's in Glynwood hospital. After all, he may be more hurt than I think.'

She chewed her fingers. 'No. Don't say anything. I could be wrong like you said. But I'm sure I'm not. How may red Fiats do you see with a black stripe like that? I noticed the car because of Minty's.'

Mention of their daughter's name gave him a lead to change the subject and her face brightened as he told her he'd met Minty's husband in town that afternoon. With an inward sigh of relief he kept the conversation going until Cynthia's favourite cookery programme began. And she vaguely waved him away when he said he'd got some work to do in the den.

His study was at the back of the bungalow. It was a small room with bookshelves along two walls. The desk was large and although the blotter was changed as soon as it showed a trace of ink, Cynthia had learned not to disturb any of his papers. He sank into his favourite chair with relief, sighing and wondering once more what on earth life would be like when he retired. But no use to think of that yet. Who knows? Maybe Cynthia would be a little better by then.

He closed his eyes for a while, but the image of the young man at the wheel of the hurtling car intruded. It was no use. He'd better phone Sylvia while Cynthia was engrossed in that programme.

He hunted out the number and dialled. Lawrence Armstrong answered, surprise in his voice when George spoke, for it was usually Cynthia who called, maddeningly often. 'Why George, how are you?' Then there was apprehension in his voice. 'Is Cynthia alright?'

'Fine thanks, Lawrence. We're both fine. I just wanted to ask Sylvia something. It's about an old acquaintance of ours. Is she about?'

'Sure. I'll get her. Just a moment.'

There was a silence, broken by the sound of distant music. He remembered their joint passion for opera and Lawrence's vast collection of tapes.

Then Sylvia's voice. 'George?' He could hear the concern in her voice. The same concern he heard in his daughters' voices; the apprehension he secretly called 'the Cynthia syndrome'.

'Sylvia. How are you my dear?' The casual opening reassured her and she responded gaily, 'Oh, I'm fine. I've been making the most of this wonderful weather. I took the dog up through the woods today. If I walked five miles, he must have run twenty!'

He made a laughing rejoinder and then his voice changed. 'Sylvia. Something rather strange happened today and your name came up. So I thought I'd better tell you about it.'

Something in his careful words alerted her. Now her voice was puzzled. 'What do you mean? What was it?'

'A young man called here and asked Cynthia if she knew you. Naturally she asked him his name. He said it was Gregory Smith and he was trying to trace his family. Cynthia saw an elderly man sitting in the car at the kerb waiting. Well, you know Cynthia. She panics when people call. So she sent him off. But the young chap left his card.' He paused, wondering what to say. 'Sylvia, the card was from Archibald E G Smith, Chartered Engineer with a London firm' He heard the intake of breath from the receiver.

'From Greg?'

'Well, I don't know. Did Greg have connections with a London firm?'

'George. It's so many years. I don't know. But he must have retired long ago. And I can't see him leaving his beloved factory in Conborough.' She put into words what they were both thinking. 'Do you think it was Greg in the car?'

'My dear, I simply don't know. There was no reason for Cynthia to think it was. Only the mention of the name Gregory Smith. But it only says 'Smith' on the card.'

She spoke slowly, considering. 'Greg always used Gregory Smith. But you wouldn't have phoned, George, if you weren't concerned.'

'You're right. I wouldn't have bothered to call you this evening, although I'd have persuaded Cynthia to send you the card the young man left. But there's more.' And he went on to tell her about the accident he'd seen and Cynthia's conviction that it was the same car. 'So you see,' he ended, 'if there's a dog's chance that the old man taken to hospital is Greg, I thought you ought to be told.'

She'd given an exclamation of horror when she heard about the accident, and then there was a long silence. 'Oh my god!' she said at last. 'What am I to do, George? Should I visit? But what about the shock of my turning up after all these years!'

'Talk it over with Lawrence, Sylvia. He's the best one to advise you. I'm sorry to have distressed you, and it might all be a misunderstanding. I just felt you ought to be put in the picture.'

'Yes, thank you George. I'm grateful to you. And as you say, the least we can do is get in touch with whoever it was who left the card. I'll phone tomorrow and find out if there's a patient called Gregory Smith in the hospital. Obviously it's too late to visit tonight.'

They said their goodbyes and George replaced the receiver and sat back in his chair, his hands gripping the carved arms. The burnished wood beneath his palms soothed away the tensions of the day and he sighed once more. Then he turned and picked up the document which was his excuse for being in the study, opened it and began to read the paperback thriller which was carefully concealed inside.

But for once the magic didn't work, for try as he might to relax, that image kept returning, obtruding between the pages, the image of the young man at the wheel and the desperation on his face as he flung the hurtling car across the road to bounce along the wall ahead.

And that Friday evening, when Jo got back with her parents after the dinner party, she was surprised to find no recorded message from Archie. She knew it was too late to call him, and in any case his phone might not be working if the battery had run out. But he'd said he'd join her as soon as he could, so she knew he'd arrive next day. And though she was disappointed not to be able to tell him the momentous news she'd discovered, she went to bed with a smile on her face, imagining the amazement he'd feel when she recounted her astonishing story.

CHAPTER EIGHTEEN

I became aware of someone at my side. I opened my eyes and turned my head and gasped at the waves of pain the movement triggered. But that glimpse was enough to tell me I was in hospital and there was a nurse standing beside the bed.

'Ah. So we're awake at last, are we? Good. How do you feel?'

As the nurse took my temperature and blood pressure, I began to ask questions and was told to stop talking while she was busy. Then, 'Right, Mr Smith. Dr Jameson will be along presently to check on you.'

'What happened?' I tried to draw my brows together, felt the unaccustomed swelling and stopped. 'I can't remember. Why am I here?'

'You were in a car crash yesterday evening, young man. You're OK now. Got a nasty bump on your head. And a broken arm. It'll all come back to you soon enough. Better rest now though.' And she bustled away.

I closed my eyes again. Gradually things were drifting back into my consciousness. I remembered getting into the car outside that woman's house; the woman who would not take my card. There had been someone else in the car. Of course! The man who'd shown me the way! 'Nurse! Nurse, please.'

She turned in the doorway, saw me trying to leave my bed and came back. 'Now you must lie still. I just told you. What's the matter?'

'My passenger. The man who was with me in the car. I was giving him a lift. Where is he?'

'A lift, was it? Some lift!' She laughed. 'Don't worry,

He's alright. Just a few bruises and shock. He'll be going home later today.'

Relieved, I lowered myself gingerly back on to the pillows. My chest hurt, breathing was difficult. And there was plaster on my right arm which weighed a ton. I closed my eyes. Yesterday evening, the nurse told me it had happened. I was supposed to call Jo sometime, leave a message if she was out. Whatever would she think! I struggled up again, determined to get a phone.

'Better lie still, mate,' came a voice from the next bed. 'The big chief is on his rounds. He'll be here in a minute.'

And as he spoke, the consultant with his entourage came striding in, moving from bed to bed. My turn came. I was examined by firm but gentle hands and presently the doctor told me to lie back and relax. 'You'll feel rough for a day or two, but you've no serious injuries. You have a broken right forearm, three cracked ribs and you were concussed. Can you remember yet what happened?'

I shook my head. And regretted the movement.

'Tell me what you can remember,' the consultant prompted.

'Just getting into the car. I must have driven off...'

'Yes, you did. You were lucky. It seems your brakes failed and you hit a wall. You'll probably remember a bit more later. But as I said, you'll be good as new in a week or two.' And he nodded curtly as he moved off.

I looked down at my plastered right arm. My head throbbed and my ribs protested with every breath. But as I tentatively moved my legs beneath the restricting sheets, I silently agreed, for I had a sudden flash of memory, the vision of a wall looming, the exploding airbags and the windscreen a hailstorm of glass against my face. A few days, the doctor had said. I must phone

Jo and let her know.

And as I thought of Jo, other memories came surging. Back in the car, knowing it was about to crash... I'd thought of Jo then, thought of going into some limbo of death and leaving her. Losing her. And I remembered the flash of understanding that Jo was the most important person in my world. Much more important than my quest. Not who I was or who I might have been. Only Jo mattered.

'Can I have a telephone, nurse? Or is my mobile here somewhere?'

The nurse, a different nurse this time, middle aged and smiling, came across to me. She felt my forehead and my hand. 'You've got a holdall in your locker. They said it was in the boot of the car so it's not damaged. Is the mobile inside the bag?'

'Oh heck, no. I forgot, the battery's flat. I'd be grateful if you could get me a phone, nurse. And could you see if my wallet is anywhere?' I felt so groggy I couldn't think where it could be. Inside the pocket of my trousers, I thought.

The nurse looked in the drawer of the bedside cabinet and took out my wallet. 'Here you are. They had to cut your clothes off, you know. Luckily your legs weren't badly hurt. Black and blue, yes, and a lot of cuts. But just like these little cuts on your face from the flying glass, they'll clear up in no time. I've got another patient to see to, but I'll get a phone for you as quick as I can.' And off she hurried.

I closed my eyes again, my head hurting. I tried to breathe gently and not move until the man in the next bed began to talk to me again. I found my head swimming and couldn't follow what the man was talking about, and I was thankful when the nurse reappeared at my side. 'Here you are,' she said. 'You can't talk for more than a few minutes, because there's always someone else needing this phone.'

I thanked her. Opened my wallet and focused on the paper with her parents' phone number. Breathing carefully, I dialled. A man's voice answered. 'Oakfield Post Office. Can I help you?'

'Is it possible to speak to Jo?' I asked diffidently.

''Fraid not,' the cheerful voice replied. 'she's gone out. But she should be back by about five o'clock. D'you want to leave your number?'

'Thanks. But it's OK. I'll ring her this evening.' Suddenly reluctant to break contact, I added, 'Tell her Archie called, will you? Tell her I couldn't get to a phone last night.'

'Right-o, Archie. I'll tell her. Bye then.' And in a distant unknown house, there was the disconnecting click.

I slowly replaced the phone, disappointment seeping through my battered body. I was annoyed at my childishness. It was a stupid time to ring anyway. The nurse came back and took the phone away and I closed my eyes again and tried to sleep. Tried to escape the chatter of my lively neighbour.

Time dragged. Lunch came, a lunch I couldn't eat, nausea sweeping over me at the sight and smell of food. The clock on the wall hauled its hands reluctantly across its face from one milestone number to the next. One o'clock. Two o'clock.

At three o'clock the police inspector arrived. 'Insurance man's nightmare, you are, aren't you?'

Behind my closed eyelids, I recognised the voice from somewhere. I opened my eyes. Good God! It was Detective Inspector Green.

'What?' I tried to sit up. Thought better of it and lay back, with my hand against my protesting ribs. 'What

119

on earth are you doing here?' My speech was a lot fainter than usual.

'Well might you ask. One of the officers sorting you out of that car wreck found my card in your wallet. Thought he'd better contact me. Good man that.'

'But... A car crash. Why bother you with that?'

'Because it wasn't *just* a car crash, that's why. The recovery boys spotted it as they were taking the car away. They saw the leakage of brake fluid, and when they checked, one of the brake union joints had been loosened. They showed it to the copper on the spot and that's why he called me. Thought I must know something about you for my card to be in your wallet.' And those heavy-lidded eyes were intent as a hunting cat's, as he watched for my reaction.

'Brake union joint...' I shook my head in disbelief and winced and sank back on the pillows.

'Yep. Loosened a little. Cleverly done. Not loosened much, so the brakes wouldn't fail right away. It would give whoever did it time and distance. But every time you put your foot on the brake, it'd force a little of the brake fluid through the joint. A bit every time. Until suddenly there'd be no fluid left. And bingo. Bango.'

But though I could follow the policeman's explanation, it didn't make sense. Once again, it was why? Why?

'So it's like I said, you're an insurance man's nightmare. First you get your house blown up. Then your brakes tampered with. We'd better get to the bottom of it before it's third time lucky for the person behind it.' The inspector nodded cheerfully to my neighbour who was in danger of falling off the side of his bed, agog with interest.

'But, the car. It's a hired car. I've only had it a few days.'

'I got forensics on it right away. They say the damage is fresh. Only a day or so at most.'

I closed my eyes and wished my throbbing head would clear.

'So. What have you been up to this last couple of days?' We'll want to know everywhere the car was parked and for how long. You up to that yet?' The inspector clearly expected a positive answer.

'I'll try.' My mouth was dry. I tried to reach the beaker of water beside the bed and the detective handed it to me. 'Ribs eh? Painful. Been there a couple of times myself. It's OK as long as you don't breathe. But now then. Right back to when you collected the car.'

Slowly I went over my movements. First to St.Hayes where I stayed one night in a guest house. Drove to Conborough. Then went to Ivybridge and then the crash.

'And the purpose of these visits?'

One of the nurses came to escort my neighbour to the bathroom He went reluctantly, obviously not wanting to miss any of this interesting interview.

'Good,' said the detective, watching the pyjama clad figure disappear through the door. 'I've had my eye on those grapes of his.' He reached across and took a handful. 'Only perk you get in these places. Go on then. Why these visits?'

I took another sip of the stale-tasting water. I'd have shrugged, but everything hurt too much. Even the minimal shake of my head. 'Just trying to find the answer to the puzzle I told you before. That advert in the paper. I wondered if it was connected with me in some way.'

'And from what you've found out, is there a connection?'

I closed my eyes against that intense gaze. 'Nothing

that makes any sense. Too many missing pieces. It's all too long ago.'

The policeman shifted his bulk on the chair. Opened and shut the locker drawer. 'Nothing is ever too long ago. It's all there, my friend. Can't be changed, the past can't. You'd be surprised. You need a bit of luck, true. But if you dig deep enough, you always find the bones.'

He palmed another small bunch of grapes and was sitting with his back squarely to the next bed when the patient returned. 'I'd better be off. That sister told me no more than five minutes and I've been three times that already.

I managed a weak grin. 'Five minutes or twenty, there's nothing more I can tell you. I don't know why anyone should want me dead. And that's the truth.'

The policeman carefully removed some pips from his mouth and put them in his pocket. 'Well, I've been holding out on you a bit. 'Cos we found the guy who blew up your flat.'

'What!'

He nodded. 'Yep. Bit of luck. He was caught driving dangerously and when they checked his car, they found traces of Semtex in it. He was high on drugs and when Detective Sergeant French interviewed him down at the station he coughed to blowing your place up. Of course he retracted everything a couple of hours later, soon as he'd got his legal beagle. But it was him alright. Admitted he'd buggered up the timing.' And the policeman gave that quick grin. 'We might not be able to make it stick, but the thing is, he couldn't have done your car. He was inside until yesterday when he got bail.'

'But why? Did he tell them why he blew the house up?' I leaned forward, ignoring the burning of my chest.

Once more the policeman smiled. 'Said his mummy told him to do it.' He slid another grape into his mouth. 'And d'you want to know her name?' And without waiting for my reply, he bent his head conspiratorially. 'She's a woman called Iris Julian.'

And my cracked ribs screamed protest as I took a deep breath and slowly exhaled. 'My car was parked overnight in St. Hayes, and my landlady, who knows the woman, phoned her that evening and told her I was staying there. She tried to persuade her to let me call on her. But she hung up.'

'Aha. Sounds good.'

'But how could she have done it? A middle aged woman.'

'Her son said his parents used to run a motor repair shop for several years. She'd know exactly what to do. But there's no chance of proving it was her.'

At that moment the sister came. And despite my urgent pleas, she marched the policeman off.

I groaned. There were so many questions I'd not been able to ask. Iris Julian! And again, the biggest question, why? Why? I closed my eyes, seething with frustration.

The curtains swished around me and I grudgingly looked up. Inspector Green put a finger to his lips. 'Mean old bat, that sister. Great tits but no imagination. I'll only be a sec. Just want to tell you. I went to see her myself, that Julian woman. Got nowhere. She denied any knowledge of the explosion. Nice mum, letting her boy stew for it. But I want to warn you.' And for the first time his eyes showed concern. 'She's a dangerous woman, that. I don't know the reason why just yet, but you must be careful.' Turning to go, he looked back. 'No one else involved in this search of yours, I suppose?'

All the air left my lungs in a gasp. 'Jo! My girlfriend.'

'Ah. I think you'd better get in touch with her, my lad. Tell her to take care. Don't rattle the bars, so to speak.'

I stared at him in horror. 'She was going to find an address for me. She wouldn't have done more, would she?'

The policeman was about to speak when the curtain was snatched back and the outraged sister appeared. 'Well, really! This is too bad!'

Detective Inspector Green held out both wrists. 'I'll come quietly Sister.' He put on a convincing leer. 'You can whip me if you like. What with that, and your uniform, well...'

The sister's angry gaze faltered. Her lips twitched. Then she primly straightened the curtains. 'Out!' And he followed her pointing finger to the door of the ward from where he turned and blew the waiting nurse a loud, smacking kiss.

At five o'clock, I told a nurse I'd like to go to the bathroom. They'd said I must stay in bed for a while because of my concussion, but this nurse made no objection. She helped me out of bed and after a few steps, I said I'd make it on my own, thanks.

Using only one arm took some getting used to, but it was only when I stood at the basin to wash my one hand that I looked up and saw my reflection. For a moment I wondered who on earth it was, then I realised the bandaged head, half closed eyes and swollen face smothered in little cuts, was indeed my own. The doctor had told me I'd feel rough for a day or two. And one of the nurses had said I'd probably be discharged tomorrow afternoon. Tomorrow. Sunday. I must ask Jo if she could come and collect me tomorrow. And with that proposition in mind, I made my way back to the ward fairly steadily and as I was now on my feet, I was taken to a wall phone to make my call.

And this time, it was Jo who answered the phone. 'Oh Archie, it's you. I was hoping you'd have left a message last night! I've got so much to tell you . I'm so glad you've called! Why didn't you ring yesterday evening?'

'Long story, Jo my darling, and I haven't got much change for this phone. But first, are you OK?' And as soon as I heard her happy voice saying yes of course she's fine, I went on. 'I've something very important to say to you Jo. Most important.'

'Oh, so you've found out something too.' Her voice was light with anticipation.

'Yes. I've found out how much I miss you, Jo.'

'Why Archie! How nice! I've missed you too.' As well as her smile, her voice had also something of wonder and surprise.

'Not just missed you, Jo.' I kept my voice low in case other people in the ward were listening, but a quick glance showed the nurse to be out of earshot and the other patients talking to each other. There was a silence at the other end. 'Jo?'

'Yes, Archie. I'm here.' Her voice was quiet and serious.

'This isn't the right time or place - a telephone for God's sake, but Jo - I just have to tell you. I never thought I could say this to anyone without knowing who I am and all that,' I heard her beginning to speak, but I went on. 'I now know it doesn't matter. None of it. You are the most important part of my life. Do you think, when this is over and I'm back at work, we will stay together?'

'Oh Archie!' Her voice was full of tears. 'Archie! Of course.' Then laughter wobbled through. 'I've been hoping for the same, ever since we met, I think.'

We exchanged some loving words, then I asked her if she could come and pick me up tomorrow, Sunday afternoon.

'Pick you up? Where are you, and what's wrong with your car?'

'Had an accident, Jo. I'm OK and they've told me I'll be discharged tomorrow.'

'Discharged! My God, are you in hospital Archie?'

'Yep. But don't get upset. I've a couple of busted ribs and a cracked arm, but as the doctor said, I'll be myself again in a few days.'

It took me a while to comfort her, I could hear the distress in her voice, but just as I thought my cash was running out, I told her where to come to collect me. 'Glynwood Hospital, sweetheart. Yes, Glynwood. But I'm not in the maternity wing this time! Take care driving here tomorrow.'

'I will Archie. And I've discovered so much, I can't wait to see you and tell you.'

'Great, darling Jo.' And as we were saying goodbyes, our conversation ended abruptly as the coins inevitably ran out.

CHAPTER NINETEEN

Jo hugged herself. It was hard to believe she could feel so happy, especially when Archie'd had an accident and was in hospital. But he'd sounded cheerful and he'd said he'd be discharged tomorrow so it couldn't be anything too serious. And she had so much to tell him. She went over it all again in her mind.

On her first evening at home, she'd mentioned to her parents that one of the engineers at work was trying to trace his parentage and she'd told him she would get an address for him - the address of a retired doctor. When her father heard it was somewhere in the Brighton area, he'd laughed and said as the owner of a post office, he'd be able to get that for her, as long as he'd got the doctor's name. And he'd rung a colleague of his who was able later on to give him the address he'd asked for.

Jo had come back home to go to her parent's friend's party on Friday evening and she'd spent most of the day with her mother out shopping and catching up on things. Her mother remarked Jo was looking very happy. Anything to tell me? She'd asked. But Jo shook her head. 'Not sure yet,' she smiled and changed the subject. In the evening her father joined them and they set off together, Jo rather disappointed not to have heard from Archie. It was late when they got back and there was still no message from Archie on the recorder. Of course she knew his battery could have run out and perhaps he couldn't get to a phone. Hopefully he'd soon have bought himself a new charger and they could be in touch again.

On Saturday morning, still not hearing from him, she

127

decided she'd go herself and visit the doctor, and hopefully Archie would arrive sometime today.

The doctor's house was at the end of a street of large old houses. 'Greyroofs' was a sprawling Victorian building, the mellow slates which gave it the name covering the steep pitches and gables of the roof. Jo parked in the road and walked up the crunching gravel drive. The front door was painted a deep gleaming maroon and there was a brass door knocker of untouchable brightness. So Jo pressed the electric bell. The deep chime produced results; movements within and an elderly woman came and opened the door. She was thin and grey and looked worried. 'Well?' she snapped.

Jo fought back the conviction she'd not get past this dragon. She summoned a confident smile. 'My name is Jo Saunders. I'm doing a series of articles with retired doctors asking their views and contrasting the old ways of medicine with modern drugs and spare-part surgery. Dr Staton's name was passed to me and I wondered if I might see him. Or make an appointment if it's not convenient right now?'

The woman's eyes were cold. 'Dr Staton is in no state to receive any visitors, and certainly not some young reporter looking for scandal no doubt.' Her voice was high, almost shrill and they were both startled to hear a man speak.

'Edna, who is it? What's this about a reporter?' The voice was old but commanding. The woman turned away from the door. 'Only some young person, Doctor Staton. She wants to know what medicine used to be like. I've told her you don't want to see anyone.' Her back was stiff with self-righteous authority.

'Edna, let me make a few decisions for myself please.

I'm not dead yet,' came the grim rejoinder. 'Bring her in.'

With a look over her shoulder spiky with dislike, the woman led Jo across the polished wooden floor of the hall and pushed the partly opened door. The room beyond was large and looked as though it had once been a library. Now a great fourposter bed stood opposite the windows where heavy curtains shut out the morning sunshine. A small lamp on the bedside table gave the room its only light.

'Well, come in, come in,' the truculent voice commanded. 'And pull the curtains back please Edna. You know I hate them closed.'

'But you were sleeping so well, Doctor. I didn't want to disturb you.'

'Fiddlesticks. I never sleep well. Pull them back.'

The woman, the housekeeper, Jo supposed, pursed her mouth even tighter and crossed the room. The curtains swished back and sunlight flooded in, revealing a Wedgewood blue carpet. There was a large mahogany desk, a rank of book shelves and a number of glowing oil paintings on the pale walls. The drapes round the bed were of some heavy embroidered material of the purest white. Jo couldn't help turning her head as the beautiful room was revealed by the flooding sunshine.

'Camp, yes? But pleasant to live in as I've discovered during the last ten months since I had to move downstairs.' The voice was still grim.

Jo turned quickly to face him, smiling. 'Sorry if I was staring, but it really is a lovely room.'

'Come and sit down. I'll ring when I need you, Edna,' his remark was pointed and the woman turned abruptly and went out, closing the door behind her. 'Come on then,' his voice crackled with impatience and Jo felt a certain sympathy for the hapless Edna.

A chair stood beside the bed and she wondered fleetingly if the housekeeper sat there through the quiet afternoons or during the long nights, keeping watch over her charge. She approached the bed and looked at the man who lay there. Dark red silk pyjamas hung from his shoulders, brittle wrists and pale claw-like hands lay on the white coverlet. But the deep-set eyes belied his frailty, peering intently at her. 'Go on then. Sit down. I won't bite. Don't have the teeth for it.' And he gave a sudden bark of bitter laughter.

Jo chewed her lip in confusion. So much rested on this interview; it was sheer luck she'd got this far. But she couldn't cheat a man who was so obviously dying. So she remained standing. 'Look, I'm sorry, I'm not a reporter. I tricked my way in.' Before he could speak, she went on rapidly. 'You once owned a nursing home in Conborough. There's a mystery about a child who was born there and I think you could help to solve it. The baby's name was Archibald Ensor Gregory Smith.' There was a swift indrawing of breath from the man in the bed and Jo went on. 'If you don't want to talk to me, I'll accept that. It was unforgivable of me to lie, But now it's so important for Archie to find out who he is…' Her voice was choked and there were tears in her eyes.

The man leaning against the banked pillows now closed his own eyes and there was silence. Jo could hear the ticking of the clock on the marble mantlepiece. The silence stretched. Then the doctor expelled his breath in a sibilant hiss. 'At last! I knew it would come one day.' He opened his eyes and stared down at his hands. Jo stood still, afraid to move. Then he looked up at her. He stared for an embarrassingly long moment until he spoke. 'That hair of yours. Titian. Wonderful against the blue of the walls. Just let me see the sunlight on it before you sit yourself down.'

Astonished and bemused, Jo crossed the room and stood in front of the French window and looked out. There were green and tended lawns, many shrubs and a great tree at the far end of the garden. 'Yes,' came the voice from the bed. 'Your hair is the same colour as the leaves that will come on that copper beech. Wonderful.' Jo didn't mind what he was saying as long as he would give her some answers. 'Right,' he went on. 'Come and sit down. Obviously we must have a talk.'

As soon as she'd settled herself in the chair by the bed, he said, 'You haven't told me your name.' His deepset eyes bored into hers. Seeing the man's weakness, Jo was swamped by guilt at her intrusion, but determined nevertheless, she swallowed. Pulled out a tissue and blew her nose. 'Sorry, I'm Jo Saunders.'

'Right then, Miss Jo. Ask me what you like. I reserve the right not to reply. The right to silence, I think they call it.' And he gave an unexpected smile, the drawn face suddenly warm and attractive.

So Jo began. 'The child I'm asking about was born thirty years ago. He was taken to Glynwood hospital and left there. We know - well, we're almost certain - he was taken there by Ruby Timmins. From Conborough Nursing Home.'

'Ah!' He sat bolt upright and his grey eyebrows drew together. 'So she did it! Ruby did manage to do it. Thank God. Oh thank God! All these years I've worried and wondered...' His hands clutched at the quilt spasmodically and his shoulders began to shake, whether with tears or laughter Jo couldn't tell for his chin had sunk onto his chest.

Upset and bewildered, Jo sat quietly on the edge of her chair. She had a moment of irrational fear that when this spasm of emotion was over, he'd fall back on the pillow lifeless and they would never know the end of the story. Or rather, the story's beginning.

Presently he relaxed back on to the pillows and turned to face her and she saw there were tears on his furrowed cheeks. She pulled some tissues from the box on the bedside table and handed them to him. He took them and slowly blotted his face. Impulsively she reached out and took one of those wasted hands in hers.

He looked up. 'I'm not religious my dear, but if I were I would see the hand of the Almighty in your coming here today. I've so little time left. I don't mind that. I'll be with my David again. It'll be a relief to go. But it's been the not knowing...' His voice was suddenly vehement. 'Not knowing! That has been the torment all these years.'

He turned his head and looked at her; at where she sat, almost afraid to breathe, waiting for what he would tell her. 'To hear that name again after all these years! Archibald Ensor Gregory Smith. He was a great friend of mine you know. Not, like *that,* not like me and my partner, David. No, Greg and I played golf together. That was his main hobby. Work was his life. That factory of his. And his inventions. We were all astounded when he suddenly married that young secretary, Sylvia. And then when he found they were to have a child! Well! He made me promise to look after her when they knew the baby would be born while he was in the Arctic. And I did promise. Oh my God!' He turned his face away and Jo could see he was fighting for control.

He pressed those bony hands against his face and turned again to face the girl. 'Sorry...' His voice trailed off. Then he looked up. 'I'm going to ring for Edna. She was matron in my last nursing home, you know. A good woman. Embittered by circumstance. But good.

132

Kinder than you might think.' And while he spoke he pressed a bell.

Jo's heart sank. She was certain the housekeeper, nurse or whatever, would put a stop to the revelations she'd been so sure were about to be confessed. Damn!

But when the woman came into the room, something in the man's demeanour seemed to reassure her. The doctor asked for coffee and she presently returned carrying a lace-covered tray. On it stood a glass full of whitish liquid, a small coffee pot, a china cup and saucer and a plate of biscuits. The doctor leaned forward to take the glass. 'Ah, your special biscuits, Edna. I recommend them, Miss Saunders. Miss Jameson here is the most marvellous cook.'

The woman softened visibly and when she turned to Jo, her eyes were no longer hostile, but full of sadness. 'Try not to make him too tired. His pills won't work if you do.'

'Edna, my dear,' he reached forward and touched the woman's hand and Jo had the feeling it was a rare demonstration of affection. 'It won't make any difference. But what I have to tell this girl is necessary for my peace of mind. How else can I, what is it? Go gently into the night…'

'Oh, don't.' The woman's words were choked. She stood for a moment fighting for control and then turned abruptly and left the room.

'Poor Edna. I was a sad choice for her. A very sad choice. She refused to believe how it was with David and me all those years ago. And now… But this won't do. We're wasting time. So drink your coffee. This stuff of mine is vile but it helps to keep me going.'

And while Jo drank her cup of coffee, he swallowed the contents of the glass, dabbed his lips with another tissue and started to roll it into a ball between his restless fingers.

Then he looked up. 'It's a long story I have to tell you. But before I begin, where do you come into the picture, young lady?' And those shadowed eyes bored into hers once more.

She smiled at him. 'Oh call me Jo. Everyone does. You see, Archie, this Archibald we spoke of, is a friend of mine.'

'A friend?'

Her smile faltered. 'It's all happened so quickly. But I think I've fallen in love with him. In fact, I have.' And she went on to tell the story of the advertisement appearing in the newspaper and what Archie had discovered so far, right up to Ruby Timmins' mysterious trip to Glynwood.

'Right then dear girl. Jo. Now you must listen to my story. My confession.' He gave another of those wry smiles that lit up his gaunt features. 'My deathbed confession. Well, I must say it will be a relief. To know now that the child lived… Ah, how it has haunted me!' He indicated the bedside cupboard. 'There's a flask of brandy in there. Would you take it out please?'

Jo opened the cupboard. Standing at the front was a silver flask and he nodded when she took it out. 'Pour some into that glass for me if you will. And then leave it on the tray.' She quickly did as he asked and when she handed him the glass, he sipped and leaned back and closed his eyes and once more Jo was afraid he might never open them again.

She sat on the chair beside the bed, rigid with tension as she waited; willing him the strength to continue. And at last, he opened his eyes and began to talk.

CHAPTER TWENTY

'It was a few days before Sylvia's baby was due. I had her in early because her blood pressure was up, no doubt thanks to the stress of living with that woman, Iris Julian. Ruby Timmins was one of my nursing sisters. We had a very good staff in my Conborough Home.' There was a reminiscent pause before he went on. 'That morning, this Iris Julian came knocking on my door. She was Greg's housekeeper, you know. She walked in without waiting for my reply. "I've something to say to you," she announced and sat herself down on the other side of my desk. "You did an abortion on Ruby three years ago."

'Well. It was a bombshell. I thought no one had known. Because Ruby was the last person to talk.' He shot a glance at Jo. 'She was raped after a dance, yards from her home. And became pregnant. I only found out when I came across her going through the dangerous drugs cabinet. I was about to ask her what she was looking for, when I saw her face and guessed she was looking for a way out. "My God, Ruby!" I said. "Why? Why?" And she broke down and told me all about it. Her eyes were dark with despair. With horror. "I can't carry the child of that madman who attacked me. I know I did wrong in not going to the police, but I couldn't bear the thought of everyone knowing. Pointing me out..." Again the doctor looked at Jo. 'She was an Irish girl, a Roman Catholic. I told her suicide was not the way. What about her mother? "I know, I've thought of nothing else," she said. "But I know my mother. She'd be better able to accept my death than she would the scandal and gossip if I had this child.

She's a staunch Catholic, doctor. The child would be a little sinner to her."

'I made her sit down and told her I would look after her. I told her an abortion was the lesser of two evils for her; not killing a child, simply aborting developing cells. She was on night duty that week. So I did the abortion during her meal break when the other two nurses were on the wards. It didn't take long. It was only a few weeks development and I was a very experienced doctor.' His lips twisted in that bitter smile again. 'When I did my rounds I told the other nurses that Ruby had a migraine and I'd made her go to bed in one of the side rooms. Then I gave her a few days off. Not necessary for her physically but she'd been very badly traumatised and needed a break.' The doctor sipped his brandy again. He was visibly tiring. Jo sat rigid on the chair, willing him the strength to continue.

'But that was a few years ago. And now, suddenly, this Iris Julian turned up knowing all about it. "It's no use denying it," she went on. "I heard Ruby telling Sylvia Gregory Smith one day. They didn't know I was listening. She was saying what a wonderful man you are. Trust you with her life she would. And she told her all about it. The rape and the abortion. She said she should have gone to an abortion clinic but she didn't want anyone to hear about her rape. She said "There should have been two doctors to confirm an abortion, but you just went ahead. So now you're in for it. What you did was illegal."

'I tried to bluff it out. "And what do you propose to do with this story of yours?" I asked her, trying to remain cool and offhand. She said "I'm going to the local newspaper. And the police. When they start asking her questions, Ruby'll break down. I know she will. And then you'll have to leave all this. And you'll be in prison. And you know how they treat the likes of you in prison." Her voice was venomous. Full of hate.

'I sat still as a statue, my world about to be destroyed. I was a very good doctor.' He looked intently at Jo. 'I didn't think I'd be sent to prison. After all I'd saved Ruby's life that night. But I would be suspended until the Medical Council had considered my case. The likes of me, as she put it, are often gently caring people. And the thought of being suspended for maybe months would cost me my nursing home.'

Silence fell in the room as the dying man stared again into that old abyss.

"There's only one way out for you," she said. "That baby of hers is not to leave this hospital alive." I stared at her dumbstruck. I knew she meant Sylvia's baby.

'Presently I said, "But what you're asking me to do is murder."

"You didn't say that before, did you? Not when you killed that one of Ruby's."

'Well, I knew I would not, could not kill Sylvia's child. And Ruby's hadn't been a child anyway, just a collection of cells. But I needed time to think. Time to talk to Ruby. So after a long silence, I looked across at the woman and barely nodded my head. She could see what she'd done to me, and she thought she was going to have her way. She stood up. "Right then. She goes home alone. Or I go to the papers with the story." And then she was gone.

'After an age, I sent for Ruby. Told her all about it. She was prepared to lie. To confess to the police that she'd had the abortion done by some unknown woman. But we both knew she wouldn't be able to keep up the pretence. We had to think of a different way out.

'That night, one of my patients gave birth to a stillborn child. It gave me an idea. I kept the child's

137

body while the parents arranged it's funeral for the following week.

'We knew Sylvia was going straight from the nursing home to her friend's house, And that she'd arranged for post natal care at Glynwood Hospital which was a few miles away from her friend's home. We knew we had to remove her child from danger, because we couldn't tell what the woman would do when she heard Sylvia had given birth. So we decided Ruby would take the baby to the Glynwood Hospital right after the birth and we would tell Sylvia all about it the following day.'

Jo was tense in her chair. Sometime during the long disclosure she'd clasped the doctor's hand again and now his bony grip tightened. 'Then Ruby phoned me from Glynwood Hospital in tears. Didn't think she could leave the little baby. Suppose she was caught, it would all come out. I tried to persuade her. After all, it was only for the one night and the baby would be well cared for. Just leave the bag inside the door and go.

'Well. You know the rest of the story. That ghastly accident. There were unidentified remains and I feared she'd taken the baby with her after all. That they had both died. I phoned the hospital as soon as we heard on the radio what had happened. But when I asked was there an abandoned baby, the switchboard girl said no. Of course there was so much confusion that night. So many admissions of wounded people who'd been rescued. But a number of passengers had been killed. Including Ruby…'

He was silent again for a long while. Then he sipped the last of the brandy in his glass. 'So I had to tell Sylvia that her baby had died. I showed her the stillborn infant's body. The one I'd planned to show to that mad Julian woman. To buy time. Time to get Sylvia's child well out of danger.

'But now, Ruby was dead. And the child too, I thought. So I kept quiet. Said nothing. Did all I could to help Sylvia through her grief. But when she left the hospital, I didn't know where she went. Only that her friend lived somewhere near Glynwood. But only Ruby knew the friend's name.'

He reached for the silver flask again. His voice was noticeably weaker. But when Jo would have spoken, he shook his head and went on. 'Then I had a letter from Sylvia. Saying she hadn't called at Glynwood Hospital as she was alright physically. She hadn't left her friend's house. And she told me she was leaving Greg. There was no address. No way that I could plead for my friend. It was over. Iris Julian had won.'

Jo left the house half an hour later. In her bag was a stiff envelope and inside it a statement signed by Doctor Staton and witnessed by his nurse. A statement which he hoped would give Archie the proof he needed of his identity.

Jo couldn't imagine what Archie would say about all this when she told him the tale and gave him the statement. The statement which would prove his identity as the doctor had told her...

CHAPTER TWENTY ONE

After speaking to Jo, I found myself feeling much better. Sure, my ribs hurt, and my bruises, and my arm, but I felt such a glow of happiness thinking of Jo's loving words. We were going to stay together. To live together. We were going to spend the rest of our lives together. Fantastic. I lay back on my bed for a while and presently decided to get dressed.

I stood up and dragged my holdall out of the locker and opened it. Good. I was so pleased I'd put in this extra pair of trousers and shirt. I'd added them hoping I'd be able to go and meet Jo's parents, and now, of course, they'd have to take the place of the clothes which had been cut off when they put me in the ambulance. I spotted a male nurse and asked if he'd give me a hand to get dressed. I was able to climb into the chinos, but instead of the shirt, I decided to haul the spare sweatshirt over my head, leaving one sleeve hanging empty and my plastered arm comfortable against my chest.

Food came round and this time I was able to eat. Jo's words had made me feel so much better that as soon as the plates were taken away, I began to walk up and down the corridor until a sister told me to go and sit in the dayroom during the visitors' hour unless I had someone coming to see me. I stood up, and said I'd do that; no visitor expected this evening.

I found I was glad to sit down and rest again in a chair over by the window. There were several other patients lounging about, some watching the television, others playing cards or chatting in a desultory way. I found myself dozing from time to time.

'Oh, there you are Mr Gregory Smith. You have a visitor' There was a slight teasing emphasis on the 'Gregory' since I'd only referred to myself as 'Smith'. I opened my eyes and turned towards the nurse who was standing in the open doorway. A visitor. Who on earth… It couldn't possibly be Jo. Standing behind the nurse was a middle-aged woman who was staring intently at the group of patients who sat round the television. She was tall and smartly dressed and her eyes briefly met mine in their quest and I felt a jolt of recognition. The woman's gaze finally rested on one particular man and I followed her glance. It was an old man, white head sagging on his frail neck, hands gripping the arm rest of his chair.

I hoisted myself slowly and gingerly to my feet, turning to my visitor and I extended my left, undamaged hand. But she was not looking at me now, only staring at the old man the nurse had gone over to, saying, 'Come along now, Uncle. Time for bed.' She was helping the elderly patient out of the chair and my visitor was standing stiffly, her gaze never leaving the old man. She watched as the nurse retrieved a walking aid from the floor, wrapped the dressing gown firmly round the slight body and helped him up. But as she at last turned her patient round, saying, 'Well done Uncle Tony' with the unconscious patronising tone of a lot of the nursing profession, the strained anxiety on the watching woman's face changed to bewilderment.

I stepped forward. 'I'm Archie Gregory Smith. Would you like to come and sit over by the window.'

The woman dragged her gaze from the old patient who was being led from the room and turned to me, puzzled and confused. I took her elbow in my good hand and led her to the deep window recess where we were shielded from the rest of the room. She allowed herself to be seated in one of the big armchairs while I perched myself on the edge of another, facing her.

She seemed to see me properly for the first time. 'Oh, you poor thing.' Her hand came out as though to touch my bruised and swollen face, and she seemed aware of the other unseen hurts beyond the empty sleeve. 'But…' There was a helpless bewilderment in the word.

'That is my name. Archibald Gregory Smith. Aren't I the person you came to visit?' I smiled.

She stared at me uncomprehendingly. 'But Cynthia said there was an old man in the car.'

And I realised now who it was my visitor had come expecting to see. 'Ah. Yes, there was an old man in the car. He'd been giving me directions to Mrs Dawson's house. It's rather hard to find.'

She was looking at me now, the haunted, hunted look back on her face. I leaned forward, ignoring my protesting ribs, and took her hand. 'It's OK. That old man is alright. He went home today. But the man you were looking for, well, you don't have to worry about him any more. He's gone.'

I was sure I knew who this woman was, though I didn't know what to call her.

'What do you mean?'

'I must ask you your name. Are you called Sylvia, by any chance.'

'Yes, of course I am. I'm Sylvia Armstrong.

'I think you came expecting to see your first husband, Gregory Smith, yes?'

She nodded. 'Yes, that's who I came to enquire about.'

'Well, you don't have to worry about him any more. He died last month.'

The hand that had lain in mine moved suddenly,

142

clutching my fingers. 'Greg - dead? Oh no. And I...'
Her voice died away. For a few moments she sat as
though turned to stone, head down, her fingers tight
about my hand. Then she looked up at me, and
suddenly conscious of her fierce grip, released my
hand. She regarded me again and asked slowly, 'Archie
Gregory Smith?' Her face lightened. 'Then he did find
someone else! You're his son?' Her blue eyes met mine
hopefully.

There was a little silence before I replied wryly. 'It
doesn't look like it, although I do bear his name.
Perhaps you can throw some light on it.'

There was strain and confusion apparent once more on
her face. 'What do you mean, I can throw some light on
it?'

I was aware of the pain in my chest and leaned
gingerly back in my chair to try and relax.

'What do you mean, I can throw light on it?' she
repeated. And before I could reply, she added, 'How
did you guess my name was Sylvia when I came in?'

I chose my words carefully. I wanted to say 'I
recognised you. Those eyes look at me every morning
when I'm shaving. Can't you see who *I* am?' Then I
remembered the battered visage I'd seen in the mirror
today and I'd hardly recognised myself. So I just said,
'Well, it had to be you. Just before the crash I'd been to
see your friend Cynthia Dawson to ask about you. I
gave her my card and asked her to contact you. I guess
she read about the accident and had spotted my elderly
passenger in the car. Did she tell you it was your first
husband, because of hearing his name?' I gave a little
smile. 'I can understand now who you expected to see.'

She shook her head. 'I don't understand any of it.
What is your *real* name?'

I'd stuck my wallet in the pocket of my trousers and

now I took it out and withdrew my driving licence. I handed it to her. She took it and read it - the full name with its tedious data which I so rarely used.

'But that was *his* name entirely. What relation are you then?' Without waiting for a reply, she rushed on. 'Yet Greg said he had no family at all since his brother died.' Her face brightened. 'Are you Hannibal's son then?'

'I'm afraid it doesn't look like it. Hannibal died four years before I was born.'

'I don't understand.' She said once more, clenching her fists in her lap and giving them a small frustrated shake.

I cleared my throat, my hand against my protesting ribs as I spoke. 'It's a long and confused story and I don't know where to begin.'

She smiled suddenly, her face softening into beauty as the tension vanished. 'Try starting at the beginning, that's what I always used to tell my daughters.'

I gave another wry grin. 'That's just it. I don't know where the beginning actually started.' I glanced round the dayroom, deserted now, even the television set which had flickered non-stop all day, was grey and silent. 'I suppose I must start here, in this hospital. It's where all I know about myself, began.'

She said nothing, but gazed intently into my eyes.

'I was found here, left abandoned in the maternity wing on the twenty-sixth of June, nineteen eighty-six.' I was aware of the little sound she made, but went on. 'I was well dressed and cared for and had a note carefully pinned on the shawl I was wrapped in. It said 'I am Archibald Ensor Gregory Smith. Take care of me for my mother.' I was a few hours old.'

'How strange. But couldn't they have traced the

144

person who left you? Someone must have seen something.'

'They did. They remembered seeing a woman leaving the foyer quite soon before I was found. She was wearing a distinctive multicoloured headscarf and a dark coat, but she was never traced. And that same night, a coach crashed through a bridge and there were many deaths and injuries. It took all the hospital resources and of course the newspapers concentrated on that big story. One abandoned baby warranted very little space with all the sad stories that were published.'

A nurse entered the room and glanced round. She smiled brightly at us, a pair who sat talking so intently, picked up a couple of magazines and left, feet clicking on the hard floor.

'What happened then?' Sylvia Armstrong asked as soon as we were alone again.

I gave a shrug, winced and pressed my hand once more against my chest. 'Well, they tried - plenty of local advertisements after the horror of the bus crash had died down. They published the baby's name in full, you'd have thought it might have raised some comment, but nothing came of it.'

There was silence in the big impersonal room. We heard the visitors' leaving time from the corridor but neither of us took it in. The woman was silent again, her eyes never leaving my face.

I gave a tired sigh. 'That's it, really. I was taken into a children's home. Once or twice I was fostered with a view to adoption. The first time I was adopted for two and a half years, but then my adoptive mother died. And I never wanted to be adopted once more and made sure it never happened again.' I gave a bitter smile. 'You might say I wouldn't settle for second best. I had this dream, you see, that one day my real parents would

145

come to claim me and I didn't want to be involved with anyone else.' My face was downcast as I readjusted the position of my plastered arm inside my sweatshirt.

'How sad. Did you try to trace yourself when you grew up?'

I looked up and gave a small grin. 'With a name like Smith, where do you begin? I did try though. I assumed the 'Smith' was just a, well, an alias. So I tried all the other names as surnames, thinking there must be a reason for lumbering a child with so many.' I paused, remembering the years of searching. 'Ironic, isn't it? I never tried my own name. This last bit of record searching has been so incredibly quick and easy. But of course, I'd been given a newspaper cutting with my namesake's death notice.'

There was a silence between us. Then she spoke. 'That date - the day you were born. You probably thought you might be Greg's love child. Well, our own baby was born that day. And I know Greg wasn't unfaithful to me at any time. Indeed the opportunity wasn't there. For our honeymoon we sailed on a merchant ship to Sri Lanka and that's when I became pregnant. But in any case, apparently Greg hadn't shown interest in any other woman as he was totally involved in his work. And off on expeditions to the Arctic and so on.' She paused and then continued, 'He was the inventor and maintenance engineer of equipment used on Arctic expeditions.'

I nodded. 'So I've discovered.'

'You've been to St. Hayes, then?'

'Yes. As soon as I saw the notice in the paper.' I stopped and took out my wallet again and pulled out the now crumpled cutting. Sylvia took the piece of paper and read it. When she handed it back to me, I saw there were tears in her eyes.

She shook her head. 'You may think it silly, hypocritical even, to be upset after all this time. But I am sorry. Sorry for the way I left him. But I know I'd still do the same thing again. It would have been different if our baby had lived.' She was quiet again, looking out of the window over the hospital gardens towards the setting sun. 'Do you know you were born on the same day as our child?'

'Yes. That was something I found out in my inquiries.' I looked at her directly as I spoke. 'That was what made me feel there might have been a switch of the babies.'

She stared at me blankly. 'A switch? But my baby died.'

I was silent for a while, then I looked up again. 'Forgive me, but you're sure, you're totally sure your baby did die?'

She stared at me in obvious distress. 'Of course! They brought him to me, didn't they? How could I ever forget!' She suddenly buried her face in her hands, remembering. Remembering her own anguished cry to the doctor 'That's not my baby! That's not my baby!' And then Doctor Staton had given her an injection and she had drifted off.

'I'm sorry. Please, Mrs Armstrong, I'm so sorry to have upset you like this. I never meant to hurt you.' I leaned forward again as I spoke, ignoring the surge of pain, overwhelmed with remorse for causing her such distress.

Sylvia Armstrong fumbled in her handbag for a tissue. 'No, I'm sorry about that.' She looked at me again. 'I quite understand your need to find out all you can. Your name, and the birth date and so on, it's all a remarkable coincidence. But there's no link, is there, between Conborough where my baby was born, and

147

this hospital here where you were found?' She was in control again, a mature and sensible woman, trying to look back on a tragic incident with some detachment.

She was looking at me again, with that direct blue gaze I found so disconcertingly familiar. And I thought of the link I'd found; of Ruby Timmins who had died just a few miles from this very hospital. Remembered the brightly coloured scarf which lay in a place of honour in her mother's house in St. Hayes.

While I wondered what more I should tell her, she spoke again. 'You know, what you said just now about your childhood. It may sound strange to you, I know it's selfish, but you see, I mourned my baby for years. Even today, looking at my lovely daughters and their children, I wonder what my son would have been like…'

I watched her, knowing in my very bones who this woman was; knowing also that it lay in my hands whether we would ever meet again.

She went on, 'What I'm trying to say is this - if by some strange set of events, you *had* been mine, I don't believe I could bear to think of my child and Greg's, needing us, wanting us, and yet growing up with strangers!' Her voice broke. 'We both wanted him so much, you know. If he'd lived I'd never have left Greg. He didn't deserve it. But I couldn't go back to that house with that ghastly woman…' She blew her nose vigorously in her bundle of tissues. 'Sorry, you won't know what I'm talking about, but anyway, I did leave him. I came to Cynthia and she was marvellous and made me work and I met Lawrence.' She stopped abruptly, then gave him a shaky little smile. 'That must all be quite baffling to you, but I do want you to understand.'

'I do. And I know what you mean about the Julian

148

woman.'

'You've met her?' She exclaimed in astonishment.

'Well, hardly 'met'. But yes, I did try and talk to her. But she just hung up each time.' I paused, 'I've met lots of people you might have known, Reg Barrymore, Mr Evelyn the solicitor, old Mrs Timmins.'

'What, Mrs Timmins! She's still alive! She used to help me in the house until her husband became crippled. That's when the Julian woman came. I was still working as Greg's secretary. My choice, I can tell you.' And she smiled. 'But how was Mrs Timmins?'

'Pretty frail. All she talks about is her daughter Ruby.'

'Ah Ruby! We were such good friends. I was tempted to write to her but I was afraid my whereabouts might get back to Greg. I knew he'd come and try and get me back. And I couldn't face him; I was so muddled and confused.'

'I'm afraid Ruby died in a traffic accident a long time ago. And I don't think her mother has been normal since it happened.'

'Oh no! Poor Mrs Timmins. Ruby was her whole world after her husband died.'

There was real shock and distress in her voice and I paused before speaking again. I knew I must choose. Should I tell her, tell her that I had discovered Ruby was indeed the link. How Ruby had for some strange reason brought a new born baby nearly a hundred miles to another hospital? But now I thought of Sylvia's new family. They were complete and whole. I had been loved and mourned. Surely it was better for her, better for all her family, to leave it now. To leave the matter here. I myself now had Jo. I'd gone far enough with this quest of mine. I still didn't know why it had all happened, but I knew this nice woman was my mother and that was enough.

I was just about to speak again when the nurse came back. 'It's getting late, Mr Smith. The others have gone a long time ago.' She smiled at Sylvia Armstrong who was getting to her feet with an apology. 'It's alright, we don't mind family and you're Mr Smith's only visitor, but Sister will be on her rounds soon and she's a bit of a stickler.'

So we both stood up. 'I'll walk you to the lift.'

'There's no need.'

But she didn't protest and we moved together slowly along the polished corridor to the landing where the lifts waited. I pressed the button and we stood in silence, watching for a light to come on. Presently one flickered into life and we heard the click and whirr of the approaching lift.

She spoke quickly. 'I didn't ask you, are you married?'

I smiled at her. 'Not yet, but my partner is a girl called Jo. A redhead. We're living together permanently when I'm out of all this.' I indicated my plastered arm.

'I'm glad.'

I smiled at her again. I wanted to say, Don't go. Not yet. We've only had an hour with each other. Can't you see who I am? Like I can, like I feel, in my very bones? But I said, 'Thank you for coming and listening. It's been great meeting you.'

She stood looking at me, puzzled again, and uncertain, tears not very far away. She seemed about to say, you're very easy to talk to, but suddenly she showed fear and bewilderment once more. I was, after all, a complete stranger. She'd never set eyes on me before. So she said, 'I hope you'll soon be better. I'd like to meet your Jo. Perhaps you'll ask me to your wedding.' And as she spoke she looked surprised at what she'd just said. How stupid!

The lift arrived, its doors opening with a swish.

I looked grave. She took my bruised face gently between her hands and kissed me, sudden tears starting from her eyes. I stood still, my good arm stiff by my side.

She stepped quickly into the empty lift and the doors closed and she was gone.

I leaned against the cool, cream painted wall, weak and shaking. My injuries were painfully apparent and Sister would soon be around with my tablets. But just a few minutes, just a short time alone. I'd be alright then.

For thirty years I'd longed and sought for my mother. And now we'd met at last, and talked and she was kind and loving and gentle. Everything I'd dreamed of. And I hadn't told her. Hadn't put the facts before her. Because it was quite clear, my mother didn't really want to know.

The whirr of the returning lift stung me into movement. I pulled myself upright and turned slowly back to the ward, no longer aware of the protest of my bruised and damaged muscles and ribs, trying instead to cope with a new and painful void which had suddenly opened up within my battered body.

CHAPTER TWENTY TWO

Sylvia turned her car into the drive and methodically garaged it. She locked it and went slowly up the steps to her front door, letting herself in with her key. In the hall she paused and listened. Her dog Benji came to greet her, wagging his tail and she automatically let him out into the back garden and stood in the doorway staring into space until he came rushing back inside. With some relief she took off her coat and made her way to the kitchen and automatically switched on the light.

It was a large old-fashioned kitchen; deliberately old-fashioned since last year when they'd bought a Belfast sink and installed it where one would have sat many years before, now gleaming against the wooden work tops. A large Aga stood beneath the mantelpiece in a recess and beside it was an old rocking chair with a patchwork cushion. A comfortable and practical room; her kitchen, her domain.

She went over to the rocker and sat down, easing off her shoes and leaning back with her eyes closed. Lawrence should be home soon. She ought to be preparing a meal but just now the thought of food revolted her. It must wait.

She sat, rocking herself gently, arms clasped across her breast, noting vaguely the spasms of trembling that swept her body from time to time. The clock ticked in the warm, quiet room. A magazine lay on the big pine table where she'd dropped it last night when George Dawson had phoned with his strange news. She stared at its bright cover. When she'd been reading it, she'd been a normal happy woman with two grown-up daughters and three grandchildren. Now, perhaps, she had a son. Or did she? A thirty year old stranger whose presence had disturbed her greatly. Who was he? How could he be hers, that baby she'd held so briefly after his birth. And then later, a small bundle, pale and still. And she had cried 'That's not my baby! That's not my baby!' and there'd been an injection and a merciful oblivion.

She heard her husband's car and Benjie ran happily to the front door to welcome him. Still she didn't move. Couldn't move. She listened while his key fumbled in the lock and heard him speak to their dog which came running into the kitchen as if to tell her Lawrence was back. He came into the kitchen and when he saw her sitting so quietly in the rocking chair, he crossed to her side straight away.

'Sylvia! Darling! What's the matter? What's wrong?' He stooped forward and took her hands in his.

'It's alright, Lo,' she used the diminutive, shaking her head and smiling weakly to allay his fears. 'It's alright, really - the girls, the children and all. It's just that I've had rather a shock.'

He pulled a kitchen chair round and sat beside her. 'What do you mean? You're not ill, are you?'

Again she shook her head. 'Oh no. I'm not ill. It's just...well, such a strange story I hardly know where to begin.' She realised she was using the very words *he* had used when he'd started to tell his tale. 'It's to do with Gregory.'

'Gregory? That story George Dawson told you last night, have you been following it up?'

'Yes I have. But we needn't think Greg had finally tracked me down. He's dead, Lo. He died last month.' Her voice trailed away again, she was reluctant to put into words the story she must tell.

'I'm going to make us both a cup of tea. You stay there.' Lawrence got to his feet and went to put the kettle on.

Sylvia started up, suddenly aware. 'Oh Lawrence, you'll want to eat and I've not made a meal or anything!'

'It's alright. I did eat - a large business lunch. I was hoping you'd not have prepared a big meal. A slice of toast will do later on. But I'd like a hot drink.' He took two mugs from the dresser and made tea in a small brown teapot which he stood on the hob of the stove while he fetched milk from the refrigerator concealed behind the kitchen panels.

'There,' he handed her one of the mugs. She took it thankfully, cradling it against her breastbone where she could feel the warmth seep through her jumper and her hands.

'It's about the baby, Lo. The baby I lost - you remember, just before I came to stay with Cynthia.'

'Of course I remember, sweetheart. You were such a desolate little thing, so vulnerable, so alone. What on earth can that mean today, though?'

'Well, it seems it *might* be that my baby didn't die. That there was a switch. Today I met the young man who thinks he might be that baby.'

'What! Oh my god. What are you saying? Who is the fellow who told you this? Where is he? I'll see him myself. He'd no right to contact you with such a story when I'm not with you!'

'He didn't contact me, Lo. He's in hospital.' Briefly she recounted George's phone call the previous night and her subsequent trip to the hospital this evening. 'I thought it was Gregory I'd find there, Lawrence. I felt if he'd been looking for me and was injured and in hospital, the least I could do was to go and see him.

154

And find out what he wanted.'

Lawrence Armstrong sat absently stirring his tea, the spoon swirling the brown liquid round and round. Sylvia felt a sudden surge of love for him, for her loyal and devoted partner, husband in all but name for so many years.

He turned his dark eyes towards her. 'What happened?'

'I found that the Archibald Ensor Gregory Smith who'd been admitted, was a thirty-year old man. He seemed to know who I was and that I'd expected to find Greg. He told me then that Gregory was dead and he took out a newspaper cutting - from the personal column of a newspaper.'

Lawrence cut in. 'Are you sure? I don't remember seeing anything like that in our newspaper.'

Sylvia's tired face lightened for a moment with a smile. 'When did you last read the personal column, Lo? When did I? It's not our local paper is it?'

'Well, go on. What did he tell you?'

She rubbed her hand across her eyes. 'Not much really. That he'd been left in the Glynwood Maternity wing when he was just a few hours old. That he'd seen the newspaper advertisement with his complete name, the name that was pinned to his shawl when he was found. Naturally, after seeing that a namesake had died, he's been trying to see if there's a connection. He's been to the solicitors in St. Hayes but they couldn't help him much without real proof of his identity.

'Oh, so that's it, is it, after part of the estate? A glib tale to try and get his hands on someone else's money.' Lawrence's face was grim.

'I thought that too, at first, but he showed me his driving licence with his name in full. And at least, Lo, having read the newspaper announcement, we now know that Greg has indeed died.' She looked meaningfully at him with a little smile. He stared at her for a moment, uncomprehending, and then his face lightened.

'My God! So we can be married at last! Well, well,' his face broke into an engaging smile and he came and stood before her. 'Do I make a formal proposal or what? I'm a bit out of practice!'

She laughed. 'Idiot! But I'll be glad though, won't you? I've called you my husband all these years. I don't feel guilty about it these days, like I used to, but I still think it'll be good.'

'How could our marriage,' he stressed the word faintly, 'be better than it is, sweetheart? Better than it's always been. We'll get a licence of course, but I can't see how it can make any difference.'

Sylvia spoke a little shyly. 'Well, we can make the girls - legitimate.' The word came with something of an effort.

He snorted. 'Legitimate be dammed! Of course they're legitimate. They've had my name ever since they were born. You too, are legally Sylvia Armstrong. By law. By deed poll.'

'I know, but...' her voice trailed away once more.

He suddenly dropped to his knees before her and took her hands in his. 'Sylvia, my dear girl. We'll get married as soon as we can at the Register Office. But I meant what I said. Our life together couldn't be happier. Now could it?'

She leaned forward and kissed him. 'Darling Lo. No, it couldn't be more happy. You're a wonderful husband. The best in the world.' She leaned back. 'Perhaps we ought to stay just as we are and not bother with a wedding ceremony.'

He pulled himself to his feet and smiled down at her.

'Well, it's certainly shutting the stable door after the horse has bolted. But we'll do it anyway. Sort of tidy up the loose ends, eh?' His face broke into a laugh. 'Where shall we go for our honeymoon?'

She got to her feet, smiling. 'I'll give that some thought. But right now I'm going to get you something to eat in case you change your mind! An omelette perhaps?'

'Mm, that'd be nice. But only if you feel up to it.'

While she cooked, he continued his restless walk round the kitchen, and she knew he was thinking about the death notice and its implications. He paused by the stove, took a china ornament off the mantelpiece and inspected it absently and replaced it. Through her distress and uncertainty, Sylvia found herself smiling fondly. Lawrence's habitual fiddling with things when he was disturbed was a family joke.

Presently they sat at the big table, he with a large mushroom omelette on a brown earthenware platter, she with a corner of it on a small plate. He picked up his fork and began to eat. After a while she felt his eyes upon her and she looked up, her fork absently chasing the food round on her plate. 'It's no good. I can't eat a thing, Lo. I keep seeing that boy's face, all bruised and cut.' Her voice broke. 'Who is he, Lo? How can we ever know?'

He put down his own fork. 'I don't know, but I intend to find out.' His voice was grim. 'He could be a con man you know, that driving licence could be a forgery. Someone who goes after advertisements like this one where there may be money at the end, with whatever story he can come up with.' His jaw set. 'This is about as far-fetched a yarn as any I've heard.'

Sylvia propped her elbows on the table and leaned her head on her hands. 'I know. I've thought all that. But,

157

there's something about him I can't explain... Suppose it is true!' She raised her head and regarded him miserably. 'Just suppose it was my baby left in that hospital all those years ago! Oh my god, it doesn't bear thinking about!' Her arms dropped to the table, and she sank her head on them, her shoulders heaving as sobs wracked her body.

With an exclamation that was a mixture of anger and pity, Lawrence came to her side.

'You're overwrought, Sylvia darling. And no wonder after hearing such a story. I'm going to give you a stiff whisky and you're going to bed. And tomorrow I'm going to see this chap and get to the bottom of it. Right? Now, off you go to bed and I'll bring you the drink when you're ready.'

'Alright, Lawrence,' she gulped and rubbed her sleeve across her eyes, childlike. 'I'll go on up. But I'd just as soon have a hot drink.'

'OK. I'll make it a hot toddy. Go on. Off with you.'

At the door she turned and looked at him. He smiled and held out his arms and she went into them and pressed her face against his shoulder and burst into tears again.

'It's alright, Sylvia. It's alright. It'll pass. Tomorrow we'll look into it and it'll all be sorted out. You'll see.'

'But suppose,' she raised her tearstained face, 'suppose it's true. That he's,' she found it hard to get the words out, 'that he's my son.'

'Sweetheart, *if* he is, and it can be proved by DNA, then we'll accept that we have a grown-up son. And the girls will have a brother. They always wanted one. Come on now! That's not a disaster is it?' He smoothed back her hair.

'Not a disaster. Of course not. It's not the present or the future that's upsetting me. It's the thought of a little

158

boy growing up and needing me and wondering why I didn't come. And me all the while being totally oblivious.' She looked at him, her eyes shocked and desolate.

'Sylvia.' His voice was stern. 'What's the use of thinking like that! Go to bed. Think of tomorrow if you like, or next week. But put those thoughts out of your mind. If this young man is genuine, he certainly wouldn't want you brooding over the past like this. And if he's not genuine, we'll soon find out. Now, off you go!'

She nodded her head slowly. 'You're right. I'm being stupid. It's all been such a shock, hearing about Greg and all. It's brought it all back somehow.'

'Yes, I know. Your feelings of guilt. Our feelings of guilt, I should say. But we've been over it many times, my darling. And there were faults on Greg's side too, remember.'

Sylvia Armstrong pulled out another tissue and blew her nose. He could feel her shoulders squaring. 'I'm alright now. Poor Lo! What an evening for you. And football on the TV too!' She smiled shakily.

'Oh! I'd forgotten that. You can whistle for your hot toddy! Go on. I'll be with you in a minute.'

She kissed him tenderly. 'I'm a very lucky woman to have you. Such a lucky woman.' And comforted, she turned and went up to their bedroom.

CHAPTER TWENTY THREE

Before Jo left home to go and collect Archie from Glynwood Hospital, in Devon, she told her parents about her relationship with him. Her mother hugged her tearfully and said she'd thought there must be a man in Jo's life because she was so much happier than she'd been for such a long time. Her father too showed how pleased he was that she'd found someone and they let her know how delighted they'd be to meet him. Of course, Jo had said, it might be a week or two before he was ready to travel after his accident, but she knew he was keen to meet them as well.

She phoned the hospital and was put through to Archie's ward and the sister said he'd be discharged that day when the registrar had completed his morning rounds. If not, she would be able to collect him the following day. Jo thanked her and said she'd call at the hospital that afternoon and stay overnight if it should prove necessary.

When she arrived at the hospital she made her way to the reception desk and asked for Archie's ward number. The receptionist repeated her request. 'Archibald Gregory Smith? Yes, he's in Ward Four on the second floor. But you can't go up until after two thirty as the patients are resting.' Jo thanked her and made her way across the room to the group of chairs.

A woman standing nearby followed her and as Jo sat down, she came and stood in front of her with her hand outstretched. Smiling, she said, 'I heard you ask for Archie's room and I think you must be Jo. Yes?'

Puzzled, Jo agreed that, yes she was and looked at the

woman enquiringly. Then, as the woman shook her hand, Jo looked at her directly. Those darkly fringed intensely blue eyes were so like Archie's. Could this possibly be the person Archie was searching for?

Before she could speak, the woman introduced herself. 'I'm Sylvia Armstrong. I met Archie yesterday evening and he told me about you. I knew you must be Jo because of that wonderful coloured hair he told me about. And I felt I must come and see him again before he leaves. I believe he's probably going home today?'

Jo smiled and said, 'I hope so. I've come to collect him. But you...' She let out a huge sigh of astonishment. This was Sylvia. This was Archie's mother. But it doesn't look as if Archie had told her that she was. She seemed very anxious and uncertain and eager to have someone else beside her when they went to see Archie. And in Jo's handbag was that envelope so full of astonishing evidence...she wondered what to say.

She patted the chair next to her and the woman sat down. Jo leaned forward and put her hand out again. 'This must be terribly traumatic for you. I've been thinking about it a lot. I just don't know how I'd cope with a situation like this.'

Sylvia looked at her with an expression of relief on her face. 'I can't tell you how I feel. I hardly slept at all last night. Half of me doesn't believe that strange story he told me he has discovered. *Can't* believe it. And yet part of me feels it might be true. I don't know who could have done such a wicked thing, or why.' Her eyes were dark with misery. 'And the things I said to him. You wouldn't believe what I said to him yesterday evening.' Her voice was anguished.

Jo put her hand on the woman's arm and squeezed it with wordless sympathy. The older woman looked up, tears welling in her eyes.

'I told him I'd rather he had died! Words to that effect. Oh God, what is happening to me! If you only knew how I'd longed for that baby.' She fumbled in her bag for a tissue.

'Don't distress yourself about what you said. Archie has had quite a lot of time to work it all out, but you had this crazy story sprung upon you. No wonder you're confused.'

'I told my husband Lawrence all about it last night. He was angry because I was so upset. He thinks it's some kind of elaborate hoax. Do you mind my saying that?' She looked at Jo anxiously.

'No, of course not. It's what any intelligent person would be bound to think without any proof to back up the story.'

'Yes, I said something like that to...' She stumbled over the name. 'To him, to the young man,' she went on, 'that there's nothing to link it all together.'

'And what did Archie say?'

'That's just it. He seemed to change the subject, but afterwards, last night, I kept thinking he'd been about to tell me something - something that maybe would have convinced me.' She stared into space, shredding the tissue in her hands. 'What do you think?'

Jo stood up. 'I think it's time we went up to see him. Come on.'

But Sylvia Armstrong shook her head. 'You go up. I'll stay here for a little while.'

'You will come up though, won't you?' Jo asked. 'You will come to see him?'

There was a pause. 'Yes. I'll come. I know I must speak to him again before he leaves. In fact I don't think I could have stayed away.' She gave a little laugh, the first Jo had seen and the resemblance to Archie was stronger than ever.

'OK. Shall I tell him we've met?'

'No, please don't say anything about me.'

'Alright. But he might be ready and waiting to leave, so don't be too long.'

Jo crossed the foyer and took a lift to the second floor and quickly made her way to Ward Four. She passed through the swing doors with an eager step and a few moments later she found Archie, sitting in a large chair beside his newly made bed.

She stopped abruptly. Although the swellings on his face had subsided, the skin round his eyes was darkly purple and pocked with small grazes. He was wearing his own trousers, but the plaster on his arm meant he was in his sweatshirt with one sleeve dangling empty.

'Archie!' He looked up and the next moment she was on her knees by his chair, tears coursing down her cheeks.

I laughed, a little guardedly, one hand on my ribs. 'Come on, Jo, I'm going home in a minute when they've brought my medication pack. Don't I get a kiss, then?'

Jo's laugh was shaky. 'I don't know where to aim, Archie. You look so - sore.' But we embraced and shared a cautious, tentative kiss, then Jo's wet cheek was against mine. I pulled her down on to the chair beside me, her hands still clinging to my uninjured arm. Then we sat, heads close together, Jo's questions about my injuries, about the accident, a confusion of words tumbling out.

I told her all I could about the accident, repeating what Detective Inspector Green had told me about Iris Julian being behind the explosion of the flat, and that she was probably also responsible for the brake damage to the car I'd smashed. Jo wept again hearing about the car crash, knowing it could have ended so tragically. Like losing her first husband I guessed.

While I was comforting her, I looked up and saw Sylvia Armstrong standing hesitatingly in the ward doorway. I smiled and pulled myself out of my chair, drawing Jo up beside me.

'Well, this is a surprise. Come and meet my Jo.' My face must have been split with a grin of sheer delight. Both women shook hands and smiled, and I could see Sylvia was glad there was someone else with us. She, like Jo, looked emotional. And Jo wiped her eyes, took a deep shuddering breath and held my hand as she sat down again. A nurse brought another chair for Sylvia and told us the pharmacy was so busy it would probably be another half an hour before my medication arrived.

'Good,' said Jo. 'We've a lot to talk about.'

We all sat down and for a moment no one knew what to say.

Sylvia began. 'I had to come back. There's so much you haven't told me.' She looked at me again. 'Please don't hold back because of my reaction yesterday. It was all so incredible. So totally unexpected.' She paused. 'But if,' again the pause, 'if you are my son,' she stumbled over the words, 'then I am entitled to know everything you have found out.'

Jo looked at me, this guy she herself had so newly discovered. I picked up Jo's hand absently while I thought. Then I gave a sudden grin. 'There's a lot I don't know either. And much of what I've found out is pure guesswork - nothing concrete. Nothing that completed a picture.'

Jo spoke quietly. 'Well, I've found out some things that might mean a lot to you both. But…'

I squeezed the hand which still lay in mine. 'Go ahead, Jo. If it'll clear things up, then I suppose we should both be told.' I looked questioningly at the woman who nodded, tensely twisting the strap of her handbag on her lap.

So Jo began to tell her story.

CHAPTER TWENTY FOUR

Jo went through her story as briefly and succinctly as she could. Several times Sylvia or I myself exclaimed or asked a question. But for the most part, Jo told her tale without hesitation, her eyes preoccupied, seeming to feel herself back in that lush bedroom full of sunshine and flowers and the imminence of death that she'd described so clearly.

Her voice broke for the first time as she finished her story. She blew her nose and picked up her bag and took out the envelope with Dr Staton's statement in it. Sylvia still sat rigidly; tears had been flowing down her cheeks, but she'd shaken her head and told Jo to go on whenever the girl had looked questioningly at her, ready to pause. I too, felt weak and shaken. I'd been sure of my identity for some time now, but all these details of the tragedy were new and disturbing.

Together Sylvia and I read the doctor's brief and concise statement and handed it back to Jo who folded it carefully and put it back in its envelope.

Presently Sylvia spoke. 'Poor Dr Staton,' she said quietly. 'And poor Ruby. She was such a sweet girl. But to think they were caught up in such a…' Her voice trailed off as the enormity of the tragedy struck her. She was about to speak when a nurse approached.

'There's only supposed to be two visitors to a bed, but although you're ready to leave, Mr Smith, the pharmacy has been delayed and it'll probably be a bit longer still before they bring you your pack. So you'll have time to see this gentleman.' She turned towards the door and waved to the man who was standing there.

I looked across and saw a well-dressed, middle-aged

man approaching with a stern, set look on his face. Sylvia too, had turned and gave a gasp of surprise. 'Lawrence!' she exclaimed. 'What are you doing here?'

He said nothing to her, but stopped beside her chair and placed one hand on her shoulder in a proprietary manner, glanced briefly at Jo and then stared hard, glared, at me who returned the look for a moment, and then, grinning wanly, struggled to my feet. I held out my left hand. 'I'm not surprised to see you here Mr Armstrong. You must wonder what on earth is going on.'

The older man hesitated briefly, then took my proffered hand and shook it awkwardly with his right. 'You're right. I'm sorry to come barging in like this but Sylvia was so distressed last night. I came home early this afternoon to be with her, but when I found her car gone, I guessed she might be here. In any case, I needed to see you for myself.'

'This is Jo, my partner.' Lawrence Armstrong shook her hand gravely and observed Jo's strained smile. He could see Sylvia's pallor and tear-wet eyes. Whatever had been said here in the last half hour had taken its toll on all three of us. I knew from shaving that morning that I was beginning to look a bit more like my old self and I wondered if any resemblance to Sylvia was beginning to show. I'd bet part of him was sceptical and angry, but maybe there was something that disarmed him.

'Sit down, Lawrence.' He found the chair Sylvia had indicated and brought it to the bed, sitting down beside her.

Sylvia spoke again. 'What I told you last night - I didn't believe it either. I didn't want to believe it and I couldn't. But as you know I didn't get much sleep. There was a sort of feeling, I can't explain it. I had to

167

come back today to find out what he hadn't told me. I knew there was more.'

Lawrence put his arm round her shoulders. 'It's alright, darling. I'm not going to throw him out the window - not while he's still in plaster anyway.'

We all smiled weakly at his pleasantry and some of the tension left the air. I leaned forward, winced and held my ribs and settled back in my chair. 'It's a long and strange story. If you choose to disbelieve it, I wouldn't blame you. I've been thinking hard all night too. And for me, for myself, this search I've been making is over. I've found out all I need to know. About myself and about Jo and about...' But I stopped short of saying 'about my mother'.

I smiled at Sylvia. 'The past is over. We can't change any of it. When I leave here, as soon I'm back at work, Jo and I are getting together. Permanently I hope.' I gave a sudden grin. 'You two had better do the same I think.'

Sylvia laughed and a faint blush tinged her cheeks. Lawrence lost his man-of-the- world air of sophistication and looked startled and embarrassed. Then he grinned. 'I won't ask you how you knew that, but you're right. That's what I've been doing this morning.' He withdrew a piece of paper from his pocket. 'Date of our Register Office, appointment, sweetheart. Have you decided yet where we shall go for our honeymoon?'

Sylvia looked smilingly up at him, patting his sleeve. He glanced down at her hand and then at mine which was lying extended on the arm of my chair. We had the same pointed index finger, the remaining finger tips square, and long curved thumbs, Sylvia and I. Then he looked at my face. He would see we had the same blue eyes, the same straight black brows. I felt the shiver of

168

his recognition, feeling he'd know now that Jo and I were not the couple of scheming fortune hunters he'd thought us to be. And he suddenly seemed not to know what to say.

Jo spoke up. 'Look, if Archie has to wait yet another half hour before he gets his medical pack, I think he should lie down and rest. You really do look exhausted, Archie, and we've a drive ahead which won't be very comfortable.'

Sylvia gave an exclamation of distress. 'Of course. How could we be so thoughtless! We'll go at once.' She stood up, paused for a moment uncertainly, then stooped and brushed a kiss on my cheek. Lawrence nodded gravely, his penetrating gaze on my face, no longer hostile. 'We'll wait downstairs to see you both before you leave' and Sylvia's smile included us both.

'I'll be back in a minute,' whispered Jo and she followed them down the corridor.

I sank back against the chair and closed my eyes and kept them closed until a persistent young nurse repeated several times, 'Here's a nice cup of tea for you Mr Smith.' Wearily I opened my eyes and took the cup from the kind nurse. I sat holding it absently until presently Jo returned.

'They wanted our address.'

'What do you make of it all Jo?' I asked quietly.

She sat down beside me, placing the cup safely on the bedside table. 'Her husband had doubts at first, but I think he's coming round now. Sylvia of course, believes it. She knew Iris Julian only too well. But believing it is one thing, accepting that you suddenly have a thirty-year old son can't be easy. She's in almost as much state of shock as you are, Archie my love.'

'Can we go home, Jo?' There was a quiet desperation in my voice.

'Yes, we can as soon as they bring that pack. I've just been talking to the sister and she told me she'd wanted to keep you here for another night. But she said as long as I drive carefully it'll be alright for you to leave. I must contact your doctor as soon as we get back and report any change you feel.'

She hauled my holdall from the locker and took my remaining possessions from the bedside table while I slowly drank the cup of tea, leaning back with my eyes closed once more.

'Here we are sir,' a young man had arrived by the bedside. 'Here's your pack. The tablets and dressings are inside. And we'll be contacting your doctor of course to bring him up to date with your injuries.'

Down in the foyer, Sylvia and her husband were waiting. They stood up, and we checked and exchanged telephone numbers and made some small talk.

Jo went off to bring the car round to the collection point and Sylvia and Lawrence accompanied me and while waiting, my mother turned to me.

'Archie, I know you'll need a couple of weeks at least in your own place to get over this, but when you're well, perhaps you and Jo would come and stay with us for a break?'

I smiled. 'Sounds great. But as you say, I've got to get my act together first.' I turned to Lawrence and held out my free hand again. 'Thanks for coming to see me. And you too,' and I put my arm round my mother's waist. She hugged me gently, so aware of my injuries, and tried to hide her tears again.

As we walked outside to the pick-up spot, I was thinking if Jo and I came to stay with them, I'd have to meet my half-sisters and their families. I wondered how I'd cope. If indeed I would cope. I'd been a loner all my life until meeting Jo. And Jo was everything to me now. I was glad to have met my mother, but didn't know if we would need to be part of each other's future. Or how her daughters would cope with meeting me.

Jo's car pulled up and I hauled myself on to the passenger seat, wanting more than anything to set off on the journey to her flat. Part of me felt guilty to want to leave so fiercely; to part from the woman I'd spent so much of my life longing to meet.

Lawrence put my holdall into the boot and Jo called her goodbyes and moments later the car was driving off. Looking in the rear mirror, I saw my mother turn to her husband who took her into his arms.

And I bit my lip feeling guilty at what my search had done to her.

CHAPTER TWENTY FIVE

It was evening by the time we got back to Jo's flat. To our relief, Gloria wasn't there; she'd left a note to say she was staying with a friend in Yorkshire for a couple of days.

'Jeeze!' I exclaimed when Jo read me the message. 'Just you and me. Jo, I can't tell you how much that means to me.' And she agreed, steering me into the sitting room to lie on the couch.

'Now, stay there Archie. Have a kip while I get us something to eat. No, don't say it,' she interrupted me as I began to speak. 'You really do need to rest. You've gone through so much these last few days. Go on, close your eyes,' and she bent and kissed my battered face as I settled back on the couch.

Jo took her time preparing our meal. Each time she glanced into the sitting room, she saw me lying unmoving, eyes closed, pretending to be fast asleep. When she'd finally put a chicken curry in the oven, she came back to the sitting room and sat for a long time in an armchair, thinking, I suppose. I was still feigning sleep to give her time to rest.

Presently she spoke quietly to me. I immediately opened my eyes. 'I thought you were sleeping Archie. But since you're awake, I'll tell you what I've been thinking about. All your life, you've been alone. And now, not long after meeting me and finding out the delight of having a partner, you've been plunged into other relationships. I know you've always longed to find out who your parents were; perhaps to meet them, and I know you were deeply moved on discovering Sylvia was indeed your mother. And yet I could see

172

how much you wanted to come away and just be with me.'

She got up and came and sat beside me on the couch, careful not to press against my ribs. 'It's going to take a bit of getting used to, when you meet your half sisters and their children. And I know you would like to meet my parents. But at the moment you are both physically and mentally battered by all that has happened and all that has come to light.' She took a deep breath. 'So I'm going to keep you to myself until you're able to cope with your injuries, and not until you are better will I let you meet the new people who want to get to know you. So there.' She smiled and leaned across and kissed me.

My voice was husky when I told her how much her plans meant to me. How I agreed I needed time to get my head round all that we'd discovered. And all the proof that she had found. What a girl!

The phone rang. It was her mother, and they spoke for good while, her mother agreeing with Jo's decision to guard me against new meetings until I was better. This was despite her wanting to meet me herself, but she could well understand my need to recover from the injuries I'd got from my accident. Jo saw I was listening while she was on the phone, but she carried on chatting, glad to see me looking more relaxed and not minding me obviously eavesdropping while she spoke.

When she put the phone down, she came across the room and sat beside me.

'That was nice of you, Jo. What you said about not letting all my new relations meet me just yet. It practically overwhelmed me this morning, meeting my mother, again. And her husband.' I'd stumbled over the word 'mother'.

She lay down on the couch alongside me, still so careful not to press against my ribs. I stroked her hair with my good hand. 'Just you and me, Jo. I feel better already, being here with you. They'll be expecting me back at work on Monday though, so I'd better phone David in the morning. And I'll have to go and see my doctor and find out how long before I'll have this plaster off.' I touched my chest and grinned. 'And how long before I can breathe properly again.'

'Good idea to phone David.' She turned to look at me. 'I don't think you'll mind if your work pals come to see you, will you?'

I looked surprised and nodded. 'You're right. I won't mind anyone coming who I've worked with over the years. What will be a big strain is meeting members of my unknown family. Feeling like an unwanted intruder. After all, they never knew I existed and I'm sure they'll wish I'd never turned up.'

Jo looked at her watch and stood up. 'Dinner's ready, Archie. Make yourself comfortable at the table while I fetch it. OK?'

'Definitely OK.' And I got to my feet as Jo went into the kitchen.

I'd been surprised that Jo and her mum were in agreement to give me plenty of time to recover from my injuries before planning a meeting. I felt sure I'd be ready to meet her parents quite quickly, much sooner than my own unknown siblings and their families. And to my relief, just as I began to fret about that, Jo came in with the mouth-watering meal. I was feeling hungry for the first time since the accident and what made it so good was being alone with Jo.

We watched television for a while and went off to bed earlier than usual. Jo helped me get my sweatshirt off as I undressed and I was glad to lie down once more in her bed. I'd taken my medication and Jo had checked my many stitched cuts and the bruises and dressed them as directed on the medical pack. Then she came and lay alongside me, her bare skin against mine, careful not to lean against my painful chest and tender wounds. She'd told me how thankful she was that I was at home with her. It was only yesterday she'd got the shock of hearing about my accident. And now here I was. With her. And she presently fell asleep. I felt overwhelmed by her gentle care and drifted off to sleep while Jo lay next to me.

In the morning, just as we finished our breakfast, Jo's mobile rang. She answered it, looked surprised and handed it to me. 'It's Inspector Green, He wants to talk to you, Archie. Here you are,' and she handed the phone to me and started to clear the table.

'Oh yes, I gave him your number when I saw him in hospital,' I said as I took the phone from her. Then, 'Good morning Inspector Green.'

'Morning, Mr Smith,' replied the policeman. 'Got some more news for you. That woman's son who blew up your flat, Cyril Julian, has got his legal beagle running round in circles. Says Cyril is the son of your namesake who died recently. Says his mother told him to get rid of you before you took over the dead man's estate.'

'What!' I gasped. 'Good God, whatever has he been told! And anyway, it's up to him to prove what he claims, isn't it?'

'Exactly. And the best way is using DNA. I don't know if you've been able to prove your own relationship yet but if you have, we'll need your DNA too.'

I quickly told him what we'd discovered and that I'd actually met my mother.

'Well, well. We'll need to know a bit more. And if

175

that's the case, we could do with her DNA as well. That'd prove you were the son of her husband, and would that match Cyril Julian's? Good question, eh?'

'But how would that affect the court case? He blew the place up, didn't he?'

'Yes he did. But the legal boffin would try to lessen the verdict by use of mental and emotional reasons for his act. Whatever.'

I spoke slowly. 'I'll come over to the station today, if you like. And then I can tell you all I've learned. And show you the reason for it all on a signed piece of paper. I don't like to call it a confession.'

'Great. Come in the afternoon. If I'm not here, see Detective Sergeant French. All the best.' And the conversation ended abruptly.

Jo phoned our workplace to say why she wouldn't be in, and that I'd be seeing my doctor this morning. Justin was the one who answered the phone and he was very sorry I'd had an accident and wanted to know all about it. And he reminded her that his own arm, broken while he was in Africa, was almost better already, so he said she must tell me not to worry. Jo thanked him and said I'd would give him a ring later on, after seeing my doctor so I could bring everyone up to date with everything.

After breakfast Jo drove me to the doctor's surgery. When I came out she said I was looking pale and bothered. 'Yes, well. I've got to go round to the hospital for a couple of X-rays before my doctor will see me at a one o'clock appointment this afternoon. And then I have to go and see Inspector Green.'

'That'll be OK Archie. I've got the whole day off you know.' She smiled and held the car door open as I gingerly lowered myself onto the passenger seat. Luckily at the hospital we didn't have to wait too long and Jo drove us home soon afterwards and I took a much-needed rest before we lunched together.

At the surgery my doctor was busily reading up the notes on the computer screen. 'So you got this arm smashed when your car turned over onto a rock, eh? And it smashed your ribs too. Not sure what gave you concussion, but you pretty soon got over the worst of that.' He chatted as he examined me, and found I couldn't remember anything about being freed from the wrecked car and loaded into the ambulance or about the operation which followed. I was relieved though to hear the X-ray showed my arm to be in good condition and my doctor told me how to exercise my hand and elbow regularly. The other X-ray had been on my ribs. 'Yep, three ribs broken, Mr Smith. Try and lie on that side when you're in bed. It'll make your breathing easier, and you must practise deep breathing as often as you can. It can take up to six weeks to heal your broken arm, and probably your ribs as well.' When I said I wanted to go back to work long before that, my doctor patted me on the back. 'Up to you, Mr Smith, but rest is the best way to speed up healing. Just do those exercises regularly.'

I climbed back into Jo's car carefully and told her what the doctor had said.

'Well, let's just wait and see how you're feeling over the next couple of weeks. You may be well enough to go into the office by then. I know how keen you are on your work, Archie.'

I gave a rueful grin. 'You're right. I know I won't be up to much practical work for a while, but there's plenty of other stuff to do in our business.'

At the police station I was glad to be met once more by Detective Inspector Green. The policeman was intrigued by the story that had come to light. As he read the doctor's 'confession', he muttered, 'I'm sorry for the old boy who wrote this statement. Sometimes people are stuck in an impossible situation. See it often in my job. Anyway, we'll get this DNA thing sorted out. And you will phone your mother today?' He peered intently at me as he spoke.

'Yes, I will. As soon as I get home.' And I did.

Sylvia was very pleased to get a call from me. 'I was dying to phone you, Archie, but afraid I'd wake you up or something. How are you? Are you feeling any better yet?'

I brought her up to date with my medical visits, and then told her about the talk with the policeman about Iris Julian's son.

'What nonsense!' she exclaimed. 'Iris Julian was married for years and the child was about seven when she and her husband moved into the gardener's cottage on Greg's land. I'm not sure where they'd come from, but they certainly weren't local. But yes, I'll let them have my DNA too.' She suddenly laughed. 'It'll put paid to my daughters' doubts too. Mind you, as soon as they meet you, they'd have to believe their eyes. Even Lawrence can see a resemblance despite your black eyes and cuts and grazes!'

When I put down the phone, I found I was more relaxed than I'd expected. But I still didn't want to meet the rest of the family until I felt better.

And after the two medical visits and the meeting with Inspector Green, I felt I certainly needed to rest for the remainder of the day. Jo agreed, and we spent another evening half watching television and half dozing. And after a number of calls from my colleagues, Jo finally switched off the phone and packed me off to bed. I, a man who'd always been in charge of my life, was glad to be treated like this for once and I lay awake waiting for Jo to come and lie down beside me. Which she did and we both slept deeply until the morning sun awoke us.

CHAPTER TWENTY SIX

Gloria arrived back at the flat the following morning. 'Good Lord!' she exclaimed when she found both Jo and me there, and gave a little scream when she saw my blackened eyes and plastered arm. Jo made coffee and as we sat down together, to our delight, Gloria told us she was planning to move in with her boyfriend. And Jo was especially astonished to hear that the boyfriend she'd been seeing lately, was actually her ex. 'And we've decided to live together once more. And this time forever, we hope.'

We both congratulated her and Jo wanted to know exactly where they'd be living and the two girls kept chattering away excitedly. 'Can you take over my share of the rent here, Archie?' Gloria suddenly asked me.

'Well, of course I can, Gloria. I've already settled this with Jo, despite her arguing against it. Anyway, we wish you and your boyfriend the very best. And as soon as I'm up to it, I'd like to cook a meal for you both. How about that Jo?'

She laughed and agreed and wrote down Gloria's new address and they both went off to Gloria's room and began to pack all her possessions. They made several trips down to her car and I felt frustrated because I couldn't carry her suitcases down the stairs. They shooed me out of the way as I loomed over them and I could see they were both happy about Gloria finding her partner and a new home.

After we'd waved her goodbye, we strolled back upstairs.

'I'm going to have to go back to work tomorrow, Archie. There's a lot to be done and I don't mind leaving you alone now that Gloria won't get her hands on you!'

Jo took me downstairs to meet her Great Aunt Matilda, and as the sun was shining, her elderly aunt invited us to spend the day in her walled garden, a sun trap that was sheltered from the spring breeze. Jo started up the barbecue and I managed to grill several mackerel with my one hand, a job I'd always enjoyed.

Matilda praised me for my success in cooking the fish. 'This is my favourite food, as a matter of fact.' She thanked me and turned to Jo. 'You seem to have made a very good choice, my child, in your new man friend.'

Jo smiled and helped herself to another plateful and nodded her head, her copper hair gleaming in the sunlight.

Later, when we'd finished eating and I'd cleared away the plates, 'Are you two children going to get a house of your own to live together?' Matilda asked, peering over the top of her spectacles as she spoke.

'Until I'm better, we'll stay in your house if you don't mind, Great Aunt,' I smiled. 'My own flat has been burned down, so it'll be a while until I can find somewhere else.' I put my good arm round Jo's shoulders and gave her a hug.

'Hmm. Well, I can understand that. I hope it won't take you too long to get better.'

'About six weeks, according to his doctor, Auntie,' said Jo. 'But, as you said, it's something to take our time about. Just being together is great.'

'Six weeks isn't too long,' Matilda agreed. 'It's just that conventions from the past are still part of my life. In my time, no one lived together until they were wed. Mind you, for me that wasn't a very good choice. The man my parents had suggested I should marry, was not a good partner for me. And although it caused a good deal of gossip, I was secretly pleased when he ran off with another woman. We had no children, but I made quite a good living on my own, writing for some magazines.'

Jo turned to me. 'Yes, she's a very good writer. You still submit articles to several papers, don't you, Auntie?'

And her aunt nodded shyly and quickly changed the subject while I looked round at the large house and garden and wondered if this was the result of the old lady's talent.

When Jo left for work next day, I wandered down the stairs and out through the porch into the walled garden once more. I'd taken my phone with me and just as I settled down onto a bench in the sunshine, it rang. It was David Phillips. He asked me if he could come round and see me today. I said of course he could, and it was only after the call had ended that I had an idea of what he wanted to discuss. I'd told David about the iron foundry in St. Hayes. And David had said our firm needed somewhere to manufacture a couple of new rock drills they'd been trying to adapt. I felt a tingle of excitement at the thought of going to the foundry with my boss to introduce him to Reg Barrymore. But I put the thoughts out of my head as the sun came out. The tablets I'd taken on doctor's orders tended to make me sleepy and after a short while reading a paperback, I fell asleep once more.

When I awoke later on, I picked up the list I'd made of people I'd said I would phone; people who'd been intrigued by my search. But the first call I made was to Reg Barrymore, of course, the man who'd given me the packet of letters to read; letters I now knew were from my parents. And this was something I would never tell

Sylvia. The name, Sylvia, came into my mind easily, and though I now knew she was my mother, I felt it would be better for all her family if I simply called her by that name.

When Reg Barrymore answered, he sounded pleased to hear from me. 'I won't tell you everything over the phone, Reg, but yes, I am Greg's son and I've met Sylvia. But right now I want to ask if I can bring my engineer boss to visit your foundry. They might have some work for you, but of course, we won't know until he's spoken to you.'

The manager spoke slowly. 'I don't know what I can tell you. There've been people coming here to look round and they said they're thinking of buying the foundry.'

'Christ! So we've got rival engineers, have we?'

'No, they're not engineers. They said they want the site for a big store. The fact is, it's pretty much in the centre of the town and there's plenty of parking space at the back too. So it looks like we'll be finished soon from what they said.'

I bit my lip, thinking. 'Look, Reg. I'll get back to you as soon as I can. I know it's nothing to do with me, but I'll speak to one or two people and try and find out how long it will be before the estate is settled. '

We chatted for a little longer and when we'd said goodbye, I sat with my phone in my hand for a while. Presently I called Sylvia.

She was delighted to hear from me again and as soon as I'd assured her that yes, I was getting better, I told her what I'd heard from Reg Barrymore.

'Oh,' she said. 'I phoned the Evelyn solicitors yesterday, Archie. To tell them that you are Greg's and my son. The man I spoke to was Giles Evelyn, he's the son of Greg's old friend Geoffery. He was astonished and wants me to call and see them as soon as I can. I am apparently named in Greg's will. What for, I've no idea. In any case, I really couldn't take anything from him. But I will ring Giles in a minute and ask if the foundry is going to be sold, who it belongs to now, whatever. And I'll call you back when I'm told. Will that be alright? Will I be butting in on anything? You've not gone back to work yet, have you?' They were very maternal-sounding queries and I laughed as I reassured her that yes, I was lounging in the sun in the garden and would be here for a while yet. And if my line is engaged, it's because I have a number of other calls to make.

I sat back, disappointed at what Reg Barrymore had told me, that the foundry would probably be closed. I'd have to let David Phillips know when he came round. There was no point in cancelling my boss's visit because there were plenty of other work matters to discuss when he came round.

I spent the rest of the morning phoning the people on my list and dozing between the conversations. Great Aunt Matilda brought me a cup of coffee and sat with me for a while, and we moved into her conservatory when the breeze got up.

When she offered to get my lunch, I thanked her but told her Jo had already prepared my meal and just as I turned to climb the stairs, she told me she would be out for the afternoon so I could sit wherever I wished. Seated in the kitchen eating the sandwiches Jo had made for me, I thought how nice Aunt Matilda was. And I'd also like to meet Jo's parents soon.

I was dozing once more on the couch in the living room when the doorbell rang. I clambered to my feet and made my way downstairs to the side door, and was pleased to see my boss standing outside.

I took up Matilda's invitation and led him into her conservatory and while we were settling down, my phone rang once more. It was Sylvia. She had spoken to Giles Evelyn and he'd told her that of course the foundry could not be sold until the estate was wound up. And, he'd said, it now looked as though it could all be settled quite soon, but only if she could come to the office to go through the papers with them.

'I'll go there this week if possible with Lawrence,' she said. 'I really want someone to be with me. But at least you can tell Reg Barrymore nothing can be done until the estate is settled. And though they said that could be quite soon, solicitors often say that, don't they?'

As soon as the conversation was over, I turned to my boss and told him what I'd learned during the morning. We were both intrigued and David told me we'd better not visit the foundry in Cornwall until we knew what was going to happen. 'A pity,' he said. 'I was looking forward to having a look round there. We could do with a small foundry able to spend time on our alterations. So many foundries now just go for the big productions.'

And I couldn't help agreeing with him. Phillips was quite considerate about my injuries and didn't expect me to be back at work for a while yet and we spent the next hour discussing various business matters. It was only when David left that I felt the need to go back upstairs again for a brief lie down.

Later, feeling better, I sat back and called Reg Barrymore again. 'Sylvia said the foundry couldn't be sold until the estate was wound up as you already knew. But she also said it might be settled fairly soon.'

'Well, good of you to call. From what you told me about your job, I was looking forward to seeing you again. And if this blessed place is still in business, we

185

could certainly take on the sort of work you mentioned. But there, we won't know until Mr Greg's estate is all wound up. I just hope we won't all lose our jobs too soon.'

'I agree with you Reg. And I will come down to Cornwall and see you later on. Thing is, I've had a bit of an accident. I'm supposed to take it easy for a while, got a couple of cracked ribs and a broken arm. But there, as soon as I'm better, I will certainly come and see you. I've got a lot to tell you, more than I've mentioned on the phone.'

Reg wanted to know how I'd got hurt but I simply told him I'd turned my car over. I was careful not to mention Iris Julian's name in a town where she was known. And when our call ended, I worked my way down my list of people to phone, told them as briefly as I could that there'd been a mix-up at my birth but the doctor and nurse involved had definitely done nothing wrong.

I'd left my number on Sydney Chambers' phone and an hour later Syd called back. I told him as I'd told the others, that nothing wrong had been done, that I was Greg and Sylvia's child, but I said I'd rather meet him and tell him, as I'd said to Reg Barrymore, that the rest of the story would be better told face to face.

Sydney Chambers sounded grief stricken again, but was grateful to me for my re-assurance. 'Where are you staying right now, Archie? I might be able to come and see you. I'm in London until tomorrow evening.'

I bit my lip once more. I didn't want anyone to know where Jo lived, afraid the information might somehow reach Iris Julian. So I told Sydney I was moving about amongst my friends, but would definitely come and see him within the next few weeks. We ended our

186

conversation on friendly terms and when I sat back, I felt the shiver of apprehension that came over me whenever I thought about Iris Julian. She'd tried to get me killed in that explosion of my flat that she'd talked her son into doing. And she'd damaged my car and almost succeeded in finishing me off. Inspector Green had warned me 'Don't let her be third time lucky.' So the threat still hung there and I was concerned about Jo's safety.

The doorbell went again and this time it was Tim, the young recruit at work. He teased me about the colours of the fading bruises on my face, asking what the guy who'd started the fight looked like. But despite his jesting, when he said he wanted a cup of coffee he insisted he'd make it himself. 'And one for you, you poor bugger.' And after he'd left, I found myself looking forward to being back at work. It could be stressful, but all my colleagues were easy to get along with and all shared our enthusiasm for our work. But right now, I was especially interested in what we would learn about the future of the iron foundry in St. Hayes, and according to Sylvia, that shouldn't take too long.

CHAPTER TWENTY SEVEN

The week flew by. There were many phone calls and three of my work colleagues came round one evening complete with bottles of wine and beer. I enjoyed their company - and their drinks! But between the calls and visits, there was plenty of time for me to rest, and I was feeling better every day.

Sylvia phoned in the evenings, telling Jo, who answered the phone, not to bother me. She just wanted to know how I was getting on. Jo sometimes handed the phone over to me and I'd have a chat with her, asking Sylvia questions about her daughters and their husbands and children. 'I'd like to meet them when I'm free of this plaster and all.'

And Sylvia agreed that I wasn't well enough to drive all over the place to see them.

'When you're up to it, we'll have a family party here, and you and Jo can stay over for several days if you would like to.' And I thanked her and said that'd be great.

When I put the phone down, I turned to Jo. 'Shit! Jo. Why am I so reluctant to go and meet them? You'd think I'd be dying to see them all. My own flesh and blood! Yet I want to go and see my old friend Edith before anyone else. She was so good to me. Without her, without the pressure she put on people for my sake, I'd never have been able to become an apprentice for engineering. I'd have become a misfit, like so many of the children I grew up with. We didn't really know who we were, and most of us didn't bother. We all needed someone who cared about us, and that didn't happen much.'

Jo asked me when Edith had come into my life, and as we sat together on the couch, I leaned back and told her about the life I'd lived as a child.

'I was ten when I arrived at Grange Hall. It was a big house, with a married couple in charge. They had a son the same age as me, and we didn't hit it off very well.' I gave my usual wry grin. 'I kept having a strange dream. A nightmare, I suppose. And after I'd sleep-walked out onto the main road one night, they got a psychiatrist to talk to me. He put me on tablets that made me feel really weird. But they insisted I take them. Then, one afternoon I was trying to mend the puncture on an old bike, the only one we had, and I caught my finger in the spokes. I must have yelped, because Edith, who was the cook, came to the kitchen door and saw me. "Come here," she said and made me follow her inside. She sat me at the table, inspected my hand and cleaned it up, and brought me a glass of milk and a bun. There were tears running down my face which didn't happen very often, but the tablets weren't helping me. She asked me a lot of questions and then said, "I'll make them get you a decent bike. Throw away those tablets and give yourself plenty of exercise. And every time you get back from a ride, come in here and tell me about it."

'I don't know how she managed to make them get me a good bike, but of course she was the best cook they'd ever had and she was a very domineering woman. They wouldn't dare upset her and lose her. Anyway, I used to see her reading paper backs when she had the time, and once on a bike ride, I stopped at a car boot sale and saw a couple of Dick Francis books which I knew she liked. They were cheap enough for my pocket money, so when I got back I left them on the kitchen table after I'd had my usual cup of tea and piece of cake. Edith didn't say much about it, just nodded her thanks, but I used to

189

look for more detective paperbacks when I got the chance. A couple of months later I went to the local comprehensive school. The owner's son didn't want to go there and he was able to start at a private school. It wasn't far from my school, but because there was no bus available, Granger, as we called him, drove his son every day but I had to go on my bike.

Edith was furious and told me she'd make sure I always had a decent bike. And so I did. She was so good to me, Jo. Very abrupt and bossy, but underneath it all she seemed to feel a strong sense of responsibility for me. It's thanks to her that I had a decent education. And of course, it's thanks to her sending me that newspaper cutting that I've found out who I actually am. Crazy, eh?'

'I'd really like to meet her, Archie. Perhaps we can go and see her soon?'

I turned to her. 'Jo, you're wonderful! Yes, I'd love to go and see her this week. She lives near Wittering. Not too far away.'

Jo rose to her feet. 'I'm going to get the phone for you to ring her now.'

Two days later Jo and I arrived at Edith's flat complete with flowers and wine. Edith was delighted to see us. She peered intently at Jo and suddenly smiled and gave her a brief hug. 'You'll do, my lass. You'll be able to sort him out. Good.'

Edith was no longer as strong and bold a woman as she'd been during my childhood, but we could see she was still able to make the most of her life. Her flat was comfortable and she told Jo that I'd found it for her, and still made sure she could cope with the bills. 'I've told him time and again, I don't need his help. I'm quite well off now. When my husband died years ago, I rented out our house and got work as a live-in cook. I always saved as much as I could, and when I retired, I sold the old house and was able to buy this flat that Archie found for me. It's a nice place to live and I've got some good neighbours.'

She was dying to know how much I'd learned after getting her newspaper cutting. And she was so delighted that I'd discovered my birth mother and found I had sisters and nieces and nephews. But I could see she had a wistful feeling of regret that she would no longer be a matronly figure to me.

'Edith,' I said, when I'd brought her up to date with everything else that had happened, 'you are still my number one mother figure. I'm sure Sylvia would like to meet you and learn how much you did for me as a child.'

Edith's eyes filled with tears as I spoke and I crossed the room to embrace her and she soon pushed me away and hurried off to sort out our lunch.

In the afternoon the three of us went for a walk along the beach front, Edith wanting to show Jo the places she likes to visit; spots that were near enough for her to reach, despite her troubled hip. We sat on a couple of benches during the walk, and I told Edith I needed to rest as much as she did. It was a relaxed and happy afternoon for all three of us, and driving back home, Jo agreed with me that Edith was an extraordinary woman, someone who must always be part of our lives.

Next morning the phone rang just as Jo was putting on her coat. She picked it up and turned as she spoke. 'Why Sylvia, you just caught me. I'm off to work in a couple of minutes.' She listened intently to what was being said and then called me over. She handed me the phone, smiling. 'Sylvia has some important news for you Archie. But I must be off.' She said cheerio to Sylvia, gave me a quick kiss as she picked up her bag and left.

I crossed the room to the table, pulled out a chair and sat down. 'Good morning, Sylvia. Nice to hear from you.'

'Lovely to speak to you, Archie, and I do have a lot to tell you. Are you comfortable?'

'Yep, I'm fine, Sylvia. Go ahead.'

'Well, yesterday, Lawrence took me down to St. Hayes in Cornwall to meet the solicitor, Giles Evelyn who'd asked us to come. His old father, Geoffery, was there too. Then they read us Greg's will. I can't tell you how it upset me.' She paused, and she sounded emotionally choked. 'You see, Greg had made bequests to several people he respected, but everything else was left to me.'

'Good God!' I exclaimed. 'After all those years?'

'Exactly. To his wife. And the Evelyns wanted to know if we were still officially married. That I hadn't become a bigamist. Lawrence had taken some papers with him because he had a feeling there might be an enquiry about us. So he was able to produce documents to show I'd changed my name legally by deed poll and we hadn't attempted a marriage because Greg had made it clear he would not divorce me. Of course, times have changed since then, but we were perfectly happy the way things were. Geoffery Evelyn, who'd been a friend of Greg's, said he'd told him he wanted to make sure that if something happened in my life, he would still be able to take care of me. To make up for being away when our child was born. And died.' Once more I heard tears in her voice.

'What a man.' I spoke softly, thinking this was my father we were talking about.

'The thing is, Archie, the Evelyns are the executors of Greg's will, and I told them I simply couldn't take anything from him. Not after leaving him on his own and making a new life for myself. I told them everything must go to our son. To you.'

'What!' I gasped.

Before I could say another word, Sylvia went on, 'But we're afraid you won't get a lot, Archie. The house is heavily mortgaged and the foundry is in the doldrums from what the Evelyns have learned. But, they said, a big store company is keen to buy the foundry and demolish it and rebuild a supermarket on the site. It is in the town centre, of course.'

I found my head spinning. 'Yes, that's what Reg Barrymore said. But look, Sylvia, you have two daughters and several grandchildren. Surely they should be getting their share if you won't take it yourself.'

'I know what you mean, Archie. But Lawrence agrees with me. We would both feel like cheats if we took anything from his estate. And if you get what your father left, and you're an engineer like him...' She sobbed this time as she spoke.

I spoke slowly, 'I'll be very surprised if they let you do this, Sylvia. After all, they may think I'm just someone chasing after the estate. That there may be a lawsuit about it all in the future, with the solicitors to take the blame.'

This time Sylvia gave a little choked laugh. 'You're right. Giles told me he'd met you, and thought you were probably related to Greg, but as you say, they needed proof. When I spoke to them the first time, I mentioned the DNA tests we'd had done, and yesterday Giles told me that after our conversation, he'd had an idea and looked in the bag of personal belongings he'd collected from the hospital when Greg died. In his comb there were several hairs, rooted hairs, which he sent for the test to see if they matched yours. And yes, they did, of course.'

'Phew!' I let out another sigh and tried to slow my breathing as my chest hurt. 'Look Sylvia, I'm going to have to think about this. I don't know exactly what to do.'

'Well, that's another reason I phoned this morning. The Evelyns want both of us to call at their office as soon as we can. Do you think I could pick you and Jo up one day next week?'

I bit my lip. My heart was thumping at the shock of Sylvia's story. 'I'll check with Jo. And yes, I feel well enough to go on a trip to St. Hayes once more. I'll get Jo to give you a bell this evening. OK?'

And moments later I put the phone down and spent the rest of the day wondering what on earth would come about.

CHAPTER TWENTY EIGHT

When Jo came home and I told her about Sylvia's call, she was as astounded as I still was. We talked about it for a long time, wondering if there would be anything at all left when all the debts and the mortgages had been repaid.

'But,' I said, 'if the big store that wants to buy the foundry is prepared to pay enough, we could shift all the machinery and stuff to an industrial estate. I've looked it up on the internet, and there is a place on the outskirts of St. Hayes with a couple of vacant buildings. In many ways it would be better, a good way to set up any new machinery they need. And with our firm looking for a foundry, it could be great. I keep thinking of it. I would hate to see Reg Barrymore and his men lose their jobs. To be honest, that's the one thing that makes me want to follow through what Sylvia has said. Apart from that, it all seems... well, quite unbelievable.'

Jo said, 'Well, I can ring Sylvia now if you like, and tell her I'm free next Friday. How about that?'

'Brilliant. Will you tell her I'm out with one of the guys from work, Jo? I know it sounds daft, but I don't want to speak to her just yet. I haven't got my head round all this stuff she's told me. Not now. I can't stop thinking about her daughters and how angry they'll be with her for passing it on to me when she's their mum.' I shook my head. 'But I really do want to get my hands on the foundry and make it work. See what I mean?'

'Yes, Archie. I know how important the foundry is to you. You were so disappointed when you and David were told it could be a waste of time for you to call round there. It made everything seem so flat to you that day.'

Without further ado, Jo phoned Sylvia. This time it was Lawrence who answered. He sounded very pleased to talk to her and said he was looking forward to meeting her again with Archie. 'I'll call my wife,' he laughed. 'We got married last week,' and he handed the phone over to her.

Jo congratulated Sylvia . 'When are you going for your honeymoon?' she smiled.

'In the summer, Jo. We both want to go round Scotland in a camper van, and we like the thought of the long light evenings.' She laughed as she spoke. 'But there, what have you got to tell me?'

'We can go to meet you in St. Hayes on Friday next week, Sylvia. Will that be all right with you?'

'Oh yes. I work in the local school mid-week, so that'll be great. Shall I come and pick you up about nine o'clock?

Jo paused. 'I think I'll drive us there and meet you in the town somewhere. I know Archie is dying to call at the foundry. We could stop there overnight. Will that be alright for you? You can tell us where to meet'

'That's a very good suggestion. And I think I'll book an overnight stay as well. Lawrence will be away until Sunday evening and I do find weekends on my own a bit boring. I'll book us into a hotel I know, The Kingston Arms. And I'll call Giles again and hopefully get an appointment sometime on Friday afternoon.'

They chatted a little longer, and Sylvia was pleased to hear I was out with a friend. Glad I was feeling that much better.

When she put down the phone, Jo smiled. 'I bet you wish you did go out with a pal, Archie. You're looking so strained. Are you going to phone Reg Barrymore in

196

the morning?'

I turned round from the window where I'd been staring out at the garden.

'Yes, you're right, going out with the boys would have taken my mind off this. One minute I'm amazed and pleased that I might inherit a decent sum, and the next minute I'm doubly worried; one that I could end up with a big deficit, and the other that Sylvia's girls will never be able to get over the fact that I took what should have been theirs.' I came across the room and sat beside Jo. 'What do you think, Jo? Will it work out for the best or the worst?'

'Definitely not the worst, Archie. Even if whatever the big store offers for the building is only just enough to pay off its loans, you'll be alright. You can sell the big house and surely even after paying off the mortgages, there'll be enough for you to shift the foundry and start it up. I know that's what you're itching to do. And as for Sylvia's daughters, if I ever get the chance, I shall point out to them that without you tracking down Sylvia, they would never have heard anything about it anyway. She told me the solicitors had already employed a private investigator to trace her, but without success. They would have had to settle all the debts and the remainder would have been held in abeyance for years.'

I smiled and put my good arm round her. 'You do make me feel so much better, Jo. Come on, let's go down to the pub as you said I should have done.'

'Why don't you call Tim and Justin and see if they can come over and join us?'

The phone calls to my pals worked and we spent the rest of the evening relaxing together down at the local.

In the days before the planned trip with Sylvia, I called

197

at the surgery as requested.

'You're doing very well, Mr Smith. If I remember rightly, you wanted to go back to work quite soon, and I think if you take care, you could definitely go back next week.'

I was glad to hear this, as I'd intended to start work whatever the doctor said. But it was good to have some medical support, and I thanked the doctor, telling him the exercises I'd been doing had been a great help.

On Friday morning we set off in Jo's car quite early and arrived at the hotel Sylvia had booked for us just before lunch. Sylvia was already there and climbed out of her car when she saw us. She was looking smart and attractive wearing a short grey jacket over pale trousers. She came over to Jo and kissed her on the cheek, then stood back and looked at me wonderingly. My facial injuries had healed over the last three weeks and the colour of the bruising had faded to a faint yellow and I moved about more quickly than I'd been able to when last she saw me.

She swallowed. 'You do look so like Greg, Archie. Apart from his dark eyes. If I'd seen you this recognisable when I met you at the hospital, I think I'd probably have passed out.' She took out a tissue and blew her nose. 'Sorry to be so stupid.' She gently put her hands on my shoulder and pressed her cheek against mine. I folded my good arm round her and her face dropped to my neck. I felt the convulsive sob she tried to suppress and a tightness in my own throat stopped me from speaking. It was a bittersweet moment for us both, and Jo stood back a little, openly moved.

'Lawrence has gone to France on a short business trip,' Sylvia told us as she visibly pulled herself together. 'I know he'd have liked to come with us, but I'll tell him all about it when he gets back on Sunday

198

evening. Meanwhile,' she turned her head and smiled at me, 'we can enjoy each other's company.'

We entered the building and followed Sylvia up the stairs to a long old fashioned room with a balcony overlooking a rushing, boulder strewn river and after collecting the menus, all three of us decided it would be nice to sit outside on the balcony where the sun was shining. We were early and had plenty of choice to find a table and settle into the comfortable chairs.

'This is nice,' said Jo, standing by the rail and stretching luxuriously. When the waiter came along we gave him our orders and he presently brought along our wine.

When we were alone again, Sylvia turned to us both purposefully. 'I know you've already met both the Evelyns, Archie, and you know what you're going to hear when he reads the will again. He was planning a visit to the foundry auditors when I last spoke to him, so you'll have a better idea of what you'll get.'

'What's the house like?' asked Jo.

Both Sylvia and I looked at one another and simultaneously shook our heads. 'It's a barn of a place,' said Sylvia, remembering the house with evident dislike. 'So cold and draughty and full of sounds. I never liked it. But Greg had grown up there with his brother. From what he said they spent more time in the grounds than in the house. The garden is quite large and there was a copse and a big shrubbery. But as I said, we'll have to find out from the solicitors what the actual estate is worth. I should imagine though, that it will give you two a decent start in your life together.'

I was staring into my glass of wine. I bit my lip. 'I just feel your family are going to think I'm a terrible intruder, taking a legacy which should be yours. And theirs.'

Sylvia shook her head dismissively. 'When I tell them that the estate is laden with debt, and an iron foundry they know nothing about, they won't be so keen. And in any case, Lawrence, their father, is one hundred per cent on your side, Archie. He told them it's only because of your search that the solicitors found me. So I'd never have known that Greg had died, even. Come on, let's change the subject. What do you think of the view from here, Jo?'

'It's lovely,' Jo laughed. 'And I like what you said, Sylvia. Oh, great, here comes our lunch.' And the rest of the meal proved to be pleasantly relaxing as we ate and chatted animatedly, a happy trio. We lingered over our coffee until Sylvia glanced at her watch. 'Heavens! Look at the time! We'd better get going or we shall be late for our appointment.

CHAPTER TWENTY NINE

We reached the main car park at St. Hayes soon after three o'clock and walked along the street to the solicitors' office. At three thirty we were shown into the room where Giles Evelyn received us with warm hospitality.

'It's not every day we get a problem like the one this estate has given us!' he exclaimed as he shook our hands. 'My father will be here soon. He's not been able to talk about anything else since this matter came to light!'

While waiting for the senior partner, I introduced Jo, and Sylvia gazed round the room exclaiming with delight as she recognised the Georgian side table and the series of oil paintings on the faded wallpaper. 'It's all exactly the same! I can't believe it! I remember this room - always so warm and comfortable.'

Just then, Giles's aged father, Geoffery, arrived. He took Sylvia's hands in his and smiled at her fondly before kissing her cheeks. Turning to me, where I was standing to one side, he stared at me for a long moment before muttering his name and extending his hand to be shaken. 'I'm so sorry I didn't encourage you at all when you called at my house Mr Smith. I felt there was some connection between you and Greg, but I couldn't make any sense of it, and was relieved when you left. I do apologise once more, my boy.'

I shook his hand and thanked him and stood back as Giles came over. 'Come on Dad, there's work to be done. You can make yourselves properly acquainted later.' He grinned at me as he led his father to the big leather chair at the end of the conference table which dominated the room. 'But before you sit down, Dad, you must meet Archie's partner, Miss Josephine Saunders.'

With old-world gallantry, the old man took Jo's hand, smiling with pleasure as he gazed at her smiling face crowned with its bright tresses. 'Delighted, my dear. Delighted.' Then, aware of the others, 'We'll talk later young lady, after our work is done.'

Although the senior partner sat at the head of the table, it was the younger man who opened the file before him and withdrew a document.

'This is the will of Archibald Ensor Gregory Smith. He drew this one up six years ago, although the content has hardly changed from the previous one. It's perfectly straightforward so I'll read it to you. Here goes.'

He read. The afternoon sun streamed through the large windows illuminating the room with its clutter of heavy dark furniture and I noticed Jo was staring out into the garden, a shrubbery filled with the spring-flowering shrubs, aglow with colour.

Giles Evelyn's voice changed slightly. He'd completed the formal opening of the will and was listing the minor bequests. 'To my friend and colleague, Reginald Barrymore, works manager of my iron foundry for many years, the sum of five thousand pounds. To Harold Thompson, foreman of the said foundry, the sum of three thousand pounds. To Mrs Iris Julian, the sum of one thousand pounds and the tenancy of Primrose Cottage, (known as Gardener's Cottage), for her lifetime, after which it would be returned to the main beneficiary. The remainder of my estate, after payment of all the outstanding dues, mortgages, bank loans, etc, I give entirely to my lawful wife, Sylvia Gregory Smith in grateful thanks for our time together. Should she sadly have predeceased me, then to her heirs and assigns, I bequeath the aforementioned.'

Sylvia's face was pale and drawn, eyes dark and tear-filled. She shook her head slowly from side to side. The simple message enfolded in the formal language had found its way through her guard. She pulled a handkerchief from her bag and dabbed at her eyes. Presently she recovered herself, conscious of everyone's eyes on her.

'Giles, you know what my husband and I said must be done.' She turned to his father. 'I expect he's told you we had a long chat when I was here with Lawrence. So what must I do now?' There was a moment's pause in which I clearly heard the tick of the grandfather clock which stood beside the door, 'I wish to pass everything to my son - to Archie.' She reached across the table and laid her hand on the fingers which extended from my grubby plaster cast.

The old man looked troubled. 'My dear, Gregory was so insistent and explicit. He wanted you, his wife, to benefit.'

'I haven't been his wife for thirty years,' Sylvia's voice was shaky. 'You know that, George. I've been Mrs Armstrong for most of that time. I did try several times to get Greg to divorce me, but he never would. That's when I changed my name by deed poll.'

The old man spoke so quietly that we all leaned forward slightly to catch his words. 'I know that, Sylvia. He came to me each time you wrote, and despite my pleas he was very definite. You must understand,' his voice became stronger and authoritative, giving the hint of the strong young man of the past, 'he was not being deliberately obstructive. Oh no. He said that he was your legal husband and he wanted to give you the protection of his name should you ever be left in need. The very last time we met, he talked about you. He said "Our son would be a young man now, had he lived. I blame myself for not having stayed with her. Maybe if I'd got someone else to take my place on that expedition, if I'd stayed at home, perhaps she would have been happy. Perhaps the baby might even have lived."

He looked gravely across the table at Sylvia's white strained face. 'He always carried that feeling of guilt and remorse. He, a much older man leaving such a young bride alone in that gloomy house with the Julian woman. He said once that he felt she might have interfered with the mail. Apart from one or two of your letters it seemed you hadn't heard from him, though he regularly sent letters on the supply plane.'

Sylvia nodded slowly. 'I think that was true. I only ever received the one letter. I thought it was a case of out of sight, out of mind. I did feel - abandoned.'

Geoffery Evelyn sighed. 'Well, it's all too late, much too late now.' His head drooped and he seemed to retreat into a world of his own, a shrunken shell of the man who had been Ensor Gregory Smith's friend. He raised his head and looked round the table. 'I'm afraid I must leave you.' He stood up slowly and stiffly. 'You must excuse me, my dear,' he took Sylvia's hand in his, 'and you young people too.' He made his way round the table to shake our hands in turn. 'I'm not too well, you know. Old age and infirmities, all too many!' He smiled at us. 'You two, I hope you'll be very happy together. Gregory's son. Imagine. If only he could have known.' He looked across at Sylvia. 'And it's a good thing, what you are doing. I can see now that Greg would indeed have approved.'

He hobbled slowly across the room and his son went with him and held open the door. 'The car's waiting, Dad. I'll come round and see you later. I'm very glad you were able to come.' He leaned forward and dropped a kiss on the old man's head and I felt a lump rising in my throat. Maybe my father would have expected something like that.

The door closed quietly and Giles Evelyn returned to the table and resumed his seat. 'I've got the papers drawn up for you both. It makes no difference in a case like this, the passing of a legacy from one member of the family to another, no difference regarding death duties and so forth.'

'I still feel you should have your share, Sylvia.' I was frowning.

Once more she shook her head. 'No, it must all go to you, Archie. From what Giles has said, there might not be that much anyway.' She turned to him again. 'Do you know the state of the factory, Giles?'

The solicitor furrowed his brow. 'It depends what Archie wants to do with it. The works manager insists it's still a sound business, but over the last five years, since Greg was unable to go to the continent drumming up orders, it's gone down badly. That's why Greg sold all of his oil paintings. And he mortgaged the house to the bank.' He looked grave. 'If it was all sold as it stands,' he turned to me as he spoke, 'you wouldn't make a lot. There's the house, of course. Even after repaying the mortgage there'd be something. But a lot more if the foundry were to be sold for building development. It's in a choice place.'

'But I want to keep the foundry going. If everything really is going to be mine, I'll do whatever I possibly can to keep it viable.' I didn't appear to be addressing anyone in particular, I seemed rather to be thinking aloud.

Silence fell in the sunlit room. The warmth of the sun on the burnished table released the smell of polish which wafted through the air like a strange incense.

'Well, goodness me!' the solicitor smiled. 'Mr Barrymore will be delighted to hear that. I know he's been a very worried man. That foundry means a great deal to him.' He looked at me again. 'You know, when you're talking of the place, you do remind me of Gregory, there's a very strong resemblance at times.'

I moved uncomfortably in my seat, not looking at Sylvia, unsure of her reactions even now.

Sensing my discomfort, Jo began to ask about a picture over the mantelpiece which had attracted her attention, and after some more general conversation, Giles produced the necessary papers for Sylvia and me to sign. He looked a little troubled. 'The only thing is, Sylvia, I'll have to use your legal name, that will be Sylvia Armstrong, will it not?'

Sylvia smiled. 'Yes, you're right. And now it's not just because of the deed poll, I am a legally married Sylvia Armstrong at last. Lawrence got the Registrar Office date as soon as he heard that Greg had died and we were married a couple of weeks afterwards.'

'Well, well! Congratulations anyway. I don't suppose you feel any different after all those years, but it makes it neater for us, if you see what I mean. And in any case you were still Greg's legal wife when he died, so that's alright,' and he beamed across at her. 'Now then. I'll need your full name and address, and yours too,' and he smiled at me.

'I'll have to give you Jo's address. I'm house hunting at the moment.' I still spoke in a preoccupied manner, like one in a dream.

'As soon as probate is complete, which shouldn't take too long, this will all be settled. It'll be a great relief to wind things up. Unresolved estates lead to enormous problems. Thank goodness this one will have a happy outcome. In the meantime, if you go to the foundry, we'll be quite happy to back up any plans you make.' And the genial solicitor beamed as he ushered us through the hall and down the steps into the pale sunshine.

We walked along the pavement, all three of us quiet, wrapped in our own thoughts. Jo, not as emotionally involved, glanced at our strained faces and suggested a cup of coffee and Sylvia responded with a smile of relief. 'I'll take you along to the café I used to visit with Ruby. That's if it's still there after all this time!' She led us along a narrow street which took us to a large square where an ancient church stood. Amongst the surrounding shops, she pointed out the café.

'Well!' she exclaimed when we went inside. 'How it's changed.' The walls now were panelled and the overhead beams exposed. 'When we used to come, there were spanking new tables and tiled walls. We thought it was the last word!' She smiled reminiscently. The coffee, when it came, was hot and aromatic. I was still preoccupied, and I leaned back in my chair sipping slowly while Jo and Sylvia chatted, friendly and relaxed with one another.

'Penny for them, Archie' Jo smiled at me. 'No, don't tell me. You're rearranging the plant at the foundry.'

I grinned back. 'Not quite. I know you women like to shift furniture all the time, but it's not so easy uprooting all the machinery at Gregory's.' I was suddenly conscious how easily the name had slipped from my tongue. Gregory's. *Mine.* I wondered how soon matters could be settled and I could really move in and take charge.

On the same wavelength, Sylvia mused, 'When we get back to the car park, I'll phone Giles and ask if you could go along to the foundry today to have a chat with

Reg. He didn't say we shouldn't, did he?'

I shot her a grateful look and tried to make an effort to follow their conversation with some semblance of interest. Sylvia's next words, however, promptly drove all thoughts of the foundry from my mind. 'I'd like to go and see Iris Julian right now. How about it? Or would you two like to have a wander round the town while I go. This is a lovely old place.'

Both Jo and I immediately said we wouldn't let her go on her own. 'But do you think there's any point is seeing her, Sylvia? Remember what a dangerous woman she is.' My voice was grave and I know my eyes were troubled as I leaned across the table to speak to her.

She looked back, her gaze travelling over my face. Her voice when she spoke was tight in her throat. 'I know what you say is right. But we will be taking her by surprise. All I want to do is confront her. Face her with what she did. Face her with you, if you like. My moment.' She paused. 'Can't you see it's necessary for me? A climax, if you like.'

'Come on then,' I rose from the table and took her hand, pulling her to her feet. 'You too, Jo. This is a family affair.' I was smiling but there was an undertone in my voice that showed a depth of feeling.

We walked quickly to the car park, all three of us seeming to share a sense of urgency, of wanting to get unfinished business over and done with. Complete.

Sylvia told us we must come in her Rover with her. When she unlocked the car, she picked up her mobile to call the solicitor and I told her it'd be best to leave it until after we'd seen Iris Julian. She agreed and put it back into its pocket and started the car. There was no chat between us as the vehicle negotiated the narrow streets leading to the outskirts of the town, and as we swung onto the dual carriageway, there seemed to be a strong sense of foreboding among us. Sylvia suddenly said, 'It's just a mile ahead, you'll see it when we pass the old school,' I felt my heart miss a beat and shivered with sudden fear. The Julian woman had an awful lot to account for. How might she react to our visit?

CHAPTER THIRTY

A few minutes later, Sylvia pulled up at a small lay-by. I recognised the entrance to the house. 'Why don't we just drive up to the door?' I asked.

She sat, hands on the wheel. 'I don't know. I feel she might be expecting a car, and well, news of some kind. I'd like to take her by surprise. Do you think I'm silly?' She turned a troubled face towards me.

'I don't think anything to do with that woman is silly. Come on, let's go.' I clambered from the car, less awkward now, but still cautious of twisting, my ribs protesting at too sudden a movement. I opened the rear door for Jo.

She got out and stood facing me. 'If you don't mind, I'd rather wait around.' She bit her lip and turned to Sylvia. 'It's just, well, very personal isn't it? I think it would be better if I kept out of it.' She stood, looking at us, from one to the other, her hair swinging as she turned her head.

I reached out a hand and touched the bright locks. 'OK babe. You can call the cops if we don't appear in half an hour or so.'

'Don't joke.' Jo's voice was tight and strained. 'Go on, get it over with. And don't be too long - I'm dying for a good meal.' Her attempt at lightness was only too apparent, and as we turned into the dark and overgrown drive, clouds drifted across the sun, and glancing back, it seemed to me that the only colour and warmth to be seen, was the bright mane of Jo's hair as she stood beside the car, a suddenly small and forlorn figure who responded to my wave with a half-hearted movement of her hand.

I turned away and fell into step with the woman who was my mother; sensing the pointlessness of this visit and yet its inevitability. This would in some way mark a turning point in our relationship; of that I was certain.

We made our way along the unkempt drive. Broken boughs torn from the trees in some winter gale rotted alongside where they'd fallen, sprouting a growth of ferns and fungi. This had once been an impressive entrance and my heart jolted as I knew this would now be mine.

As if she'd read my mind, Sylvia spoke. 'You'll soon be able to get this back into shape. That's if you want to live here. It's not a place of pleasant memories for me, but maybe you could change that.' She shivered. 'I wish I'd brought my other coat. It's cold.'

'Have mine.' I paused and began to struggle with the coat fastened round my shoulders.

'No need. Look, we're here now.'

We'd rounded the bend as she spoke and the house lay before us, shuttered windows reflecting the blowing clouds. 'We'll try the back door.' Sylvia strode firmly towards the rear of the house, and as before, I spotted a milk bottle standing at the head of the steps, a mute sign of human occupation.

I pressed the bell, a shiver of apprehension running down my spine, knowing how this woman had nearly killed me. We didn't hear her approaching footsteps; the door opened silently and unexpectedly and Iris Julian stood there.

She stared at us, her impassive face betraying no emotion, neither surprise nor animosity. 'What do you want?' Her voice was sharp.

'To talk to you.' Sylvia was quiet and controlled.

I thought she wasn't going to let us in, that the door would be slammed in our faces, but after a long moment of silence, she slowly stepped back and we followed her, and I closed the door behind us.

We were in a narrow passage with a door on either side and a glimpse of the main hall and stairs at the far end. The first door on the right was open and Sylvia turned her head to look again at the kitchen, large and old-fashioned, as it had been when she lived here so long ago.

But Iris Julian led us past that door and into the hall, dark and gloomy with the shadowed stairs sweeping away upwards in an elegant curve. We crossed the polished floor, footsteps echoing, and the woman opened a heavy panelled door and pressed the light switch. The brilliance of the chandeliered lights was dazzling for a moment as we followed her into the large drawing room.

I glanced around. It was a well proportioned room with a white marble fireplace flanked by a pair of sofas on an Aubusson carpet. There were several tables, large and small, bare of ornaments and pictures, as were the walls, though patches on the faded flock wallpaper showed where some had lately hung.

Sylvia too, gazed around intently. She obviously saw how the room had been emptied but we both noticed the surfaces of the mahogany tables gleamed, and there was a general absence of dust, a feeling the room was well kept. She crossed to one of the large windows as though about to open the shutters, recollected herself and paused.

'The shutters are kept locked. Mr Gregory was concerned about his paintings. I never open them now.'

Sylvia stood still, gripping the back of a small delicate chair. 'We want to know *why*. Why you lost me my son.'

Iris Julian remained stolid and unblinking. 'I didn't do

anything. Ask Dr Staton.' She spat out his name.

I spoke. 'We have done. He told us all about it, about your blackmail and threats, about Ruby's death on the coach, everything. Only he didn't know until he was told that Ruby had left me, the baby, in a safe place before she caught that bus.'

Iris Julian's face at last registered feeling. Her eyes widened and her gaze flickered between our faces as we stood before her. I saw a beading of perspiration on her upper lip.

'And we know about Cyril causing the explosion at my flat. And someone,' I emphasised the 'someone', 'damaging my car and causing this,' and I lifted my plaster cast.

Now her fear was evident. 'My Cyril had nothing to do with anything. Of course he didn't. He's a good reliable son, he'll do anything for me, for his mother. I can't run this great house without Cyril. I don't know where he is now, but it's because you told the police about him. You, *you...*' Her voice had risen and words came out automatically, all on one level like a poorly recited speech.

Sylvia spoke quietly. 'We didn't go to the police about anything. They found out for themselves. In any case, we see no point in going to the police about what you did to us as a family. That is beyond punishment. You deprived Gregory and myself of our own son, you deprived our son of his parents. You condemned him to childhood in an institution. There is no punishment for that. And no forgiveness or understanding.'

I looked from one woman to the other, both pale under the blaze of light. Sylvia Armstrong standing, brittle and stiff, Iris Julian tall and stolid before us, her eyes flickering constantly from my mother to myself. She's not listening, I thought. She's not taking it in at all.

213

How could anyone hear such condemnation and heartbreak and not react? She must be mad. Quite mad.

Her eyes were now on me and I saw growing determination behind the blank gaze, a strange determination. There was a moment of silence in the room, silence broken by the steady ticking of the clock on the mantelpiece.

Sylvia's voice broke the silence. 'Why? That's all we want to know. Why did you do it? Just why?' Her voice had lost its brittle control and broke on the last word.

Iris Julian was looking at her now. 'Because you had no business here, nor any child of yours. This place is rightly Cyril's. And mine. He should have married me, Cyril is his brother's boy.'

'That's not true and you know it. Greg's brother was in Africa until a couple of months before your son was born. Greg told me that. He said he'd heard you'd put out a rumour about that. But it was impossible.' She paused, waiting for a reaction but there was none. 'You were already married and pregnant when Greg's brother came back here to live.'

'Liar!' the voice came like a whiplash, its vehemence the more startling after the dull monotone which had gone before. 'Liar! This is my house and Cyril's. What do you know? Fools! That's what you are. Two fools who don't know anything.' She turned to me. 'And you. Who do you think you are, coming here like you did, banging on the door, saying what you did on the phone. Saying you're Mr Gregory's son! Liar! That baby is dead and gone, dead and gone where he should be. Where you should be, both of you.'

She looked at my plaster cast and suddenly her mouth twisted into the semblance of a grin. 'Car brakes fail, did they? I wasn't sure I did it right. Finding the car parked round the back of her B & B.'

Sylvia had stepped close to me at the beginning of the diatribe. 'Come on Archie, we'd better go. We'll get nowhere.' She turned to the woman, 'I feel sorry for you. I don't know why after all you've done, but I do. Very sorry.' And we turned towards the door.

But Iris Julian moved swiftly before us and stopped as she opened the door. 'Wait here. Wait. I've something to show you. You'd better see it now, you won't get the chance again.'

'Of course we will, it's Archie's house now.' Sylvia spoke as she moved towards the door.

'What? What did you say?' Her voice was a rasping whisper and her face was white and wild. 'His house? No, it's mine. It's mine.' She whirled to the door, opened it with a wrench and flung herself through, slamming it behind her.

I ran after her and gripped the doorknob. I turned to my mother. 'She's locked it! What the hell is she up to now? The woman is quite mad!'

'I know. She's deranged.' Sylvia came towards me. 'Let's get out of here.' She crossed to the shutters once more and tried to open them. 'Damn! They are locked as she said. Can you force them, Archie? We've got to get out. It doesn't matter what damage we do. Put a chair under the doorknob in case she comes back.'

I swiftly wedged a chair against the door and paused. I put my ear against the massive door. 'Christ! I can hear water. Water being splashed on the floor. What is she doing?' I stood there uneasily until Sylvia called me to help her again.

The shutters had been fitted with a modern safety lock and wouldn't respond to our joint tugging. I looked round the room for a lever and spotted a set of brass fire irons in the hearth. I crossed the room and picked up the heavy poker. Back at the window I tried to force the end of the poker into the joint of the shutters, using my broken arm in clumsy conjunction with my good arm, but the poker merely bounced and slid away. I glanced back across the room to the door. 'What's that? Bloody hell, what is she doing!' I ran past the bemused Sylvia towards the door. A narrow stream of liquid was seeping towards the carpet from the gap beneath. I sniffed, bent down and put my finger into the liquid. 'Petrol! Bloody hell! She's got us trapped!. Quick!' I ran to the window and started to tug at the heavy velvet curtains. 'Quick, we've got to plug the door.'

Sylvia dragged a chair to the window, leapt up and swiftly removed the curtain from the rail. The heavy hooks rattled as she tugged the curtains off. I dashed across the room again, and using my good hand, pushed the material hard against the crack under the door, stemming the seepage for the moment. I piled the second curtain against the first. 'We'll need another to stifle the flames as they start.' Silently and swiftly we took down all the other curtains and draped them over a chair.

'Now, work this time for fuck's sake!' I took the poker to the shutters again and tried frantically to lever the hinges, but got nowhere. I struck the poker against the wood, the loudness of the noise deafening in the empty room.

And as the echoes died, we both heard something else; the roaring of flames.

Sylvia made a small sound in her throat and stood, rooted with terror in the centre of the room. I looked wildly round. Grabbed a wooden chair that stood near the window and lifted it, holding it, beating it against the unyielding shutters, clumsy with my damaged arm but finding strength in panic. The chair crashed again and again against the shutters, the echoing slams drowning all other sounds until finally a leg cracked off the chair.

I turned, sweat pouring from my brow. 'It's no good!' I flung the chair down. 'Come on, there must be something in this room we can use to open those shutters with.'

'Look.' Sylvia's voice was hushed. Blue smoke was floating into the room through the cracks round the door. 'Oh God! I left my phone in the car.'

'Phone! Hell, why didn't I think of that.' I snatched my own phone from my pocket. 'I'll call Jo,' and I quickly called her number. 'Blast! It's engaged. She must be chatting to someone.' I dialled nine nine nine and was answered immediately.

'We're in Keyes Lane House and it's on fire. And we're trapped in a room with shutters across the windows. And I don't think we'll have very long before the room's ablaze.'

'Yes sir. We've already been informed of the fire and the engine is on its way. Try and keep calm…' There was a loud explosion at the back of the house as we spoke, and I dropped the phone. Cursing, I snatched it up from the floor again and found the call had ended.

CHAPTER THIRTY ONE

Jo was leaning against the car for a few minutes after Archie and Sylvia left and suddenly felt guilty at not going with them. She stood upright and decided to catch them up. When she turned into the long drive, they were already out of sight. She hurried along but still couldn't see them by the time she reached the open space in front of the house. She stood and stared at the building. It looked such a large and deserted home with the downstairs windows all shuttered. And it was so quiet. She decided to go round to the back, as Archie told her he'd done on his first visit. Perhaps she might catch them up on the doorstep.

When she reached the back door where a milk bottle stood, it was closed and there was still no sign of her companions. She supposed they'd already gone indoors to talk to the Julian woman. Not wanting to knock and have to introduce herself, she looked round at the out-buildings opposite the house. There was a woodshed, a large car port with a white van inside, and alongside a garage with an up and over door. She crossed the yard and wandered along, interested in an old building which could have been a stable when the house was built. There was a date engraved in some stonework, and as she paused to try and make it out, she heard the back door open. She darted in through the open door of the woodshed and peered out, wanting to see who it was before she made herself known.

A tall, well built woman was crossing the yard, and for a minute Jo thought she'd been seen. But the woman swung open the garage door and came out a minute later carrying a large petrol can. What on earth

218

could she need that for, thought Jo. Iris Julian was talking, talking to herself, as there was no one else in sight and as she swung the garage door closed, she gave a wild laugh. 'This'll show 'em. This'll teach them a lesson. Serve them right. Serve them right.' While she spoke she hurried back across the yard, and Jo could see the can must be full from the way the woman was carrying it. She went back inside the house and slammed the back door shut behind her.

Jo ran across the yard herself, not caring if the woman saw her now. She knew what Iris Julian was about to do. Without wasting another moment, she grabbed the door and pulled it open. As she did, there was a loud whoosh and a burst of flame at the end of a passage. She shut the door swiftly, knowing she mustn't make the fire worse by giving it more draught, and she instantly pulled out her mobile.

She rang the emergency number and yelled for help. For the fire engines. And the police. They asked for the name of the house and the address, and she was in such a panic she found herself stumbling over those essential details. But soon they said they knew where she was and told her to keep well away from the burning building. 'But there are people in there. Three people. You must come quickly. Please.' Then she rang off for she must phone Archie. If only he had his phone switched on. If only...

Thankfully Archie answered her. Both were overwhelmed with relief at hearing each other's voice. 'Where about in the house are you, Archie? I'm outside.'

'We're in the room to the right of the front door, Jo. Can you find something to smash a window and then break open the shutters?'

'Yes, I'm at the back but I'll be there in a minute.' She

shoved the phone into her pocket as she ran across to the woodshed, hoping he'd hear her running and would know help was on its way.

In the room Sylvia spoke again with terror in her voice. 'Look, Archie. The door is so hot it's beginning to smoke.' I ran across the room and began to trample on the curtains which were smouldering. I knew we'd have a very short time before the door burst into flame and let the fire in. The room was hazy now with smoke. It was seeping through invisible cracks and from the surface of the door itself, blue wisps were curling. Sylvia and I looked at one another. When the door caught fire, we'd have very little time left. I went over to her and gave her a sudden hug and turned in renewed desperation to the window.

'Right you bastard. Open!' I pressed the point of the poker under the lock, and gaining purchase, I levered my weight against the shutter. But I still couldn't force it open in spite of my desperation. Then, there was the sudden sound of smashing glass and a great thump on the shutters on the adjoining window. Jo had found us! And found something to break the shutters. What an amazing life-saver is my Jo!

There was another smash and an axe head appeared. An instant later the shutters swung open and there was Jo wielding the axe, aiming now at the sash window with desperate strength. I grabbed one of the curtains we'd left on a chair back and flung it over the broken glass on the sill as Jo forced the bottom half of the window upwards. As she did, the door, reacting to the rush of air, ignited with a roar and a ball of flames curled into the room.

'Quick!' Sylvia was already clambering into the window space and I hurled her through and flung myself over the sill behind her. We both landed in a heap on the ground beneath the window.

Jo's eyes were terrified in her chalk white face. 'Run! Quick! Quick!' We picked ourselves up and all three of us fled across the gravelled drive to the overgrown lawn at the front, and flung ourselves down in the long grass. Gasping, we lay there, my good arm stretched across the two women's shoulders. As we regained our breath, we turned round and looked back at the house. Already it was ablaze. There was another explosion in the building and flames came roaring through the window we had just left. The upstairs windows, too, were exploding with the heat and flames were leaping through the gaps. The window from which we'd escaped now belched clouds of dark smoke and the roof slates had begun to explode in a series of cracks.

Then, over the roar of the burning building, there was the sound of the fire engine's siren as it raced up the drive.

Shakily we looked at each other, Sylvia's pale face was streaked with black and I supposed mine was too, while Jo's freckles were standing clear above her pallor. By common consent we all three rose and quickly moved farther away from the fire, and perched ourselves on a low garden wall, well away from the house.

The fire engine screeched to a halt, the men leaping from the machine even before it had stopped. One of them spotted us and while the rest of the crew sped into their much practised routine with the hoses, he came running across to where we sat.

'Anyone inside the house?'

We looked at each other. Where was Iris Julian? I answered. 'There was a woman in there. But she must have got out before the fire took hold. I don't think there can be anyone still in there.'

The fireman looked grim. 'No one alive anyway, that's for sure. Thanks mate. Keep well clear.' He ran off and disappeared round the back of the fire engine.

The men fought the fire with disciplined efficiency. Soon they were joined by another engine, with a police car and ambulance following. We three remained, mesmerised by the scene, not seeming to have the energy to go back to our car.

Together we watched. The house began to die before our eyes. Part of the roof fell in. More windows burst asunder. The massive front door blew out. And all the time the professionals fought grimly and steadily, gradually bringing the fire under control.

The fireman who'd first spoken to us suddenly reappeared at our side. 'The woman you spoke of, who was she?'

'The housekeeper, Iris Julian. She lives here.'

'Well, I'm afraid she didn't get out.' He spoke slowly. 'We've told the police. I expect they'll want a word with you. Must go.' And he left us as abruptly as he'd arrived.

We looked towards the police car which had moved some way back up the drive. Beside the car was a knot of onlookers being firmly dissuaded from getting any nearer to the inferno. And coming across the grass towards us was an ambulance medic.

He came to a stop and looked down at us. 'Well, well. Very lucky people to have got out of that, eh? But you'd better come with me. We'll take you over to the hospital for a check-up and then the police will be able to have a chat with you and find out what happened. OK? Can you make it to the ambulance? We don't want to bring it any nearer.'

All three of us got to our feet, surprised at how weak

222

and shaky we were feeling. We followed the man who'd introduced himself as Terry, and he helped us climb into the ambulance and settle down. Moments later the vehicle was reversing until it found a space in which to turn, and soon we were racing along the road.

When we arrived at the hospital we were treated as emergency patients. We all had several cuts from the broken and flying glass of the window, and they removed my arm plaster which to my surprise was badly damaged by the way I'd bashed it against the poker, when I'd used it as a hammer. I was unpleasantly aware of my battered ribs and held my chest carefully as I breathed.

Sylvia had noticed my arm. 'Oh Archie,' she wailed. 'All that hammering and swinging that chair! What has it done to you? You look dreadful.'

Jo butted in. 'He'll be OK. He's tough. It's much more apparent than real.' She leaned forward and kissed my smoke blackened face. 'Nothing a long soak in the tub won't put right, eh?'

I smiled at her, and I could see in a reflection on a glass wall that my teeth gleamed very white against the blackness of my skin.

'We'll give you another X-ray, Mr Smith, and see if your arm can do with a different plaster.' The doctor was young and helpful and an hour later, he told us we could all leave. I now wore a plaster that was in two parts and could be opened and removed and fastened back on again as long as was necessary.

There were two policemen waiting for us in the hospital foyer as they'd promised us they would.

'My car is in the lay-by near the driveway entrance to the house? Can you drop us there?' asked Sylvia.

'Better than that. Tell us where you're planning to go and we'll get the car taken there for you. You're in no state to drive, you know. None of you. Anyway, we've got to ask you some questions,' and the sergeant led us into a side room.

Jo told them what she'd seen the Julian woman doing, carrying the petrol can into the house, and the fire she'd seen through the back door moments later. And I told them the woman was quite demented and had locked us in the room before we knew what she was about. And it was thanks to Jo that we'd escaped as we did.

Sylvia told them Iris Julian had really lost it when she was told she would no longer be able to live in the house. 'We suppose she thought, if she couldn't live there, neither should we.' Sylvia sounded very tired and sad.

The two policemen completed their interviews eventually and told us they might as well take us off now. As they escorted us out of the hospital and ushered us into the police car, there were flashes from the cameras of waiting journalists. 'Fuck sake!' I muttered. 'Don't tell us we'll be in the papers tomorrow.'

'Don't know about the newspapers, sir, but I expect you'll be on the local television news tonight.' The sergeant smiled at us as he spoke. 'Never mind. You're all OK and that's the most important thing.'

Sylvia gave a sudden giggle. 'Looking like we do, d'you think they'll let us back into the hotel?'

The sergeant laughed with her. 'We'll make sure they do,' he said, and ten minutes later we were dropped at the hotel where our rooms had luckily been booked for the night.

CHAPTER THIRTY TWO

The hotel manager was waiting for us in the reception foyer, having already learned about the disastrous fire and his customers' involvement. 'What on earth happened, Mrs Armstrong?' he asked Sylvia as we were escorted indoors.

She told him as little as she could, having been advised by the police to be careful about what we said. 'We got locked in a room by mistake and then the place caught fire,' she said.

'Good God!' he exclaimed. 'What a terrible accident. Would you like to come and sit in our private lounge, for a while?' he asked.

'To be honest, all we want is to go upstairs and have a shower,' Sylvia spoke gently to the manager whom she'd met before, 'We really must go up to our rooms, Mr Jones. You can see we all need a good clean-up!' and he quickly agreed and escorted us across to the hall.

'You'd better use the lift,' he said. 'There's bound to be a reporter in the lounge,' and as we by-passed the reception, there were more camera flashes and a man came hurrying towards us asking questions. 'Not yet,' the manager held the reporter back as we three took the lift. Much as he would have liked a good chat with us himself, he could see we were feeling very weak and shaky and wouldn't be giving him all the details he'd have liked to hear.

I guessed the hotel manager would certainly give the reporter all the news he could, and I couldn't blame him for making the most of the hotel's publicity. 'Come on, you two,' I said as the lift stopped on the upper floor, and as we stepped out, I steered them to the safe haven of Sylvia's bedroom.

We sat around for a while, dirty and exhausted, but loathe to leave one another's company. At last Jo stood up. 'Come on Archie, you're for the bath. I'll run it for you.' She looked at Sylvia who lay back in her armchair. 'Then I'll come back and run one for you too, Sylvia. Just stay there until I come.'

Sylvia smiled tiredly at her. 'I don't think I could move if you paid me, right now.' But a quarter of an hour later, when Jo went back, she told me Sylvia had called out from her bathroom that she was fine. 'Go and look after Archie and I'll join you later.' she'd said.

Jo told her that of course she must, and reminded her of our room number before coming back to our bedroom. I was in the bathroom, already soaking in the hot tub.

'Great that you can remove that plaster now and then, Archie.' Jo smiled at me.

I nodded. 'The arm's a bit sore still, and I'll certainly fasten the plaster on again, but right now it's the first time for weeks that I've been able to have a decent bath.' I looked up at her, my eyes intent. 'Shit, Jo, what a near miss we had!'

She came across and perched on the side of the bath, touching my shoulder. 'Yes, I know. I go cold every time I think about it.'

'Thank God you came looking for us. If you'd stayed by the car, we'd have had it.'

'Oh stop, Archie. I can't bear to think of that.' she was soaping the sponge. 'Let's just get you clean and dressed and in your right mind. Then I'll have a shower.' She smiled shakily down at me. 'I'll get Sylvia to join us when we're ready and we can all tell each other exactly what happened. What we told the police was pretty brief, wasn't it? But come on now, let's get this grime off you.'

And glad not having to reach round and scrub my back, I laughed, 'I don't remember ever having been bathed by someone else. Keep going Jo. This is great.'

Half an hour later, Jo having overruled my suggestion to get dressed again, I lay propped up in bed, Jo perched on the foot in a pair of pyjamas, and Sylvia comfortable in her dressing gown in the sole armchair.

Just as we'd made ourselves comfortable, there was a knock on the door and the manager called out, 'Can I come in? I've a tray to leave with you.'

Jo hopped off the bed and let him in. He put down the tray on a side table. 'There. Some nibbles for the three of you. I know you said you wouldn't want a meal tonight, but a little snack might go down well with the tea and the brandy!'

And just as we thanked him, he went on, 'If you like, I'll get your clothes laundered overnight. You were apologising for the smell of smoke when you arrived, and I should think washing would get rid of it, wouldn't it?'

We were delighted with his suggestion. 'I thought we'd have to go out first thing tomorrow and buy some new clothes!' Sylvia exclaimed.

After he'd let himself out, we drank the tea laced with brandy and alone now and cleansed of the smoke which had wreaked our hair and skin, we sipped our drinks, revelling in the warmth and comfort of our surroundings.

'Right, Jo. Tell us your side of the story.'

She wrapped her arms round her up drawn knees, a bright figure on the pale coverlet in her red pyjamas. 'Well, I know you joked about getting the police if you

227

were away more than half an hour, but the whole thing worried me. I was really concerned from the moment you left. I had a feeling something awful would happen.' Her grey eyes were dark with remembrance as she spoke. 'After a bit I couldn't stand it any longer, so I left the car and walked up the drive.'

And for the next half an hour, Jo told us what she had done. That she'd come round to the back of the house and was looking at a wood shed when Iris Julian came out. And Jo had quickly hidden herself in the shed. We were amazed to hear she'd seen the woman grab a can of petrol and Jo could hear what Iris Julian was going to do. And she'd run after her to the back door, opened it, seen the flames and quickly closed it. And Jo had dialled 999 and called the fire station.

We kept interrupting her, telling her how much we owed her for what she'd done. She smiled and said her next call was to my mobile and when she found it engaged, she wondered if I was calling the police. Then she dialled me again and this time I'd answered and she shuddered as she told us how terrified she was that we might not be able to escape. That my mobile might not have been switched on. But when I'd told her we needed to have the window shutter broken open, she was so glad she'd hidden in the wood shed where there was an axe, the strong axe that did the job.

'And we know exactly what happened after that. Thank goodness!'

Jo's face was still pale and her eyes enormous as she stared unseeingly before her.

I reached out for her hand and she came and leaned against my shoulder. 'You're truly a life-saver, Jo. We were trapped and the door was burning…'

'Don't!' she shuddered again and buried her face in the hollow of my neck.

'Archie's right, Jo,' Sylvia spoke intensely. 'Thank God for your resourcefulness and courage. If you'd waited by the car...' She too, left the sentence unfinished. She pulled herself up. 'I'm going now. I want to phone Lawrence. He usually rings about nine o'clock when he's away. I must ring him first before he finds out I'm not at home.' She gave a little smile and stood up. She put her arms round Jo and held her tightly, then walked round the bed to my side.

'Lean forward, your pillows aren't right.' She pummelled them to her satisfaction and shook them into place. 'There, that's better,' Leaning forward she gently embraced me and I felt her tears against my face. 'Goodnight Archie, my darling.' Her voice was choked with emotion and she turned her head away as she crossed to the door and did not look back as she left.

Next morning the manager in person brought all our laundered clothing back. It was a great relief that we didn't have to go out smelling like cave people. Sylvia was wearing a different blouse, one she'd packed in her overnight bag. Jo and I also had clean tee shirts; thankfully we didn't have to go and buy new trousers.

Before yesterday's terrible event, we'd planned to stroll round the town and I'd wanted to visit Reg Barrymore. And we'd have left to go home on this Saturday morning. But now I definitely intended to meet Reg.

Not long after we were seated at the table for our breakfast, the manager came across once more. 'A message for you, my friends. Someone from the police station will be calling to see you about ten o'clock. I hope that doesn't upset your plans too much?'

I answered. 'No. We had planned to leave this morning, but I've a visit to make. In fact,' I turned to

Jo, 'I think we might need to stay over again tonight. What do you think?'

She nodded. 'I felt we'd need a bit more time here after all that has happened. What about you Sylvia?

'I think I'd rather like to go home today. Last night I had so many phone calls! My daughters told me we'd been photographed climbing into the ambulance and it was shown on the national news. And again when we arrived at the hotel with the policemen!'

'Wow!' exclaimed Jo. 'I'm glad Mum and Dad were out with their friends last night. I left a message for them and they called back later and I brought them up to date. And you spoke to your friend Edith, didn't you Archie?'

I nodded, glad I'd talked to her, glad Edith had not been worried if she'd seen the event on the TV.

'Both my daughters and several of my friends and neighbours who had my mobile number called me.' Sylvia smiled. 'So I switched the thing off after a bit. I'd already spoken to Lawrence for quite a long time. I thought I'd better tell him we were OK in case one of my girls called him. He was horrified to hear what had happened but very glad I hadn't gone on my own to see the woman as I'd intended.'

Just then the hotel manager came across to us again, holding a couple of newspapers in his hand. He beamed at us. 'Look, here you are ladies and gentleman. Photos in both these papers. And I've already banned several journalists from pinning you down. When you leave I suggest you go via the back entrance. Meanwhile, when you've breakfasted, if you go along to the conservatory, I'll make sure no one else goes there. Apart from the policeman, of course.' He laughed as he turned away, shaking his head at our thanks.

After we'd eaten - and I ate a full English breakfast,

suddenly very hungry - we did as he'd suggested and found our way to the conservatory.

CHAPTER THIRTY THREE

When we'd settled down in the comfortable chairs, all three of us spent a lot of time making phone calls. Sylvia had learned the hard way not to leave her mobile in the car again and Jo chatted to her parents once more.

I spent a long while on the phone to Edith as my call to her last night had been quite brief; I'd been too exhausted to say a lot. She too had been concerned when she'd seen our photos on the news channel, but knew from my call to her that I was OK. Now I'd be able to bring her up to date with everything. I stepped out into the garden as I talked to her, not minding the light drizzle, liking to speak to her privately. I told her about our visit to the solicitor and the possibility of running the iron foundry. She was very pleased and quite moved to know I'd be 'stepping into my father's shoes', as she put it. Just as I ended my conversation with Edith and stepped back into the conservatory, a member of staff tapped on the door, opened it and said I had a visitor. I looked round and to my astonishment, Detective Inspector Green stood in the doorway.

''ello, ello' he was saying, imitating an old-time television policeman. 'Good to see you made it third time lucky, my friend.'

'Christ! It's great to see you Inspector, but what on earth brought you here?'

'That story on the news last evening. I recognised you, and of course I'd already called at that Cornish house to speak to Iris Julian. But what really caught my eye, was the white van in the car port. Some bloke with a camera had followed the firemen round the back and I recognised the number plate.'

'But that was Iris Julian's van, Inspector. Her white van.'

'No, it was her son Cyril's. We had his vehicle number in his file from when they'd found that semtex in the boot. He's been out on bail since that explosion and was supposed to sign in with us regularly. And the last few days he hasn't. After seeing that van, I checked with the St. Hayes police and they looked inside the garage, and yes, her white van was also there and they confirmed Cyril's number was the one on the van in the carport.

'Fuck's sake! Was he inside the house too?' I gasped.

'I asked if the firemen had checked and they said their inspector would be going over the place again this morning. And he did. They'd found Iris Julian's body yesterday at the bottom of the stairs. And this morning they found another, almost certainly Cyril's. His body was in the servant's wing of the house, buried under the fallen roof which was too hot and smouldering to be checked yesterday.'

Sylvia and Jo were just as shocked as me. I introduced my companions and Inspector Green became a polite and sincere gentleman, someone I hadn't known before. I thought, what a weirdo he was! What an actor!

Soon, after some coffee and a lot of biscuits, the police detective inspector stood up. 'You are a very lucky man, Mr Smith. These last few weeks it's been interesting to hear about your search for family history. I seem to remember warning you about the Julian woman. Like I said, it's been third time lucky for you. Definitely not for her. And it's good to see you've found your mother. Madam, you too are fortunate to have such a smart son and his courageous partner.' He shook hands with them and I walked out into the foyer with him.

'I sure do have to thank you, Inspector. You've kept me up to date with all the things Iris Julian did. I know it was a terrible end for her, and for her son as well. But it definitely was third time lucky for me.' I shook the man's hand once more and as the Inspector left the hotel, I spotted a journalist peering through the door and quickly shot out of sight and back to the conservatory.

Minutes later, Lawrence Armstrong strode into the room. 'Good heavens, Lo! How did you get here?' Sylvia flung herself into her husband's arms.

'I caught a plane back last night after our conversation. Cancelled today's meeting.' He held her tightly to him. 'I had to come and make sure you really were alright.' He smiled across at Jo and me. 'We'll come back and see you presently. I just want to take my wife for a walk round the garden and hear everything again. OK?' As they set off Lawrence removed his coat and draped it round Sylvia's shoulders and a few minutes later they settled in an arbour, sitting close together as they talked.

Jo and I decided to go into town and called out to Sylvia we'd be back in time for lunch. As we walked through the foyer, the manager caught us up. 'No reporters now to bother you, my friends. They've been told the story won't make television again. And they know they can get what facts they need from the police.'

As Jo drove out of the car park, I said 'I think I'll phone Reg Barrymore. I know it's Saturday and the foundry won't be open, but I do need to talk to him.'

'Good idea. If he wants you to call at his home, I'll drop you off and go shopping and you can call me when you're ready to be picked up.'

Reg answered and told me he'd be delighted if I came round to his house. He was still shocked at what he'd heard about the fire at his old boss's house and wanted to hear all about it. Jo dropped me at his gate and for the next hour, once I'd told him about the fire, the two of us were able to talk about the future of the foundry. Reg was glad to hear all the estate would go to me, and astounded at the thought of the machinery being moved to the Industrial Estate. 'What a good idea. There are so many obstacles in our old foundry. Because it's been extended over the years, we don't have all the open spaces we need.'

'I won't be leaving my firm, Reg, but I know my bosses would like to have a permanent spot to go to with their inventions and adaptations. And I will obviously come down regularly to catch up with everything. And I know now I can fly down to Newquay and hire a car from there whenever. We'll check your salary soon, as I'm sure you'll need a decent increase, Reg. You really do deserve it for the way you've been keeping things going.'

After we'd caught up with all we needed to discuss, I shook Reg's hand and thanked his wife for the tea and went outside where Jo had just arrived after my call. She told me it was now her turn to go and get a cup of coffee, while I filled her in with the news.

I dropped a kiss on her cheek as she pulled into the town car park, and we strolled up the main street together until we found a coffee bar. It was good to be alone, just the two of us once more. Yes, there were other people at the tables, but we were in a world of our own.

When we got back to the hotel, Sylvia and Lawrence were sitting in the conservatory with her overnight bag alongside. Lawrence stood up and held out his hand to me 'Glad you've got back. We're just about to leave, Archie.' And he turned to Jo and gave her a hug and kiss, thanking her once more for what she had done.

Sylvia too, stood up and hugged Jo, unable to speak as tears filled her eyes. They held one another for a long minute. Then she turned to me and held out her arms. I drew her to me, my face in her hair. I swallowed hard before I released her and was able to wish them a safe journey home. And promised to come and see them again soon. And to meet the girls and their families. Just let me get rid of this plaster first, yes?

Our odd, choked conversations ended and we went outside with them. We waved them into Sylvia's car when Lawrence drew it up at the front steps, and waved again until they had gone out of sight.

That afternoon we had to call at the police station to sign another couple of statements which Sylvia had already done, and afterwards we drove up to the Keyes Lane House. We chatted to the fire inspection people who were still poking round in the rubble and then we went off for a walk. We circled the building and followed a path through the copse at the back. Soon we came across the gardener's cottage where Iris Julian had lived until she moved into the big house. Jo was surprised at the extent of the garden. 'If this place gets sold to a developer, Archie, they could build a number of houses. I bet, after paying off the mortgage, you'll be quite well off.' She sounded a little shocked.

I put my good arm round her. 'I don't care, Jo. All I want is you. And the foundry. If there is a decent bit of capital, it'll be needed to get the foundry re-equipped on the industrial estate. And it'll be an expensive place to run for quite a time. So you and I will have to go on working as we do. And that's what we both like, don't we?'

She wrapped her arms round me. 'Good. I don't want you to become a play boy!' And we both laughed as we hugged each other.

Back at the hotel, a reporter wanted a few words despite what the manager had said. We did answer him, but very briefly and without mentioning Iris Julian's responsibility for the fire.

The day fled by and, still sore and tired, I suggested going to bed early. Jo agreed. She too hadn't slept well the previous night, so shocked and appalled by what had happened.

In our room, as I chatted to her, I told Jo that Edith was so glad I'd met 'that lovely girl' as she'd called her. 'She said she hoped we'd always be together, and that we'd have a family of our own. I told her I would like that too, but it would take a year or two to come about!'

Jo laughed. 'Yes, a year or two before we start a family. But actually, we are able to practise in the meantime, aren't we?'

'Well, yes. I know I've got a busted arm and dodgy ribs and we've both got cuts and bruises. But hopefully we'll both be fit enough in a couple of weeks to practise!'

And still laughing, Jo came to me and put her arms round me, so gently, knowing exactly where my ribs and arm would hurt. 'I don't mind how long it takes, Archie. Just being with you, and sleeping skin to skin is wonderful,' and I hugged her as tightly as I could, so glad that I was no longer having to sleep alone.

It was a while before I went to sleep. Jo had dropped off very quickly and I lay alongside her, leaning back on my pillow with my eyes closed.

What a difference my life was now. A few months ago

I was virtually alone in the world. Yes, I had my work friends, but often I was overseas, once more with strangers. But now, I knew where I truly had come from and I couldn't help thinking what my life would have been like if the series of events had not occurred – having been abandoned at that hospital as a baby. I felt so sorry that I'd never met my father, and even more sad that he had never known I was still alive and well. A real shame.

But I have now discovered that I have a mother and two half sisters as well. And I have a future I could never have imagined, full of love and promise. A family I belong to.

A smile crossed my face. I opened my eyes and reached for Jo's hand as she lay so close to me. I will have her family in my life as well.

At present we are utterly exhausted from our recent experience, but we are both full of anticipation for our coming future. Our future. Together.

About the Author

After various occupations, Enid Mavor started teaching for some years. Upon leaving, she wrote her first novel, Portrait of Polwerris, which was then published. Several short stories were also published and broadcast on Radio Cornwall, together with some award winning poetry. Her second novel, Flood Tide, was published prior to this book.